Braverman
Confessions of a
Jewish Teenage Drug
Dealer

A work of fiction based on a true story.

Jeffrey Wachman

&

Travis Montez

DEDICATION

For my mother, Sheila

ACKNOWLEDGMENTS

Thank you to all who believed in me and this project . I love you all. You know who you are.

PROLOGUE

I am Inmate 700455EE.

I have been Inmate 700455EE for over eleven months now. And if the State of New Jersey has its way, if I don't convince them that I have pulled my act together enough to be discharged to a halfway house, I will continue being Inmate 700455EE for another five years. But it could have been worse.

See, before I was just another number to check off at evening call, in the mid-90s, until I got caught trying to buy two keys of cocaine in The Garden State in 2008, I was one of the cockiest, flashiest drug dealers New York City had ever seen. On top of that, the streets of Brooklyn had nicknamed me "Jeremy" after the big-dicked porn star of classics like King Kong's Long Dong 2, I Love Juicy and I Ream A Genie. That's because, I also had a reputation for being well endowed and quite the ladies' man. And I used it to my advantage at every turn.

I started dealing drugs when I dropped out of junior high school by selling weed to my former classmates and other people in the Brooklyn community of Midwood where my family lived. It was a working class, religious Jewish neighborhood that really didn't want us there because we were not religious at all. I quickly worked my way up through the ranks until I had my own territories and a crew of dealers that worked for me. By then, I was selling much more than marijuana. As a white teenager from a working class Jewish family, holding down a significant part of the drug trade in and around Brooklyn, I had to handle my business to keep people from trying to take what was mine. And I definitely handled my business. People knew me and knew not to mess with me. And, of course, the cops knew me. The poor schmucks spent years trying to lock me up. I got arrested, tried and even did little stints in lockup for assaults, drug offenses, even attempted murder. But I had high paid lawyers and a lucky streak that

1

made me think I was untouchable.

Turns out I wasn't.

On October 18, 2009, I am Inmate 700455EE. My older brother, Scott, always warned me that drug dealing wasn't going to last forever. "If you gonna live this life," he'd said to me more than once, "you gotta be prepared to do serious time or die." I was too young and conceited to think either of those things could happen to me. And now that it has, now that I am facing six years in prison -- feeling lucky because it could have been 20 with all the charges they had me on -- I haven't spent my time locked up feeling sorry for myself or worrying about the business Ron Jeremy is losing while I am away.

I am spending my time as Inmate 7000455EE figuring out how to become Noah Braveman again or the Noah Braverman I should have become.

As Noah, I was the youngest child of seven – six boys, one girl -- who all grew up in a one-bedroom apartment. I was the one Ma called her favorite. Before the sex, drugs, and gangster lifestyle. Before the guns -- before the arrests and the court dates. Before the New York Times articles about the trouble I caused in the neighborhood. Before I had to see my parents looking old and worn out at all my court dates. I was the golden child, and then something went terribly wrong. Out of desperation I turned bad. The truth of the matter is, I was so good at being bad, that being good, will be the hardest thing I'll ever do.

PART 1
CHAPTER 1

The belt snapped as it hit my thigh, sending a sharp hot pain down my leg. Stunned, I shot up in bed and could hear myself scream as more licks kept coming. My arm. My shoulder. Up and down my legs. My thirteen-year-old body jerked from the pain. My face was still covered by the fucking blanket, but instinct had me scoot away from the lashes until my back hit the wall.

A hand gripped my upper arm and yanked me off the bed onto the floor. The thin, fraying rug of our bedroom provided no cushion as I landed on my stomach and chest, just missing a pile of dog shit probably left by Dutch, my 70-pound pit bull.

The belt again bit into my back. I tried to roll away, but the space between the twin set of bunk beds was too narrow. I managed to scramble away from the beating just far enough to free myself from the blankets.

Maybe if she could see me, see how sorry I was, it would stop. But, when I looked up, it wasn't Ma. My father was standing over me with his thick belt, the one he wore with his work uniform. He was ready to strike again. Fuck. Why wasn't he at work? Another sick day? He was having more and more of those lately.

"How many times does your mother got to tell you to get up?"

Crack. The belt came down like a bolt of lightning.

"Huh?" I cried.

Crack. It made a sound like thunder.

"She gotta ask you to go to school?"

Crack. It stung like a bee.

"You think you gonna lay around here all day like some fuckin' bum?"

My legs felt like a three-alarm fire. My Arms. My shoulder. My back.

3

But mostly my legs; I think he chose them because I was wearing a t-shirt and underwear, so my legs were bare. You could already see angry, red welts rising on my skin.

"I'm sorry," I croaked. "I'm going. I'm going." The tears ran down my cheeks.

Dad gripped the back of my neck and pulled me off the floor. My father wasn't tall, but he was a solid guy. Despite being ill, he lifted my skinny teen-aged body with no trouble. His fingers dug into the flesh of my neck. I had to fight the urge to push him away. Fighting back only made things worse. I'd seen what happened to my brothers when they'd made that mistake. Like getting hit with a bat, or my brother Scott getting a remote control cracked over his head. Ma would hit me with anything she could get her hands on -- a hanger, phone-cord, shoe or bat.

If I put my hands up to block her, she would call my father and say I was trying to hit her. Then, all hell would break loose and my dad would just beat the ever-living shit out of me.

"You better be out of this house in ten minutes. You better get straight to school. No more of your bullshit! You understand me?"

I nodded and managed a whispered, "Yes, sir," as he threw me against the wall.

He left the room without another word. Standing there, sobbing, I started to pick my way through the stacks of worn out clothes on the floor to find something to wear. I pulled on a pair of jeans and a long-sleeved, shirt to hide the welts. Then, I noticed Ma standing in the doorway. Had she been there the entire time?

"Ten minutes, Noah," she hollered. Then she padded away in her old, green slippers. And I heard the springs creak as my parents sat down on the couch to watch their favorite morning TV beginning with The Today Show, then Let's Make A Deal and The Price Is Right.

****

I should have fuckin' expected it. Earlier that morning, Ma had come into the bedroom three times, just to wake me up for school. The last time she even tried to yank the covers off of me.

She yelled, "Noah Braverman, you've been out of school two days this week already! Get up!"

"Maaaa, I don't feel good," I whined, struggling to keep the blankets over my head. "My stomach hurts."

"My twat, your stomach hurts," she had said. "Funny how your stomach keeps you from going to school, but doesn't keep you from going over to Alyssa's or Caitlin's." She was right. That was my plan: to stay in bed all day and get up around the time my two best friends got out of school. Then, I'd head over to one of their houses before Dad got in from work, hang out, stay for dinner, then come home when it was time for bed.

"You little punk, you're going to school today. Whether or not you go in one piece is up to you. Now get up you little fuck!" She screamed

My head was still under the blankets when she stopped tugging, but I peeked out just in time to see the back of her Wu Tang Clan tee shirt storming out of the room.

My brothers usually had something to say about everything. But they knew to keep quiet when Ma was on the warpath or her wrath would turn on them. She was bound to come back and with more than a fist. Or worse, my father to do her dirty work. I must have started to doze off listening to my brothers bump into and trip over each other getting ready for their day: work for Jared, school for David, Special Ed class for Adam and the usual trouble making for Scott.

"Mom's gonna kill you" Adam shouted, waking me again. Meanwhile, my brothers were still on overdrive, pulling jeans, shirts, and mismatched socks from piles of clothes on the floor. One wall of the bedroom that we all slept in was covered from one end to the other and from floor to ceiling with bags of clothes and other shit. Even though there were 5 boys, it was mostly my sister, Sara and her daughter's crap that overwhelmed the entire room. It was impossible on most days to tell what shirt or pair of jeans belonged to whom, and no one gave a crap. Our basic rule was, if you could fit into it, wear it. It would eventually be yours through our hand-me-down system, anyway.

I hated the house because of how we had to live. In addition to the double set of bunk beds, the bedroom had one dresser and no closet, because it was turned into a room where my older brother slept. And besides the wall of bags, there was a wall covered with posters of Dr. Dre, Janet Jackson's sexy ass, 2Pac, Aerosmith, Ice Cube, and girls from the Sports Illustrated Swim Suit editions. The posters were more than just decorations; they hid holes in the walls. Lots of holes – from punches thrown by one of us boys or our mom but mostly Adam, who would throw fits sometimes on account of his being emotionally disturbed.

I heard Ma pull plates and bowls out of the kitchen cabinet, spoons out of drawers and set the table for breakfast. From the smell of it, I could tell she was making the Quaker Oatmeal knock-off that Adam had every morning. Then, I heard her stirring water into the powdered milk my brothers would use for cereal. I must have dozed off again because I didn't hear them eat or make plans for after they got out of school. I didn't hear them pick on each other. I didn't hear my mother tell them to stop behaving like animals. I didn't hear any of the normal sounds of what happened when us boys were around the table. I was still asleep and ma wasn't happy. So she sent my Dad in to beat the shit out of me.

****

Still feeling the burn from my father's beating, earlier that morning, I went into our tiny kitchen to make myself something quick to eat. Flicking on the light, I ducked into the bathroom – empty for once – giving the roaches in the kitchen that crawled on the counter tops and floor a chance to run for cover. I stepped carefully through the newspapers soaked with dog piss and shit that blanketed half the floor and began my search for breakfast. With 3 dogs and 10 cats my whole house was a minefield, especially the kitchen. As always, my choices were limited. I found some Wonder Bread with the discount orange sticker that meant it was close to its expiration date, a huge block of American 'welfare' cheese and a generic brand of mayo my parents would put in the year old Hellmann's jar, in a poor attempt to trick us. The cereal was gone. Anyway, I hated the fact that we never had real milk, only the powdered kind. But we considered ourselves lucky if there weren't any roaches feasting in the box. The oatmeal was Adam's … he'd throw a fit if it was touched.

The roaches were really bad in our house and I never understood why nothing was done about it. Until one day when my mom was rushed to the emergency room with a terrible pain in her ear that turned out to be a roach stuck in her ear canal. The next day there were exterminators at the house, but only because the landlord thought my mom would sue, which she threatened but never did.

So, I choked down a cheese sandwich. As I ate, I stood in our small kitchen and watched my parents sitting on the tattered couch that pulled out into a bed where they slept at night. The folding cardboard table we ate on was up in front of the sofa, partially surrounded by plastic milk crates that my mom would send us to steal, so we could use as chairs. The 1-800 number was still stamped on the sides, to call and return if found.

It was crazy hot, and I was sweating my balls off, but I had to wear a long-sleeve shirt to cover my welts and some older bruises. Sometimes it was roasting in the apartment, to the point where you could barely breathe. A lot of times us kids would pile into the living room and sleep on the floor because it was the only room with an air conditioner. You couldn't run two air conditioners at the same time in the shit-hole without blowing the lights. But normally, the four of us boys, my sister, Sara, and my niece, Melissa, piled into the bedroom, with me, the youngest, always having to share a bed.

I glanced again into the living room at the two lumps huddled on the couch. I pitied them, but felt more sorry for myself. I ate in silence and left without saying a word. The movement of walking downstairs caused the welts to sting, especially the ones on the back of my legs. As I stepped out onto the sidewalk and headed to school, I hoped that no one could tell I'd been crying.

In 1993, public school 99 in Brooklyn was a plain brick building covered with fading paint and sorry attempts to cover the graffiti, which you could see right through the fresh coats of enamel. It looked like any other New York City public school at the time, worn and dreary. But to me, walking into that place was like going to my death every day. I hated everything about it. I hated getting up in the morning. I hated the teachers. I even hated my classmates. I had to fight with myself (and my parents) almost every day just to get there.

I was 13 and in my second year of junior high school. I was an awful student and my teachers never missed a chance to point that out to me. And everyone else. In one way or another, they all let me know that they thought I was a troublemaker. And in return, I did everything I could to live up to the reputation. If it was time to be quiet, I was talking. If it was time to sit in a seat to do work, I was up flirting with some girl, out in the hall messing around with my friends, or outside the school completely. And I don't think I ever took a book home. I never did homework. Which obviously was part of the reason why my grades were so terrible.

Another reason for my poor marks was that back in first grade; I was kept home a lot because I had really bad asthma. Sometimes my mother would beat me until I had an asthma attack, then I would have to be on a nebulizer. And because I even hated school then, I always complained about being sick just to stay home. As a result of missing so much school, I got held back a year. I don't know if I just got used to the habit of being absent all the time or what, but I never fell back into the groove of regular school attendance. I never felt like I belonged in school with those normal kids.

To me back then, the normal kids had decent, new clothes for school. They had money to go on school trips and lunch every day. They had real milk at home not the fake kind, and they didn't have to beg for food from the Catholic Church even though they were Jewish. One time when I waited on a line that wrapped around the block to get can goods and cheese from the church, some of my classmates saw me and didn't miss the opportunity to make fun of 'the begging Jew on the church line'.

'Normal' certainly wasn't the Bravermans. My dad had always been a hardworking man, busting his ass at 2 jobs -- foreman for the Trailways bus company and a security guard in the Hospital for Joint Diseases. My mom had always been a housewife. It was a full-time job taking care of all us kids.

We were always struggling financially, even when my dad was working, we were poor. By the time I was in junior high, he'd been in and out of the hospital he worked in with heart problems and wasn't really working any more. What little money had been coming in for all of us before he got sick was gone now. All of us existed on his Veteran's disability and my mentally challenged brother Adam's Social Security disability checks. We never qualified for welfare because the household received too much money. On top of all that, was the constant thought in the back of my head that my father's heart could fail at any moment and that one-day he would go to the hospital and not return.

Being the baby of a large, broke family meant that everything I owned, except for sometimes my shoes, had at one point belonged to one or more of my brothers first. I wore nothing but hand-me-downs. My junior high school classmates noticed my worn, outdated clothes and made fun of me almost every day. On most days I responded to being teased with a joke of my own and kept it moving. Some days though, the teasing led to a fight.

"Yo, Noah, you sure you American?" this Italian kid, Anthony, asked me while we were sitting at lunch. There was a bunch of us boys just hanging around, eating, talking bullshit and listening to music on somebody's Walkman headphones.

"What?" I said confused, thinking maybe Anthony had managed to get high before lunch and was just rambling some nonsense like he did sometimes. "Are you sure you American?" he repeated in a louder voice that got all the other boys to pay attention. He had this grin on his face that let me know a joke was coming. "Yeah, I was born right here in Brooklyn just like yo' guinea ass. What about it?" I said, daring him to crack a joke on me. "I don't know, my man. Wit' them 1980s high-waters on and yo Air Mikey's, you be dressing like them ESL kids straight off the boat!". In those days everyone who was cool talked like they were black and into Hip Hop. Talking like the black kids meant you were street and tough, soft core ghetto. I could feel everyone turn and look down at my shoes. They weren't name brand. They weren't even from Pay-Less. They were what my parents could afford. Some shit sneakers from 'Favor' stores called Olympian. My jeans and faded knock-off Polo shirts from the flea market were donated from friends, and had been worn by at least two of my four older brothers back when they were in junior high school. My clothes weren't anything like what most of the boys were wearing.

Hip Hop style was the only style back then. Which meant guys my age wore trendy clothes like baggy jeans and shirts, Timberland boots or super clean, Adidas pumps or Nikes. If you didn't, you were lame because everyone dressed like that. Everyone except for me and the ESL (English as a Second Language) kids, who had just come to the United States and didn't know our style. They didn't even know English! Of course, the other guys at the table laughed like there was something funny about me being poor.

This wasn't the first time Anthony or someone else in junior high had made some comment about my clothes. And it wasn't like I didn't expect it. I knew every morning when I got dressed in those worn out clothes that someone at some point would say something. That's how kids are.

But on that day, it got to me.

I'd just had enough. I was tired of being broke. I was tired of wearing clothes that hadn't been cool since the 80s. I was tired of corny punks like Anthony getting laughs off me. I couldn't do anything about being poor, but I could do something about Anthony. I remember him pointing at my shoes and laughing that snorting, nasal laugh of his. I remember the other guys joining in. And, I remember hearing the sound of my chair scraping the floor as I jumped out of my seat. The rest is a blur. I know I grabbed him by his shirt. I remember the feel of it ripping as I yanked him across the lunch table. I remember how big and round his eyes got when I shoved him to floor and pinned him down with my knee across his chest. I started throwing punches at his face. I wanted to smash it in. Destroy it. Destroy what made him rich and me poor. Destroy what gave him the right to laugh at me. Then there was blood coming from his mouth. And more of my punches smeared it across his cheek.

Someone broke us up, and I bounced before the teachers came. I ran out of the lunchroom, down the main hall, and out of one of the side doors of the school. My face was so hot I knew it must've been red. I was breathing hard, and my heart roared in my chest like the D train on the Coney Island Line. Tears of rage and embarrassment stung my eyes, but I wasn't going to let them fall. Not over Anthony and a stupid fight. When I reached the sidewalk, I looked back at P.S. 99.

"Fuck it," I whispered to myself as I turned and walked down the block. I was never going back to school. I didn't know how I was going to keep my parents from finding out or what I was going to do instead, but I knew for a fact that my days as a student were over. Walking up the block, I was trying to figure out where I'd hide out for the rest of the day until it was safe to go home. Deep in my own thoughts, I didn't see the tall, skinny kid rounding the corner, headed in the opposite direction. I plowed right into him and nearly knocked him off his feet.

"Vhat the fuck, bro? Vatch where the hell you going!" he said.

"My bad, man. I wasn't payin'…"

The words stuck in my throat when I realized that I knew the guy. Slavic was an older teenager, originally from Russia and moved into our neighborhood when he was 12 years old. And was friendly with my brother, Scott. Shit! My mind started spinning trying to think of some way to explain why I wasn't at school or at least some way to convince him not to mention to Scott that he caught me skipping. Now, Scott was no angel, and I knew for a fact that he'd done his share of cutting school. But any time I acted up or did something that upset Ma, he was on me like her enforcer, and I would get my ass kicked! "Hey, Slavic," I said. "Sorry, about that. I'm not feeling well so they let me go early. I was just tryin' to rush home."

Slavic folded his arms across his chest and raised both his eyebrows (which were just as unruly as his stubborn black hair), into what looked like twin bushy question marks. He had this smirk on his face that let me know without a doubt he wasn't buying my story. But hell, Slavic didn't finish high school. He and Scott ran around getting into all kinds of trouble together. He should understand my situation and keep his mouth shut, at least until I let my brother know myself. So, I told him everything. I told him about how I wasn't meant for that school shit. I told him about those teachers giving me a hard time. I told him about the fights. And, I told him about the hand-me-downs and getting made fun of for being poor while Dad was in and out of the hospital.

"So, vhat you gonna do?" Slavic asked when I finished.

"I dunno. Find me a job. Anything to put money in my pocket. Then, I can help out with bills at the house and stuff."

"Well, if you vanna make some quick money, I got something for ya."

I'd like to say Slavic had to convince me to do it. I'd like to tell you that I had all kinds of issues with what he proposed for me to do to make some cash. But, that would be a lie. Slavic was a drug dealer with Russian mob connections. He sold weed mostly to other high school dropouts and people with jobs who liked to get high on the weekend. He thought I would be the perfect person to help him expand his business. Being 19, he really couldn't hang out around junior high schools during the day without making teachers, parents, and cops suspicious. But, I could. And, the truth is I was more than willing.

The first morning of my new "job" – my test run – Slavic gave me a quarter of an ounce of weed (seven grams), divided up in to nine, nickel bags. This, he told me, was worth 45 dollars total. After selling it all, I was to give him back 30 dollars and keep 15 for myself. That day turned out to be one test I could actually pass. I sold the nine bags in less than two hours. Slavic was impressed, and I was happy to be good at something that put money in my pocket so quickly.

After that day, my routine was simple: I went to school in the morning to sell to kids before classes started. After the morning bell rang, I stayed close by P.S. 99 or, on rare occasions, went inside the school to sell to kids at lunch or while they skipped classes throughout the day. Then, after school I would sell more weed to kids on their way home.

After only a couple of weeks, I was already up to selling an ounce of weed (twenty-eight grams), worth 180 dollars. My cut was 60. Not too long after that I was moving about two and a half ounces a week, making at least

120 dollars! To a broke thirteen year-old, I felt like Donald Trump. A feeling like none I'd ever had. I was finally . . . somebody.

Word got around that I was the guy for kids to come to for marijuana. I sold more and more weed and made more and more money. And, I rewarded myself. I got new clothes. I got name brand shoes. I got a pager. Sometimes, I sneaked money into Dad's wallet so he'd think he just had $20 dollar bills in there he'd forgotten about or that he was going a bit senile.

The kids that made fun of me for wearing my brother's clothes weren't laughing anymore. Now, I had better gear than they did. I came and went as I pleased, no matter what teachers told me to do. And I was cool. The fact that I sold weed and that I always had weed to sell, made me popular. I was the guy you wanted to skip school with. I was the guy you wanted to invite to that party you were throwing when your parents were away. I was the bad boy other dudes wanted to know and that girls wanted to date.

To me, after just four weeks, my life was different. I was making money. My own money. And money seemed like the answer to everything. Yeah, it let me get the clothes and other nice things I'd always been jealous that other kids could get. But it also put food on the table for the whole family. And it helped pay bills that my parents were struggling with. Having money gave me power that I didn't have before. And that new-found power was more addictive than anything I was selling to my classmates.

CHAPTER 2

"You sure, Noah? I don't wanna get in trouble for stealing shit." Of my brothers, David, with his dark striking looks was the angel of the bunch and the closest to my age.

"Ain't nobody stealing. Get whatever you want. You too, Adam. It's on me."

I couldn't help but chuckle as I watched them stare at the candy display of the bodega -- practically drooling. Had my brothers ever been told to get whatever they wanted?

Adam, who was like the Eveready battery, first fingered a candy bar, took his hand away, and then touched a bag of sour candy. Come to think of it he was like an addict when it came to candy. Maybe that's why he was so hyperactive.

The Pakistani clerk behind the counter eyed us suspiciously. I knew he was about to tell us to buy something or get the fuck out of his store. I could see it in his sneering brown face

"My man, how much for two of all your candy bars?" I asked

"All? They are 50 cents each." He didn't sound sure. I did the math in my head. There were about 20 different candy bars. I told my brothers to get two of every candy bar, two big bags of Doritos, and two sodas from the refrigerator. I handed him two 20-dollar bills, got my change, and we made our way to the schoolyard.

It was still early evening, and the sun hadn't gone down just yet. Most kids were home for dinner so the playground was empty. But dinner time wasn't at a strict hour in the Braverman house, so we had a bit of leeway.

David and Adam wasted no time tearing into their candy and chips. They guzzled their name-brand sodas. David had a Coke, Adam a Dr. Pepper. I know Ma would of warned them that they would eat themselves sick if she could see them. But any sick was worth Adam's laughter and the chocolate smeared across his face.

"Thank you, Noah!" he said between chomps on a Hershey bar. I hugged him and sat down between my brothers.

"Where did you get all that money?" David asked. "You had a knot of twenties!"

"I got a job. But don't tell Ma or Dad." I answered.

"It's a secret. If you tell them, they'll make me quit."

David looked at me. I could tell the moment he decided it was better not to ask me anything else about where the money came from. The corners of his mouth were orange from the chips. He popped another in his mouth and let his crunching fill the silence.

The truth was: I was selling too fast for Slav, as he was called for short.

After just a few months of dealing, it became obvious that I could easily move more weed than he could give me. A lot of times I would sell out, go give him his money and get more weed, only to find that he had run out too.

I couldn't deal with Slav's low supply for two reasons. First, once I got a taste of it, I needed to keep up the lifestyle that being a teen-aged drug dealer helped me achieve. There was no way I was giving up the freedom and power that having steady money in my pocket gave me. Having weed and money made me popular. People looked for me, asked about me, asked for me to come to places so that they could be around me. I was a fucking star.

The other, increasingly important reason Slavic's empty hands didn't work for me was that after a few months of selling marijuana, I had developed a pretty serious weed habit of my own. With or without friends, I was smoking two blunts a day. So, when Slavic ran out of weed, not only did I have none to sell, I had to go looking for other dealers to fill my personal stash.

I guess you could say that is how I got to know my competition. And buying from them, I quickly realized that the nickel bags I got for myself were a lot bigger than what I was selling to customers for Slavic. I figured out that these other dealers must have been getting their weed cheaper. If I could buy from their source or a better one, and sell on my own, I could make even more money (and have more weed to smoke).

What did I need Slavic for?

He couldn't keep up with my customer demand anyway. There were times when entire weeks went by and I didn't hear from him at all. And those were weeks that I lost money as far as I was concerned.

During one such week, I asked a friend of mine, a black guy named Rendell who was a devoted weed head and lived near me, where I could pick up an ounce to resell. Rendell was a big guy. He was about 6ft tall and about 200 lbs. No one really messed with him because of his size, but I knew he was no tough guy, anyone who really knew him knew that. Rendell introduced me to the world of Crown Heights, Brooklyn, specifically the area around Franklin Avenue and Eastern Parkway.

Crown Heights is located almost exactly in the middle of Brooklyn. It's divided into two distinct sides, one made up of black people from the Caribbean or who came up from "down South," the other of Hassidic Jews. Some might say that my being Jewish meant that I was visiting the wrong side of Crown Heights, but in the months to come, I would start to feel as comfortable in the black parts of Crown Heights as I did in my own neighborhood.

But that comfort came later. In the spring of 1993, when I made my first trip out there, the only thing I knew about Crown Heights was that there had been a riot in the area that lasted for 3 days a couple of years before.

During that summer of 1991, a driver in a motorcade for a Hasidic leader supposedly had a car accident trying to make a stop-light. Two black children, on the sidewalk where his car wound up, were pinned under the car. Things were already tense between the Black and Hassidic communities, so the accident, combined with the decision of emergency responders to remove the Hassidic driver from the scene first, instead of the children pinned under the car, was like throwing gasoline on a barely contained fire. When one of the children, seven-year-old Gavin Cato died, riots erupted for three days that summer.

I remember the story that had my parents up at night was the murder of a young Jewish student, Yankel Rosenbaum, who was supposedly surrounded by twenty young black men, stabbed and severely beaten. I remember Dad telling my brothers to be careful because even though the riots were there, the anger was such that people not even living in Crown Heights were going there looking for Jews to hurt there and all over the rest of Brooklyn too. There were Israeli flag burnings, attacks on synagogues and people marching through the streets screaming "Death to all Jews!"

So, two years later a white kid -- particularly a Jewish white kid -- probably shouldn't have been hanging out in Crown Heights if he wanted to live to see his next birthday. But I was on a mission.

Rendell was gonna set me up with some Jamaican cats. From them, I would be able to pick up an ounce of weed for 60 bucks and sell it for $180. My profit from those sales would be $120, double what I was taking home hustling for Slavic. Buying from them would also allow me to supply other dealers in the neighborhood.

You would think that going to this not-so-great neighborhood with a bad reputation for racial tension, to buy drugs from someone I never met before would have made me nervous. It didn't. I was excited. It was business. And it was a win-win for both sides.

As far I was concerned, going to Crown Heights meant expanding my hustle and making more money. The money excited me. It was all I thought about. I got an adrenaline rush, a different kind of high from going out and making my own, independent drug deal.

Rendell and I took the D train from Ave M and caught the shuttle at Prospect Park. You could clearly see the difference between the trains when you got on the shuttle. The D train was kept relatively clean. The shuttle smelled like piss and had lots of graffiti. Mine was the only white face on that train, except for the conductor.

The shuttle made three stops, but we got off at the first one by the Brooklyn Botanical Gardens. As soon as we got off the train and walked up the stairs from the station, it seemed like there were people standing all over the sidewalk looking to meet the same man Rendell had brought me to see. Some dudes asked us if we wanted to buy pot. Some other guys offered to sell us stronger drugs. Rendell didn't give me a second to interact with any of them.

"Keep it movin'," he said, not even looking in their direction as he pushed me down the block.

Soon, we were in front of a corner store on Franklin Avenue, just off Eastern Parkway. It was supposed to be some kind of crockery store, but all I really remember is that there was a single line of people and bullet-proof glass everywhere. The only contact people outside the store made with people inside the store was through a thick, revolving window. It reminded me of cheese day at the church or the check-cashing place on the first of the month when Social Security checks arrived in the mail.

Eventually, Rendell and I were at the head of the line. Rendell was standing slightly in front of me and spoke through the bullet-proof glass to a huge, dark-skinned guy with long dreadlocks almost to his waist. I couldn't understand a single word being said in their thick island accents. When they finished talking to each other, Rendell and Dreadlocks turned and looked at me.

Not knowing what to say, I just told the dude what I wanted. He asked for "da doe," which I guessed meant money. I handed it to him through the window and he passed me back an ounce.

Just like that, I was in business!

I carefully stuffed the ounce deep into my pocket. As I turned with Rendell to leave, I told Dreadlocks, "You'll be seeing me again." If he heard me or gave a shit, I couldn't tell. He was on to his next customer.

After selling that first ounce and making even more money, ditching Slavic was a no-brainer. Under normal circumstances, if a street-level dealer decided to strike out on his own in the same territory and to the same customers as the guy he worked for, that dealer should expect some trouble. It's the rule of the streets. But my circumstances weren't normal. Even though he didn't approve of my getting into the drug game, my brother Scott -- who had a scary reputation around the neighborhood of his own -- wasn't going to let Slavic and his Russian gang mess with me.

After a few weeks of going back and forth to Crown Heights, my weight was up. I was moving serious amounts of weed and selling my own supply even more successfully than I had sold Slavic's. I was going back to my dealer in Crown Heights four or five times a week. For them, that was a few times too many. One day, after I had come back to Franklin Avenue for the fourth time and it was just Thursday, Dreadlocks asked to have a word with me.

Off to the side of the bulletproof window was a thick metal door. He nodded towards it and I made my way over. I heard what had to be at least 7 locks click, a chain being taken off, and a metal bar being removed before the door slid open just enough for me to step in. It slammed closed behind me, and I found myself in complete darkness.

My eyes adjusted slowly, as two men that were dark-skinned, wearing black t-shirts and pants guided me down a narrow hallway. Each was about 6 and a half feet tall and both carried rifles. Not that they needed any weapons to be intimidating. Solidly built and broad-shouldered, the men were too big to walk side-by-side and fit in the hallway. One had to walk slightly in front of me, the other slightly behind me. The sounds of their boots against the concrete floor and my breathing were all I could hear.

I was scared. Damn scared. And tried not to show it. I hadn't done anything wrong. In fact, I had, in my mind, been a great customer. I calmed myself down by convincing myself that this was just about business and I would be fine. At the end of the hall was a small room, dimly lit, with a table and chairs situated in the middle. Dreadlocks was sitting at the table, scratching his scalp with a pick. One of the guys with the rifles pulled out a chair for me.

As soon as I sat down, Dreadlocks said, "Look, I am gonna tell you this straight up. You a little white boy walking around Crown Heights, and you stand out around here. If you keep coming all the time, you gonna get noticed and make things hot for me."

By hot, he meant that my coming and going would bring the attention of the police. Police were bad for business. I thought he was going to cut me off.

"How much money you got on you?" he asked me.

Was I about to get robbed? Or worse?

I couldn't speak without stuttering and that was fine, because I didn't know how much money I had on me anyway. I just dug into my pockets and pulled out my wad of cash. I didn't count it, just handed it to him. Dreadlocks counted it, then reached under the table and brought up an unzipped duffle bag filled with bricks of weed.

He said the money I gave him was enough for a pound. But he gave me four pounds and also changed the price for me. I went from paying $60 to paying $50 an ounce, or $800 for a pound.

"The way I see it," Dreadlocks said, "if I give you more to sell, it will keep you busy, and you won't have to come around here so much."

I didn't say anything. But, I liked the idea of having more weed to sell in one shot. And it made sense. But, as it turned out, his plan didn't work. As fast as he gave it to me, was as fast as I could sell it.

With a pound at my disposal, I would almost immediately sell the amount of weed I needed to pay Dreadlocks his money. What was left over, I gave out on credit to guys I knew in other parts of Brooklyn, who then sold the shit to their circle of friends. That gave them the opportunity to get their own businesses started and created a base of dealers who otherwise would not have been able to afford the initial investment -- keeping them completely loyal to me.

By the time the next school year rolled around, I'd gone from selling ounces to selling pounds. I went from making a little over a hundred dollars a week to making thousands. I went from being someone's flunky to having kids in schools and even some adults in other neighborhoods selling for me. This was on top of what I was still dealing myself.

I was on my own, making thousands of dollars a week, getting respect -- even as a snot-nosed, white kid -- from big-time dealers. I came to believe, in those first months, that I was meant to be a drug dealer, that this life was my calling. It had all been so easy. What could go wrong?

CHAPTER 3

No one expected me to become a drug dealer. No one expected me to get into any kind of serious trouble at all. In fact, before I started dealing, I was probably one of the most sheltered kids in Midwood. I had my four older brothers looking out for me. My mom may have whipped my butt, but she watched my every move to make sure that nothing ever could happen to me.

When I was just 6 months old, my sister Rachel died two weeks before her 18th birthday. One day she complained about having chest pains. My parents took her to the doctor only to be sent home after being told that nothing was wrong. Two days later she died while visiting my mom's best friend. Turns out something was wrong. Rachel had an enlarged heart.

I don't know why the doctors didn't catch it or take her symptoms seriously. I don't know why they sent her home like that. I just know that, years later, when I was old enough to understand these things, my whole family was still devastated by the loss. Rachel, I was told, was like our family's angel. Sweet. Beautiful. Never got into any trouble. It's not hard to imagine that the time after her death was rough, especially on Ma.

Growing up, I was constantly being told that the only thing that got Ma through the rough time of losing her daughter was me. She only kept going for her baby. They say it's unnatural for a parent to have to bury a child, that there's no worse pain than losing your child suddenly.

I think that because of that loss, my mom became overprotective of me as a way to make sure she didn't lose another kid. Until junior high school, I wasn't allowed to go anywhere. While other kids were riding bikes in the street, spending the night over each other's houses or going to the park, I was kept close to home.

I loved my mom, but as I got older and saw that other kids were allowed to do more than I could, I resented being watched so closely. It was embarrassing to be treated like a baby, like some fragile doll, especially because I was a boy. And there was no hope of trying to get Dad to intervene. At some point, I think he let Ma obsess over me so she would leave him alone. The only thing that made life under Ma's watchful eye bearable was that eventually there were two places I could go to catch a break: Caitlin Pryor or Alyssa Russo's houses.

For the longest time those two girls were my only friends in the world and the only kids, not my brothers, I was allowed to see outside of school. They also happened to live right around the corner from one another.

I met Caitlin in elementary school. She was in kindergarten when I was in first grade for the second time from being left back. In fact, she was in the same class as my niece, Melissa who was just a few months younger than me. (Yeah, Ma and my older sister Sara were pregnant at the same time and had me and Melissa seven months apart). Even in first grade I was already skipping class. I would slip into Melissa and Caitlin's classroom just to hang out with them.

I remember noticing Caitlin because of her silky dark brown hair and pretty face. She would join my niece in talking to me every time I walked into their classroom. What I liked about Caitlin then, and what is still true about her to this very day, is that she was such a good girl. A true sweetheart. Something about her sweetness clicked with me instantly.

Alyssa Russo was a brown-eyed, brown-haired Italian beauty. I don't know when her family moved to the neighborhood, but I know they lived there as long, if not longer, than mine. But I didn't meet her in school. Our mothers were in the PTA together before I was even born.

One day my mother took me with her to visit her friend who lived a few blocks from our apartment. After an hour of us being there, Alyssa walked in. She was short and a bit thick-waisted and had the biggest titties I had ever seen. I was a little horn ball even back then and remember being mesmerized by her breasts. She was a couple of years older than me. Alyssa's family had a pool in their back yard. At some point during that visit, her mother said, "Alyssa, why don't you take Noah out back and show him the pool so me and Mrs. Braverman can talk."

While we were in the back yard, Caitlin showed up! That's how I learned that they were already good friends and lived just around the corner from one another. Alyssa and I became friends immediately, too.

For a long time Alyssa and Caitlin were my world. I am pretty sure the only reason my mother felt comfortable letting me go to either of their homes was because she knew their parents were as insanely protective of them as Ma was of me. I can't describe how much this surprised me. I thought I was the only kid kept on a crazy tight leash. It seemed to me we were the only three kids in all of Brooklyn who couldn't do anything. Which meant, of course, that we tried to sneak around and do everything.

When I was about 9 and Caitlin 8, I decided that she was my girlfriend. Our mother's always commented on how protective I was of her, and I said we were going to get married one day. Besides, we spent all of our time together, and I was the only boy she was even allowed to talk to. She was my best friend. The fact that I was her boyfriend was so obvious to me that I didn't even bother to ask Caitlin, or tell her. It was just a fact.

Of course, at that age, I had no idea what being boyfriend and girlfriend meant. But, I figured out that it had something to do with playing together every day, holding hands, and kissing when our parents weren't around. I was already sexually curious and wanted to try more things than just kissing. But, Caitlin, always the good girl, kept me in line. If I asked her to sit in my lap or lay down next to me and kiss (because I had discovered how good it felt to rub my 9 year-old-dick against someone), Caitlin would do it, but put a huge pillow between us to keep us from actually touching down there.

I don't mean to brag, but I was a very well-endowed even as a little boy. I showed my dick to Caitlin one day, hoping that she would be as intrigued by my hard-on as I was. Instead she was terrified. God knows what her mother told her would happen if she touched a boy's dick. But, Caitlin believed that my big dick would pop through my clothes, under her skirt, and right through her panties and make her pregnant.

Which is why she kept a pillow between us.

My relationship with Alyssa was totally different. She was like my big sister. Which didn't keep me from copping a feel of her tits here and there just out of innocent fun. But, it was never more than that. Alyssa was my conscience. My voice of reason, I guess you would call her. Alyssa was one of those people who always seemed like they were in a good mood. She was always playful and never seemed stressed. She was always laughing at something, which was like no one in my house.

I loved going to Caitlin and Alyssa's homes, not just because I got to get away from my mom, but also because their homes felt like real families - - like what I saw on television. I didn't see any arguments there. Their homes didn't seem crowded or dirty. No one seemed hungry or angry. There were no hand-me-downs. They had enough food. They had their own rooms.

And they adored me.

At Caitlin and Alyssa's, grown women would tell me I was handsome and charming. They asked me to stay for dinner and trusted me to walk around the block with their daughters like they trusted no one else. My entire world back then, before I quit school and ran into Slavic on the corner, consisted of my house, Caitlin's house, Alyssa's house and the little slice of our neighborhood that existed in between.

I never saw anything else.

It was a simple life. I had friends that loved me, and a mom who drove herself nearly insane trying to protect me. Caitlin still tells the story of the times we would tell my mother that we were going to play in the schoolyard. And since I was with Caitlin, my mom would let me go. But, without fail, after being at the park for 20 minutes or so, my mom would show up. She would claim she was running an errand or she'd be walking the dogs, Dutch our Brindle Pit-bull, Lucky our puppy Golden Retriever and our crazy-ass cocker spaniel, Skippy. I don't know why she bothered to lie. Everyone knew Ma was checking on me and would keep checking on me until I came home. Even when I was at Caitlin or Alyssa's house to play or have dinner, Ma would call a few times just to make sure I was okay.

I think her worst fear was losing me. And even after everything Ma did to watch over me and protect me, even though she kept my world narrowed down to a few blocks in Brooklyn, I took a turn no one saw coming. Not even the people who loved me and knew me best.

CHAPTER 4

You would think that since I was raised in a small apartment with four older brothers, two parents, a dog, ten cats, and an older sister with a daughter, that I would have constantly been surrounded by people and always had something to do. But most of my memories from being a little kid are of me being bored out of my fucking mind, trying to find someone to let me sleep with them since I never really had my own bed and watching my parents struggle to put a meal on the table. I remember how bad the house always smelled from the animals, but in all honesty, I was to blame for a few of them being there.

When I was a kid, I used to rescue strays from the back yard. I would throw a cat in the house, and my parents wouldn't even realize that it hadn't been there before. We would have had 20 cats, but one day when I snuck up on a little kitten eating out of the garbage, I startled it so much that when I wrapped my hands around it, the kitten flipped around and went Tasmanian devil on me. That cat scratched me so many times that my hands were bleeding from everywhere. From that day on my animal rescue days were over.

Sometimes things were so bad that we would have tuna fish and macaroni for dinner: except one can of tuna really didn't count when you had 2 bags of macaroni to mix it in. But I never really wanted to complain because I knew how hard they were trying to make something out of nothing.

Back in his day my dad was the man from what I hear. He served in the military during the Korean War and was even awarded medals for his service. Dad never talked to us kids about being in the war. The only thing he would say is that sometimes, when they ran out of food, he had to make soup in his helmet from ketchup and swamp water. That sounded disgusting to me, but Dad must have loved it because he put ketchup on everything. And, I mean everything. It was also no wonder why he never complained about the three-dollar dinners that we ate that tasted like crap.

I used to have bad dreams often when I was younger. Whenever that happened, I would wake up early and couldn't get back to sleep. Usually the only person up at that time of night would be my father.

"You had another one, huh?" he'd asked when he'd find me awake as he was getting ready for work. I didn't answer. I didn't have to, Dad could tell by the look on my face. I was probably five or six at the time. When our small apartment was packed with all my siblings, I'd fall asleep wherever I wanted. That was usually in the living room with my parents. And, I would nod my head yes. I never remembered my dreams completely, just that I was being chased by something in the dark.

Dad would pick me up out of bed and carry me into the bathroom to watch him shave and finish getting ready for work while everyone else slept. It wouldn't take long for the smell of his shaving cream and the sound of his humming some song I never recognized to make me forget about the nightmares.

"Am I gonna get to shave one day?" I'd asked once. Dad winked at me and smeared shaving cream across my nose.

"Don't be in a rush," he'd answered. "It's a damn hassle."

My favorite part was when his face was all clean and fresh looking. Dad would pull a green bottle out of the medicine cabinet, splash after-shave in his hands and then pat his face. The sharp smell of it, the scent that would always mean "dad" to me would fill my nose. Before he washed his hands, Dad would pat my face too. And then, before he left for work, Dad would put me in bed with Ma, kiss me goodbye and tell me he loved me.

As I got older and after he got sick, Dad changed. It was like he was just tuning out the world. The only thing he paid attention to was the television. Looking back, I think he became so withdrawn just to tune out my mom, and wound up closing himself off from everyone in the process. In all the noise and chaos of our home, Dad was almost always silent.

The only time my dad ever really got involved was when Ma nagged him to the point that he couldn't take anymore. And if Ma resorted to nagging Dad, it was because someone was in big trouble, the kind of trouble that came with a beating. And, I definitely got my share of those from Dad. He was big and strong and had no problem showing that when my mom got on him to get on us. The thing is I was never mad at Dad for those times he hit me. I understood Ma was really running the show. She was the one I was mad at.

Ma was the center of our lives at home. Whatever mood she was in was the mood of the whole house. When she was good, things were good. When things with Ma were going bad, it was horrible. Maybe everyone with brothers and sisters feels this way, but I felt like I was always getting hit when something went wrong, whether I did it or not. In a house with so many people, there was always something going wrong – always a mess somebody didn't clean up, something missing, too much noise, an argument happening, a sibling fight, a pet that no one walked – a million things for Ma to get upset about.

And because I was never allowed to go anywhere, I was usually the one catching the blame simply because I was there. As much as I know in my heart that my mother loved me, I caught some pretty awful beatings from her for things that weren't even my fault. I don't mean pussy spankings with her hands on my butt. I mean hard objects or cords, really anything not nailed down or too heavy for that woman to lift. I remember after getting hit with a telephone wire once asking myself: Why was I born? Why did they have me?

As an adult, I can look back and think that Ma must have been stressed from raising so many kids with no money. With my sister getting pregnant as a teenager, one of my brothers being mentally retarded and another brother committing armed robberies and stealing cars all over the neighborhood, we were more than a handful. Much of Ma's anger stemmed from us being poor. My parents struggled to make ends meet and to feed all of us even when Dad was working. Things definitely got worse in terms of Ma's moods when Dad got sick and couldn't work as much or eventually, not at all.

Sometimes, I looked at my parents when they were arguing or not speaking to each other and couldn't help but notice they had totally different personalities. I couldn't figure out how they even got together, much less had all of us with one another. From pictures, I know that they made a beautiful couple when they were young. They got married when she was 17 and he was 21. In those pictures, Ma had the figure of Olive Oil from the Popeye cartoons and Dad looked like Biff from those "Back to the Future" movies. They were young sweethearts and married for love. They moved to Midwood after having my oldest brother Jared and just stayed in the neighborhood for the rest of their lives.

Even though my parents fought a lot, and I mean a lot, it never got physical, except the one time she cracked him over the head with a lamp. But she was pregnant, so my Dad said that didn't count. One thing that stands out to me about them is that they never spent a night apart. Never. They were really old school when it came to values like that. And really, when I think of the fights between them, I remember they were always about money. Just money. We didn't have enough of it. Not enough money. Not enough food. No new clothes. And too many mouths to feed. No matter what was going on in the house, even the fun times, not having money was like this dark cloud that hovered over everything. It stained the walls. Clung to us like cigarette smoke and dampened our spirit.

Because we were poor, I didn't have a lot of toys. When I did get something, it was usually a small figurine one of my brothers bought, or stole, for me from the 99-cent store. Of course, it didn't matter to me where it came from. I was happy to have anything to play with. You would have thought those toys cost a million bucks by how I acted with them.

My brothers were always doing cool stuff like bringing me things or getting me Christmas or Hanukah presents in those years when my parents didn't really have money to do so. My brothers looked out for me. But, they were definitely characters too.

Jared, can only be described as a piece of work. He was a really eccentric guy. He spent some time, serving in the Army, and I think being in the military did something to him. Maybe it was Post Traumatic Stress Disorder or something like that. Anyways, some nights during the summer when I was a kid, Jared forced me, and my brothers, David and Adam, out to the park at midnight with our dogs. We would just stay up all night, not doing anything, until the sun came up and Jared let us go home.

My brother Scott, who was seven years older than me and the black sheep of the family, was almost never home. He was always getting himself into trouble with his friends around the neighborhood. Scott even ran a stolen car ring for a time. He also used drugs – the hallucinogenic kind.

One day, one of Ma's friends, Ms. Torresi, came to talk to Ma about Scott. Ms. Torresi and her husband ran a corner store nearby. A few days before she had stopped by, we'd heard that their store had been robbed, A group of five or six men wearing masks came in carrying guns. Mr. Torresi, at first, refused to give them any money and even had tried to go for the gun he kept behind the counter. The guys beat him bloody right in front of Ms. Torresi until she opened the cash register and the store's safe. Luckily, Mr. Torresi was just really banged up and not killed. But, Ms. Torresi came to see Ma because, even with masks on, she'd recognized one of the boys as Scott. He'd come into the store earlier that same day trying to buy beer. She'd remembered his ratty, stained Def Leppard t-shirt, ripped jeans, and his old boots. Black work boots that Ma recognized as the ones Dad was going to throw out, but Scott had begged to keep instead. And of course, Ms. Torresi knew his voice. He'd been going to that store all of his life. She was sure the other robbers were neighborhood boys as well. But Scott was the only one she'd been certain of. She came to Ma, not the police or even her husband because she knew Ma would handle it.

When Scott finally came home, Ma and Dad were waiting for him. I was sent to the bedroom, but heard it all through our thin walls.

"You could have killed him!" Dad screamed. "Do you know how you make me and your mother look? You fucking junkie! Stealing from hard-working people! And our friends!"

When he was really high or drunk, Scott found everything funny. And his laughter that night only made the inevitable beating come faster and last longer. At some point, my brother's screaming made me cover my ears. But the thing is, that didn't stop Scott. He kept right on getting high and robbing people to get money to get high. And taking those beatings like they were worth it.

Adam was born a perfectly normal baby but contracted spinal meningitis when he was 6 years old. It can be life threatening. In Adam's case, it left him what doctors called "emotionally disturbed" and what I, and others, called "mentally retarded." He was pretty much attached to my mother's hip after that. I don't know how Adam was able to tune out the awful beatings that we all got in the house from my mother and sometimes dad, but he did. Adam used to huddle in a corner looking at the wall with his hands over his ears, rocking back and forth. I know that all sounds were not blocked out by his hands, but it seemed to help him tune out from our reality.

David is the brother nearest to me in age, and I think for that reason he was the one I was closest to growing up. We played together. He used to draw things while I watched. At night, we used to do this thing where I would sing songs by Boy George, and David would be my audience. He would clap and cheer when I finished and tell me how good I was. We told each other that we would grow up and become stars.

My sister, Sara, was also a character. Like Scott, she fought with my parents a lot, but not because she got arrested or robbed anyone. Sara's offense was that she liked boys, and she liked sex. My parents threw her out of the house, the first time, after my niece was born. She and my mom always fought. Always. I think she got it even harder than Scott did.

It seemed like Ma and Sara always fought at dinner. Maybe because that was one of the only times Sara came home. One of the last and worst times they fought, I think I was seven. My niece, Melissa, was just six months younger, and she was at the dinner table with Adam and me. This particular fight started like Ma and Sara's fights usually started; with Ma asking Sara where she'd been all day and assuming that she'd been somewhere fucking a guy, who was probably black. Then Ma, reminded Sara that she already had a child that she needed to be taking better care of. And that she'd brought shame on the family by having a baby before she was married.

"I'm shaming the family? This family? Me? You know what, Ma, fuck you! Okay? So what I have a child. At least I feed her. At least I can take care of her. I don't send her out to beg for food like you do your kids! You should be ashamed of that! Just because you're married, it's okay that you had a bunch of kids you can't feed? I need to get a job? When did you ever fucking work or do a damn thing to help Dad put food on the table?"

As soon as the words were out of Sara's mouth, Ma was on her. They were pulling each other's hair. Melissa was crying. I was scared, but couldn't move. Somehow, Sara managed to shove Ma to the floor.

"You should've died. Why didn't God take you instead of Rachel?" Ma yelled. The look on Ma's face was so full of hate it's hard to believe she didn't mean it.

"Go to hell, Ma. Go straight to fucking hell." Sara was breathing hard from the fight, but there was also something sad in her voice. I could tell my sister wanted to cry. She added, "I wish I had died. Rachel was the lucky one. She didn't have to stay in this white trash shit-hole with you."

It was fast. Ma rushed up from the floor, grabbed the fork off the table, raised her hand over her head and swung down at my sister. Sara just managed to bring her own hands up in front of her face to catch the blow.

The next thing I knew Sara screamed and shoved Ma away. She grabbed her left hand with her right, but even from across the table, I could see the blood pouring through her fingers. The only reason I looked away for a second was to check on Adam, who by now was in the corner rocking with his hands over his ears and face to the wall. When I looked back, Ma was still gripping the fork as if she wanted to stab Sara again. Sara ran to the bathroom, still howling in pain with my niece crying and hanging onto her mother's leg.

Ma turned to let Sara pass. Her back was to me. I could see her shoulders moving up and down with each heavy breath. We were both motionless. Sara, through the locked bathroom door yelled, "I can't believe you stabbed me! I should have you arrested."

Dad, who'd been sitting in his chair watching television this entire time, finally turned towards us to see what was going on. He didn't seem worried or even angry. The look on his face was annoyance, maybe because things had gotten too loud for him to hear the TV show he was watching.

Sara took my niece and left, again, that night. What's funny is, in all the times that I watched them argue, all the times I heard our parents call her a slut to her face, and in all the times I saw Sara get hit, run away or get kicked out of our tiny little apartment, I never felt sorry for her. I never thought that she must be hurt or scared. I never worried about her. I thought that she was the lucky one for getting out. Sara was free.

CHAPTER 5

Ironically, growing up, I wanted to be a cop. Seriously. It was my dream for many years. I spent a lot of time thinking about what it would be like to wear that NYPD uniform and carry a badge, walk around the neighborhood with my gun on my hip and protect people. I don't know if it was from watching all those crime dramas like Miami Vice, and 21 Jump Street – but I had this idea that cops were cooler and more important than doctors or lawyers or anybody. They were the good guys. And, they had power. People had to do what they said. That definitely appealed to me. Cops didn't have to beg at food pantries or hope their friends would let them stay over for dinner. No one looked down on cops. Cops were heroes.

I knew that having that uniform and shiny badge would be something that would make my parents proud. It would make up for all the times I came home from school with a note for doing something wrong. I think even when I was very young, I could look around at my brothers and sister and know that Ma and Dad had very little to brag about.

Any time I saw police officers – driving in their patrol cars, standing inside a bodega getting coffee, twirling their night sticks, walking down the block – I watched them. I watched how they moved, demanding power and respect with every step they took, and I noticed how they talked to people with a cocky authority. Even more important, I noticed how people reacted to cops. In my neighborhood cops were put on a pedestal. People trusted and admired them. I wanted that trust and admiration. I wanted that confidence.

My love for New York's Finest lasted until I was about ten years old. By then Scott was definitely not one of the good guys. He was using drugs, stealing cars, committing armed robberies and causing all kinds of stress for our parents. I think, by then, I knew Scott could get arrested, and I even had a vague idea that he could be sent away to jail for the things he was doing. I didn't understand then that life is never really as simple as good guys and bad guys.

One night Scott and Danny, another street-running friend of his, were out to score some drugs. They were driving around the Marlboro Houses, a pretty rough housing project in south Brooklyn. Like I said, the 90s was a tense time in terms of race relations in Brooklyn, and two white boys driving around Marlboro stood out. Common sense would tell anyone that two white boys near the Marlboro projects at that time of night were either lost or up to no good.

So as luck would have it, the cops pulled Scott and Danny over, had them get out of the car and "assume the position" with their hands flat on the hood of the car, standing with their legs apart. The cops, two beefy Italian officers, patted them down and found nothing. Scott thought they were in the clear and thought the officers would warn them about how dangerous it is for white kids like them to be in the 'hood. He thought that as soon as the cops got in their car and rounded the corner, he and Danny would get back to looking for something to get high on.

"Is this your daddy's car, young man?" The older of the two officers asked Danny.

"Yes, officer," Danny answered in a more polite tone than Scott had thought he was capable.

"Did you steal it?"

"N....No officer. It's my car. My dad just helped with the down payment."

"I see," the older officer said while his partner was going through the inside of the car with a flashlight. "And what do you think your dad would say if he knew you were using the car he spent his hard-earn money helping you get to come down here and hang out with low-life, lazy niggers and gang bangers?"

Danny didn't answer so the officer turned to Scott.

"What are you guys doing over here? Buying guns? Drugs? What?"

"We have friends here, sir," Scott said. The words were polite, but the tone was Scott's own blend of wise-ass and sarcasm. The same tone that drove Ma crazy and pushed Dad into a rage on more than one occasion. The Italian cop was even less patient than our parents.

"Oh. You have friends here? You just drivin' around, trying to hang out with "yo' niggas"? You think you're one of them? You a homeboy?"

The old Italian cop's outburst made Danny's eyes go so wide with fear he contemplated making a run for it. Scott, who always found adults losing it when he frustrated them funny, laughed outright.

"Sammy, get out of the car!" The old Italian cop yelled to his partner.

"What's up, Dom?" Sammy asked after crawling out of the backseat. Officer Dom didn't answer. He opened the passenger-side door, rolled up the window, smashed down the lock, and slammed it shut. He stalked around the car and did the same with the driver-side door.

"You two smart-asses think you belong here? You think you got friends here? Let's see what the homies have to say about that!"

Scott and Danny watched confused, as the officer walked away from them, got back in their patrol car and drove off. It wasn't until Danny reached into his back pocket for his keys that he realized what Old Italian Cop Dom had done.

"He fucking locked the keys in the car!" Scott looked through the passenger window and saw the keys dangling from the ignition. Fucking pig. For all his wise-assery, Scott knew the cop had been right. Marlboro Houses was no place for a white kid to be at night, especially on foot. He thought about busting a window to get back in the car but there was nothing around strong enough to break the glass. Train station. They had to find a train station or maybe even a car service.

"Come on," Scott said to Danny as he hurried away from the car.

Marlboro Houses is made up of nearly 30 buildings that are sixteen stories high. On a summer night in Brooklyn, people are on the street to escape the heat of un-air conditioned apartments or boredom. They'd come outside to see what's going on for entertainment and couldn't be happier than to watch some white boys being harassed. It didn't take long for Danny and Scott to get noticed. The first few people they passed just stared or nudged the person nearest to them and pointed. For all the attention they got, it was like Martians had landed in Brooklyn. But that's how uncommon it was for a white person not in a blue uniform to be there.

Soon, my brother and his friend were being followed. First by one person. Then another. Then a few more. A group of young guys, mostly men.

"You lost white boy?" someone asked. But it wasn't really a question. It was a threat. The first of many. And after a few blocks, Scott spotted the entrance to the train station. There might be someone working in the booth or a transit cop on patrol, some kind of help, until the train came. But the group of guys following them had gotten larger – maybe 10 guys – and when Scott looked over his shoulder, he thought he saw at least one guy carrying a bat. Scott turned to Danny and gave his friend a slight nod. Without another word, they both started running for the train station. And maybe that's what the group wanted, because the yelling and teasing turned into cheering. Scott and Danny didn't make it far.

If you ask Scott today, he will tell you he just remembers getting hit from behind and falling. But, the falling felt like flying and he couldn't tell up from down. He fought back. Managed to get back to his feet. But then this burning feeling tore through his stomach and right side. It was a fire burning so hot it was actually cold. And Scott told himself to run, but his legs wouldn't move. He fell. And the gang of boys scattered.

I was too young to go to the hospital the night Ma and Dad got the call. It was days before I could see him. He'd been stabbed with what the doctor told my parents must have been something similar to Rambo's knife. It had torn his insides all to hell and Scott was fighting for his life. The first time I saw him in the hospital, hooked up to a lot of scary machines, I'd never seen him looking so frail, and with no promise that he'd recover. At that point, I realized just how much I loved my brother. I remember, every night while Scott was in the hospital, praying to G-d that he would live.

He lived. But, I don't know that I can say that he was ever okay after that. When he told us what happened, his anger wasn't at the guys who stabbed him. Not really. There was this fury at the white cops who left him stranded in the projects knowing what would happen. And the strange thing was, even at ten years old, I understood his rage. I think I felt it too. I felt it for him. With him.

As much trouble as Scott had been in before getting stabbed, in some ways his brush with death made him worse. He used more drugs. Committed more robberies. Even though it would be two or three years before I started my own life of crime, it was then that I decided that criminals aren't always the bad guys, and cops aren't all good just because they wear blue uniforms and a badge. Scott almost died because of the cops. Ma almost had to bury another child because of the cops. I will never forget the tears she shed worrying about my brother. Cops weren't heroes. Not to me anymore. And, in my eyes, after that, Scott could never be the bad guy. No matter what he did.

Funny thing, in the years to come, it would be Scott who would try to make me see that I'd gone too far, but by then, I'd turned him into one of my best customers. By then, he couldn't tell me a damn thing.

CHAPTER 6

"Did someone page me from this number?" I asked. It had gotten to the point that I was asking that question about fifty times a day. It wasn't unusual for regulars to call my beeper from their friends' houses. Often, with my permission, they would give out my pager number to cool people they knew who wanted a weed connect. So, when I saw an unfamiliar 718-number pop up on my pager's screen, I hadn't thought twice about calling it back.

"Is this Noah?" a very serious-sounding man's voice asked.

"Yeah, who this?" "I'm Detective Rogers with NYPD." Those words made it feel like the temperature dropped twenty degrees all of a sudden. The voice continued. "We've had an eye on your little drug operation for a while. But, don't worry. I don't care about that. Not right now. I need to talk to you about some friends of yours. Or clients, I should say. Kiki and Kimmy Cammarota.. They are in some trouble. We can look the other way about your situation if you just tell me whether or not these young ladies were with you last night. See, we think they were involved in a hold up at a bodega, but they say they were with you."

I slammed down the phone so hard, Rendell, whose house I was in at the time, glared up at me from the video game he was playing.

"What the hell is your problem?" he yelled.

I left without saying anything to him. As soon as I was outside, I started running. To where, I didn't know, I just needed to move. I ran out of breath on some random corner in my neighborhood and sat my ass down right on the curb. My heart was pounding. I felt like crying. Detective Rogers knew my name. He knew what I'd been doing. Maybe it was silly of me, but I thought with all the hiding and lying I'd been doing to my mom and dad to keep them from knowing I was dealing, I'd been pretty careful covering things up. Well, as careful as a 14-year-old could be. It had never occurred to me that anyone I sold to would talk to the cops about me.

NYPD knew about me. Had been watching me. But for how long? Had I sold to an undercover? Kimmy and Kiki were two of my best regulars. They were only in high school, but those girls smoked so much pot their brains were already fried. I was pretty sure they did other drugs as well. They spent hundreds of dollars a month buying from me. I never knew where they got their money. I didn't care where they got their money. But, I guess they figured I would just be their alibi since they were good customers.   Fuck them.

They gave my number to the cops and got me involved in some shit about armed robbery! What if the cops were watching me right now? What if they had been watching me all along just waiting to bust my ass? They could pick me up at any second and take me to Spofford, the juvenile detention facility up in the Bronx. Every kid in New York City heard stories about the bad asses who got sent to Spofford.

I tore the pager off my hip – the pager I'd lied to Ma about, telling her that my friend would help me pay for it if she just did the paper work, the pager she was thrilled for me to have so she could keep up with me now that I was allowed to leave the house, the pager Dad was furious I got because he said it made me look like a thug, the pager I needed because you just couldn't run a drug operation in 1994 without one and the pager that went off day and night with people needing me. I ripped it off my hip and smashed it on the sidewalk. Over the next couple of days I closed up shop. I had everyone working for me sell out their supply. I paid what I owed. Collected what people owed me. In the end, I had about $20,000 saved up. I kept the money where I knew no one would find it. Downstairs from our apartment there was a hallway that separated our apartment from the store on the first floor with a door that led down to the basement. The only time anyone went down there was when we blew a fuse from running the air conditioner and the microwave at the same time.   I hid all the money down there behind some dusty boxes and would just sneak down and get a little bit when I needed it.

With 20 grand stashed in my hiding place, I was all set for an early retirement from the drug game. I was afraid of getting arrested, going to jail, and having my parents find out what I was doing. They would be so ashamed of me. But, my brief brush with the law didn't scare me enough to send me back to school. It didn't even scare me enough to really stay out of trouble. It just turned me into a kid with a weed habit, a lot of money, and now a lot more time on his hands.

CHAPTER 7

Her lips tasted like cherries and she was wearing that expensive-ass perfume I bought her at Macy's. Lana (short for Svetlana) was always doing stuff like that for me. If I told her she looked pretty in something or that I liked a certain color on her, she made sure to wear it the next time I saw her.

I met her, like I met most people at that time in my life, while I was dealing. Lana was the older friend of one my regular customers, Carol, and the hottest chick I had ever seen. She was 17 to my 14, short with this tight body, and an ass that she always showed off in some body-hugging designer jeans. She had thick, long blonde hair and these blue-almost-purple eyes that were so beautiful, at first I thought they were contacts. They just seemed too amazing to be real.

Lana liked bad boys so I was perfect for her. When I met her, word was that her boyfriend was in jail for some felony assault charge. And, there I was, a good-looking kid who had spent the last few months selling a lot of weed and getting very popular because of it. I was a bad boy who was definitely tired of good girls. After all my failed attempts at trying to get into Caitlin's pants, I gave up. She and Alyssa didn't smoke weed or party at all – not like my new friends. And neither of those girls was interested in having sex with me. After I began selling, I spent less and less time with them and more and more time getting high with my new crew of guys and chasing girls who actually wanted to find out what was going on in my pants.

I had been afraid that when I stopped selling, some of my new friends would disappear. But, in some ways, I became even more popular. I had money and was more than willing to spend it on people. So, even though I wasn't selling weed, I was still buying and sharing weed. And drinking. And going to every party in the neighborhood.

The day after Detective Roberts called, I got high and stayed high. And, I continued looking for people to get high with me. Lana was the perfect companion. We started flirting with each other right after Carol introduced us. And any time either of us was with Carol, we would ask about the other and send messages until Carol just had enough of it and made us talk on the phone. After that, we were inseparable. We hung out with the same friends at the same parties. She got high as much, if not more, than I did.

And we enjoyed getting to know each other. In the beginning, she talked a lot about missing her boyfriend, Roberto. But the more we hung out, the less he seemed to come up. Until, one day we kissed. And then on another day, we kissed again. Then she let me touch her tits under her shirt. Once, I snuck over to her house while her mom was at work, and she let me finger her on the couch in their living room, which excited the shit out of me.

One day we were at Carol's house hanging out. Carol and some of the other guys were in the living room smoking weed and watching MTV. Lana and I could hear Nas, Snoop Dogg and Biggie Smalls' music videos through the walls of Carol's mom's room where we'd gone to fool around. At first I thought we would do our usual. Kiss. Suck on each other's necks. I would feel her up and finger her until she got all wet and told me to stop. And, maybe, just maybe, I could convince her to play with my dick or let me hump on her through my jeans.

She smelled so good, like honey and flowers mixed with a smell that was just hers. Like rain. Soon, we were kissing and she was on top of me. Her jeans and panties gone and she was just grinding on me. I could feel how hot and wet she was through my jeans and she was moaning through our kissing. I'd never heard her sound like that before. Then her whole body spasmed so hard, she broke our kiss and just buried her face in my neck. I didn't want to ask her what happened because I didn't want her to know I was a virgin, but I was pretty sure she came.

"I want you inside me," she whispered in my ear and started undoing my pants and pulling off my shirt. Still straddling me, Lana got my jeans and boxers down to my thighs and I pushed and kicked them off the rest of the way, as they crumpled to the carpet. She twisted out of her shirt. God, her tits were amazing. Not big, but with huge nipples that got hard and tight when I touched them. I licked one, then the other. Lana must have liked it because she whispered my name and rolled us over until I was on top of her.

I had no idea what the hell to do. Thank God she was taking the lead and used her hand to guide me. It took a few strokes for me to work my way inside her, but when I did, I closed my eyes and the world disappeared. To be inside her, that heat, that hot, slippery grip on my dick was like nothing else I had ever felt. Again, I didn't want her to know I was a virgin, so I did my best imitation of what I'd seen in porn and the rest was just instinct. I remember her repeating my name like she was saying a prayer. I remember her wrapping her legs around my waist and using her hands on my ass to pull me into her again and again. And I remember cumming hard and screaming God or Fuck or God and Fuck or something like that, because I'd never felt anything that good run through my body before.

In all honesty, it's probably taken longer for you to read this than it took for the whole thing to happen. It was just a few amazing moments that would stick in my mind forever. When I could move again, I managed to pull out and roll off Lana. She rolled onto her side and faced me, kissing my shoulders and tracing her fingers across my hip.

"That was fucking amazing," I said, hoping she would agree. With her eyes closed, she nodded her head yes, and rolled into me even closer, and started kissing my chest. I wanted to ask her if she came. I wanted to ask her if she was on the pill 'cause I nutted inside her. I wanted to ask how long until we could do it again because when she ran her lips over my nipples, I was starting to get hard again.

But, before I could ask anything, I felt something warm and wet against my leg. And felt it spreading.

"What's that?" I asked scooting back from Lana to see. She looked down too as we screamed. The white bedspread and white sheets that had gotten tangled under us were covered in blood. A lot of blood. More blood than I had ever seen. I jumped off the bed to get away from it and to figure out where it was coming from. Then I realized it was on Lana. On her thighs. She was bleeding!

"Oh my god! We gotta get you to the hospital!" I screamed, as I stumbled around the room looking for my clothes. In my mind a scene was already playing out where I had to explain to doctors, then my parents, then the police and maybe even a judge how Lana and I had sex and it was my first time so I didn't know what I was doing and I clearly broke something in her that made her bleed to death. Dressed, I turned to find Lana still sitting on the bed looking at me as if I had lost my mind.

"Can you just go get Carol and tell her I need a tampon or a pad?" she said. I could tell that she was trying not to laugh at me. "Tampon? You on your period?" I said, relieved.

"Uh....no. I just had sex for the first time. Sometimes girls bleed."

"First...You were a virg-"

"I mean, I've done everything else. Just not this. And my boyfriend is coming back soon. So I just wanted to do this with you before he got here."

And she giggled.

And her blue-almost-purple eyes sparkled and I didn't care about the mess or her boyfriend coming back or how we were going to hide it from Carol's mom. I just wanted that laugh, those cherry kisses, me inside her, and her praying my name like she did when I was making love to her.

Two weeks later, Lana's bad boy came home from prison and I never heard from her again.

CHAPTER 8

Like Rendell promised on the phone, I found the front door of our friend Kathy's house on Avenue H unlocked for me. Now that I wasn't dealing, returning pages, picking up money, dropping off weed to the guys working under me or going to school, I was free to hang out with my friends like I never had before. When I was dealing, everything, even going to parties was about work. So, five minutes after Rendell called, I bolted from my house and started over to Kathy's.

Kathy was a girl I'd met in junior high. We were just about the only two white kids in our class. Back then, she was a chunky girl with a mouth full of braces. She was sweet to me and we clicked right away. Since we lived so close to each other, we passed by each other's houses a lot and after I dropped out, we kept in touch. Her house was a free-for-all. Her parents openly drank and did drugs in front of Kathy and her friends. So, Kathy basically got to do whatever she wanted and they never said a word. Kathy's place was one of the spots I went to relax, bag up weed, and count money.

"Yo, Rendeeeell!" I called when I walked through the door into the living room and didn't see anyone. The living room opened up onto a huge, sunny kitchen, but no one was in there either.

"Kathy?"

No one answered. I thought about looking for them upstairs, but I figured maybe they had run to the store or something. Even though I'd been to Kathy's a few times, I was uncomfortable being there alone. I decided to wait on the front porch for them when I heard something, voices maybe, that made me stop. I looked around the kitchen. Across from the doorway that led back into the living room, and sort of obscured by the refrigerator, was another door I'd never noticed before. It was open and obviously went to a basement. I walked over to it and heard Rendell.

"Hand me the other spoon," I heard him say.

I started down the wooden stairs that creaked with each of my steps.

"That you, Noah?" Kathy called up.

"Yeah, it's me, sweetheart."

When I reached the bottom of the stairs, Kathy was looking in my direction and smiling. She was sitting on an old ratty couch next to Rendell.

Then it hit me that Kathy seemed to be changing, slimming down and becoming quite the hottie. I quickly changed my train of thought, reminding myself that she was just a friend.

Hunched over a coffee table was Rendell, focused on the two spoons he was holding. Looking sloppy as usual with his dark beady eyes, he reminded me of a rat going after some cheese. When Kathy turned her attention back to him, the look on her face reminded me of a little kid on her birthday when someone was about to give her a present. She was even rocking back and forth like she could hardly wait.

"What you doin' down here?" I asked as I walked over to them. Upstairs was sunny and air-conditioned. The basement was dark and musty, not the kind of place you'd want to be in at night alone. Why would they hang out down here instead of upstairs? Then, I saw a bag with a white rock the size of a marble in it. "I'm breaking up the coke," said Rendell.

"You got to put it in a spoon, then use the back of another spoon to crush it until it breaks into powder." As he spoke, he did it. I knew Rendell and Kathy did coke. I had probably even been around when they were high on it, but I'd never seen the process and had never done it with them, even though they'd asked me to.

Even though I smoked a lot of weed, a part of me didn't want to try 'real drugs'. Something about cocaine just seemed more serious to me than weed or liquor. Cocaine, from what I'd seen, got you the kind of high that drove you out of your mind. The kind of high my brother Scott got, that out-of-control shit type, that made people rob and steal for it. Dealing had kept me too busy to lose control like that. But, I wasn't dealing now. And as soon as the thought went through my mind, I realized that was why Rendell had asked me over. He had a straw cut into three pieces and gave me one.

"You go first, since you the virgin," he said as he laid out the crushed up coke onto an empty CD case and then, with his New York State driver's license, made six lines out of the pile. "Two for each of us," he said.

"Why two lines?" I asked as I sat down on the couch.

"If you sniff with just one nostril, you'll make the other one jealous," he said. "Don't want to leave one out."

Kathy laughed. Rendell smiled. And they both looked at me. Stared at me, really. Silently telling me to hurry up. The first snort burned. And so did the second. But within a few minutes the burning stopped. I didn't really feel anything. But then, I noticed this nasty dripping from my nose down the back of my throat. I told them I thought my sinuses were fucked up or something and I was going to spit it out.

"NOOO!" They both yelled at me like I was about to walk in front of a bus.

"The dripping is the best part," Kathy explained. "Just sit back and relax. Let it happen." As if to lead by example, she slumped back into the couch and closed her eyes. I swallowed the dripping and tried to let it happen, whatever it was. No one was talking. I could tell from their smiles, that something good was happening for them. But I started thinking that the coke might fuck me up real bad. What if I overdose my first time? I wasn't used to the stuff and I just put it right up my nose. What if it got in my brain? Could it make me have one of those aneurysm things where the blood vessels in your brain just explode? Or, what if we got caught? The thought got me so panicked I started grinding my teeth.

Soon it was my turn to snort again. Even with all those thoughts crowding my head, I welcomed it. When I snorted the lines the second time, there wasn't the burning like before. There was a rush of warmth. And where I had been anxious just a few minutes before, I was excited for no reason I could name. I had a sudden burst of energy. I could hear my heart beating in my ears. My entire body was tense like I was ready to fight, defend myself. And my mind was racing. I was thinking up all these new ways to make money. And then, I realized, I could sense everything. We were in the basement, but I just knew I heard someone at the front door or maybe walking around upstairs. Who was it? Clearly not friends. Friends wouldn't be that quiet, trying to sneak up on us.

"You hear that?" I asked Rendell, jumping up from the couch and going to the bottom of the stairs.

"Hear what? You bugging right now? I ain't heard nothing." Rendell said. "Ain't nobody here but us."

I heard something. A creaking noise. Light footsteps. Someone was upstairs.

"I shoulda brought my gun." I said as I turned to Kathy who was still sitting on the couch, eyes closed like nothing was going on, "Sweetie, you got a piece in the house? I'm gonna see who the fuck is playing games at the door!"

"What? Gun? What the fuck you need a gun for?" Kathy screeched.

"Protection," I announced. When I started selling a lot of weed, this guy in the neighborhood we called Dog, cause he was always looking for pussy, sold me a piece.

"You makin' money now," he had told me, "and you don't really have a crew runnin' wit' you. Eventually one of these other dealers is gonna try to test you. What you gonna do?"

I didn't have an answer. Never thought about it before. Dog pulled out a chrome gun with a black rubber handle. It was small but to me, it looked powerful. When Dog put it in my hand, I felt like The Man. He let me hold it for him if I promised to bring it to him immediately if he ever needed it. For weeks, though, I kept offering him money for the thing and after a while, I wound up giving him $400 for the right to borrow it any time I needed.

For protection. And right then, in that basement, with my first taste of coke roaring through my veins, I felt like I needed protection. What if the cops were still following me? What if another drug dealer was there to make sure I didn't get back in the game? Who the fuck was upstairs and why were they sneaking around like that?

"Coke makes you paranoid." Kathy said, as she came over to me, put her arms on my shoulders and moved me back to the couch. "No one is at the door. That's the good shit fucking with you, Noah. Try to calm down and just ride it. Don't fight it. Just relax and let it happen".

It wasn't easy. I liked the heat and the rush coke gave me. I liked the jolt my body felt, like I could do anything. I remember thinking, 'This must be how Superman feels. Invincible. Alive.' I couldn't get enough of that feeling.

But, no matter how much I used it and no matter how much I practiced focusing on the rush, that paranoia – the feeling that somewhere nearby someone was trying to hurt me or take what was mine – never went away.

CHAPTER 9

After that, to put it mildly, I couldn't get enough coke. Even with that quiet roar in the back of my mind telling me that something or someone was out to get me, I couldn't stop. Something in me just clicked when I was on it. I had all this energy. My mind was racing, but clear. The shit at home that got me down; the poverty, the having to deal to support my family and worrying about getting busted, didn't matter after a few bumps. And even though I was always looking over my shoulder, coke made me feel like I could handle anything or anybody who made a problem for me. I loved coke.

Pretty soon, Rendell and Kathy got sick of me running through their shit. So, Rendell started taking me with him when he went to see the woman he copped from. Dianna was the party girl in the neighborhood. Well, she wasn't really a girl. She had two kids, one of them a daughter almost my age and a very young son. But Dianna loved to party. I think she, at one time or another, worked at every dive bar in our part of Brooklyn and had a reputation for knowing how to get any drug you wanted. Quickly. But only if you were willing to share.

Dianna and her kids had a small apartment on Coney Island Ave. No matter what time of day it was outside that place, it was always busy and always night inside. Dark. There was always a knock on the door. Always people coming, whispering something to Dianna, and leaving with whatever package they'd come to collect.

My earliest memory of Dianna is of her opening her apartment door and poking her head out to get a look at who Rendell had brought with him. It reminded me of a turtle looking out of its shell – that kind of caution.

Her blond hair was pulled back in a tight ponytail and her green eyes seemed to look right through me. She was tall and heavyset, which struck as me odd because everyone knew she did a lot of coke. I don't know what it was that she saw –maybe that I was just a kid or another customer to pay for her high – but she smiled, laughed even, and welcomed us in.

"This is my boy, Noah. He cool," Rendell said.

"Hello," Dianna sang, more than she spoke it and kissed us both on our cheeks -- kind of like the way a mother would. It was then that I noticed her cigarette in one hand and her beer in the other. We moved around her small apartment to the tiny couch and sat down. Rendell and Dianna started talking to each other but I don't remember what about. All I remember was being afraid that this woman – this adult wasn't gonna help me get any coke because I was a kid. As I waited for her to tell me no, I worked on what I would say to convince her. I was so deep in my thoughts that I almost didn't notice that Rendell and Dianna had stopped talking and were staring at me.

"It ain't free, nigga. Give her yo' money," Rendell said, rolling his eyes at me. Apparently, they had worked it all out.

I came to learn that at Dianna's this is how it worked: You told her what you wanted and gave her the exact amount of money for it with a promise to share or you gave her some money for her to get her own. Then, she made a phone call. A few minutes later, there would be a knock on the door. It was as easy as ordering a fucking pizza.

I had no reason to worry about Dianna having a problem with my age. Her house was where a lot of kids went to party. You could get high right there in her living room, which was safer than trying to hide out on a rooftop, in an abandoned building, the park, or the back of a school where cops could bother you.

After we did some lines right there on her coffee table, our highs were in full swing. We were talking loudly and laughing about nothing really. I bent down to do my third line and when I came back up, this little boy, maybe about 8 or 9, was standing in front of me, just staring. He was blond and had Dianna's green eyes; the same eyes that felt like they were looking right through me. The way Dianna and Rendell kept right on talking and snorting, I thought that I was the only one who could see this little boy in the room and figured that the coke had finally sent me over the edge.

"Hey, my little man, when'd you get home?" Dianna finally said to the boy. My heart, that had stopped, started to beat again. He didn't answer. He just kept staring right at me.

"This is my new friend, Noah. Noah this is Kevin, my son."

"Sup, bro," I heard myself say to the kid and felt myself nod at him.

"You want another beer now, Mom?" Kevin asked Dianna, but he was still staring at me.

"Yeah, sweetie. Bring three of 'em."

He walked the few short steps to the kitchen. I heard him open the fridge, clink the beer bottles and rummage around for the opener in a drawer. Rendell and Dianna kept talking about nothing and everything. I felt like I had gotten caught doing something I wasn't supposed to be doing. I wanted to leave. I wanted to get away from Rendell, Dianna and her kid, that dreary apartment, and those sad green eyes that seemed to say: please leave my mom alone. Kevin brought us our beers and set them on the table. Then, as if he knew his mom would tell him to do so, he just headed down the hall to the back of their apartment where, I assumed, the bedrooms were.

"Nice meeting you," he called back to me and waved.

More coke and a few beers later, Rendell said he had to go. Which of course, meant I had to go. We were quiet walking down Coney Island Avenue. We were running out of our highs and had already run out of things to say to each other. However, I wanted to ask Rendell when he was coming back to Dianna's. I was already thinking about my next high. I wanted to ask, but something told me not to. For some reason, I didn't want Rendell, or anybody else, to know that coke wasn't just fun for me. There were moments when I was pretty sure I needed it, moments when I had to have it.

The need scared me.

So, I didn't ask. I decided that I would come back to Dianna's tomorrow, when I knew Rendell had shit to do in Queens. I decided that I would buy from Dianna for myself and give her a little something extra to cop for me and to keep it quiet. The thought of my next high made me happy. I started to hum some random melody as I walked down Coney Island Avenue.

CHAPTER 10

The first time me and Kathy kissed we weren't high. Not yet, anyways. We were alone in her house, her parents were gone like they were always gone, and Rendell had gone to get us some coke from Dianna. Anyone in the neighborhood could tell you that Kathy had gone from being a chubby ugly duckling with braces, to a hot girl. Kathy had long, thick fire red hair, perfect breasts, and thick hips with just the slightest chub on them and an almost perfect tight waist and that was a good thing in my eyes.

Since the thing between Lana and me had fizzled out when her man got out of prison, I flirted with Kathy a lot. More as a joke than anything else, because I didn't think she saw me as anything other than a brother. Kathy, just like Lana, loved bad boys and was going out with this older dude who was away doing a year for a robbery.

The day of the first kiss, we were on her couch watching television. For some reason, we always watched Scarface (me and Rendell's choice) or MTV's The Real World (her choice) when we were getting wasted. I don't know how or why it happened, but somehow Kathy decided to lay her head in my lap.

I didn't think anything of it at first, but I was wearing sweats. And hell, I was a just-turned-15-year-old, horny kid. After a few minutes, I realized I was getting a boner from her being so close to my dick. I tried to shift my body in a way where her head was more on my thighs so the hard-on would either go down or she wouldn't feel it, but Kathy kept scooting her head right back to my lap. It took about twenty minutes of me trying to keep my dick from pressing into the back of her head before I realized she was doing it on purpose!

When I stopped moving, she rolled over and looked up at me. She brought her hand up and started rubbing the shaft and head of my dick through my sweatpants and boxers. Then she straddled me. I will never forget the feeling of her sitting on me like that, the two of us pressed together. We kissed. I am sure I must have French kissed before Kathy. But, probably not well or at least never in a way that I liked because Kathy's tongue exploring my mouth – the taste of her and then her ending the kiss by sucking on my lips – is the first French kiss I really remember. The kiss was so hot I couldn't do anything but grab her waist, grind my erection into her and kiss her passionately. Just when I was about to put my hand up her shirt, we heard Rendell's footsteps on the porch. Kathy jumped off my lap and I ran to the bathroom to wait for my hard-on to go down, laughing all the way.

For the rest of the day, the only thing on my mind was how I was getting my freak on with Kathy, one of the hottest girls I knew, before Rendell interrupted us. I wondered how far we would have gotten. I wondered if Kathy wanted to pick up where things left off. The anticipation was killing me.

As soon as Rendell left us in the room alone again, I got my answer. Kathy whispered to me that she wanted me to sleep over that night after Rendell left. We spent so much time together, that really, no one would think anything as I practically lived there anyway, since life at home just sucked.

For the first time since I'd tried coke, I couldn't wait for us to come down from our highs, so Rendell would leave. It seemed like days, and it was dark outside by the time he finally headed home. It took every bit of willpower I had to wait for Rendell to get down the porch steps, before I started chasing Kathy through the house and into her room. At one time Kathy's bedroom had been a sun porch. I loved her room, with all its windows and her glow-in-the-dark stars and the moon she had on her ceiling. It really felt like you were sleeping under an open sky.

We turned on the radio, not to set a romantic mood, but to keep the neighbors from hearing the sounds we knew we were about to make. All of a sudden, Boyz II Men's "I'll Make Love to You" came through the speakers. That was my cue. I kissed her cheek, then her neck and finally her mouth. I worked my way down and lifted her shirt up with my teeth until I could kiss her silky belly. She squirmed and giggled. I made myself take my time. I wanted to make her moan.

I caressed her breasts more gently than I had ever touched a girl before. I licked her nipples, taking turns with each, until Kathy began to squirm underneath me. I'd never eaten a girl out before, but I knew I wanted to do it for Kathy. I wanted to know her inside and out. I licked the inside of her right thigh and began kissing my way up. When Kathy realized where I was headed, she moaned and opened her legs to make room for me. I had no idea what I was doing. There was no planned technique. I just kissed her, licked her, sucked her, let her moan and the tight circling of her hips grinding against my face guided me until she started squeezing the back of my head and telling me not to stop. Suddenly, she was shaking and her pleasure exploded. I loved the way she tasted.

I rose up, positioned myself over her, and worked myself inside her. She was wet and welcoming, moaning my name as I entered her. I felt her move her hips up to meet mine and I lost myself in how good it felt. Kathy let out a little gasp every time I hit a certain spot inside her. So, I matched her rhythm and kept hitting it.

"I'm cumming. I'm cumming," she kept repeating in my ear. Her eyes rolled up into her head. Her tiny hands gripped my biceps and she shuddered against me. Only then did I feel free to really go for mine. The release shook me. I let out a roar that I was certain the neighbors heard and just collapsed on top of her. I couldn't move. Didn't want to. In that room of windows and sky, feeling Kathy's breath against my ear, and her hands rubbing circles on my back, I fell into a sleep certain that I'd discovered the difference between fucking and making love.

CHAPTER 11

I knew Ma, Dad, and my brothers could hear me. I knew Scott would probably make fun of me, and I didn't give a shit. That's how deep in it I was. I was in the shower singing the corniest love song ever made, "I Wanna Know What Love Is" by Foreigner. And, I couldn't help myself. Kathy gave me a feeling I'd never had before. Of course I loved my dog, my family, my close friends, but Kathy was something else. Just the thought of seeing her made me get up early in the morning.

I couldn't wait to get over to her house. Standing in the shower, rinsing the soap off again, the thought of seeing her, possessing her, telling her that she was my girl was such a turn on. The rush she gave, the thrill I got making love to her, making her moan, hearing her say she loved me, was similar to the power I felt dealing. After my shower, I rushed to my room, humming because I had that damn song stuck in my head. Luckily, none of my brothers were home. But, Ma was, as usual, watching her TV. Suddenly she popped up in my doorway just as I was pulling on my jeans. She was wearing an old ratty police shirt (I think because she thought wearing it would keep us kids in line), worn-out pink pajama bottoms and her baby blue bedroom slippers that were darkened with dog shit around the edges.

"What's going on with you?" she asked. "You been walking around here smiling and singing lately. You seem different. Happy."

I knew what she was really asking me. She wanted to know if I had a girlfriend. And since every time I left the house I told her I was going to see

Kathy (who Ma loved because of her sweetness), I knew she suspected exactly what was going on. Ma would have been okay with it because she liked Kathy's parents, but I wasn't going to tell her anything. This love was all my business. I pulled a t-shirt over my head, slipped past Ma and kissed her on the cheek.

"You better not be having sex -- you're just a baby!" she said, turning to watch me skip across the living room floor.

"Don't worry Ma. I'm not doing anything wrong." I called back to her, as I slipped out the door to go get high with some friends. Like always, I was lying. And, like always, she pretended to believe me.

As I sat on the steps in front of my apartment building waiting, a familiar voice called out.

"Hey, Noah! Wassup? Where you been?"

I looked up to see four kids I knew from the neighborhood: a really short girl named Tasha we nicknamed Shorty, a girl we called KTU, Rendell, and one of my old customers, Lee. Together, the four of them had a reputation on the block for causing trouble. They would hang out at the subway station nearby and rob people for money to buy weed.

"Yo, we lookin' for some herb. You got?" Lee called out to me. The other three gathered in so close I could feel them hoping I had something on me.

"I was just here waiting on some of my boys so we could go somewhere and smoke this blunt," I said, still sitting on the step and looking up at them. "But we can go smoke it instead".

"Let's go to that school yard and do this then. You down?" said Tasha. She was so loud; I was always surprised that a voice so big came out of such a little person. It's as if someone forgot to tell her that she was practically a midget. Shorty was one of those people who just didn't give a fuck. She smoked, drank, flirted and robbed fools. She did things you just would never expect a girl that small to do.

We walked over a few blocks to P.S. 99 and sat on the steps around back to smoke the blunt. It might seem weird that an empty schoolyard is where we'd go to smoke pot, but in our neighborhood that's where shit like that went down. The walls were covered in graffiti, and the ground was covered in broken beer bottles, used condoms, and if you looked hard enough, you could probably find a random crack vial or a broken syringe lying around.

I lit up the blunt, took a couple of puffs and was about to pass it to Rendell when this beat cop who looked like he'd just gotten out of the academy five minutes ago came strolling into the school yard. My first thoughts were, "Fuck me! I knew it. I knew the cops were watching me. I knew they were going to catch me doing something stupid." Panicking, I threw the blunt away as the cop came over, completely forgetting that it was still lit. The officer smelt it burning and quickly found it right there on the ground. I was having visions of the beating my parents would give me after they got called to come and get me from the precinct.

"Whose is this?" the officer said, picking the blunt up. No one said anything and the officer took a turn staring at each of us.

"Well, whoever it is, you kids need to find somewhere else to smoke." Then he handed me the blunt and walked away. When he was out of sight, we cracked up laughing and did just what he suggested. We moved to a different part of the schoolyard, smoked that blunt quickly and went our separate ways.

Feeling buzzed, the last thing I wanted was to return to the cooped up reality waiting for me in my crowded apartment. I walked from the schoolyard towards home. The thought of listening to Ma's questions about where I'd been. Or having to hear her complain about something my brothers had done. Or her talking about her latest problems with my sister Sara, on top of Dad's unbearable silence, made me crazy. Even worse was the thought of catching a beating for not going to school or some other shit I did. Going to Dianna's for some coke was a much better option. I walked to a nearby car service and got a ride to Coney Island Avenue.

"What can I do you for, cutie?" were Dianna's first words when she opened the door.

"Can you call your guy for me? I got a hundred on me and…and here's twenty for you."

We sat and shot the shit for a while. She said she was doing fine and that Kevin was at a friend's house for dinner. Her daughter, Ariela, was also out for the night. As usual, there was the familiar knock on the door. I won't lie. The anticipation of the coke man bringing my shit made my heart race. My dick even got a little hard. But when the door opened, it wasn't Dianna's guy. It was Tasha and KTU. Apparently, Tasha's mom had gotten evicted, and KTU's mom had kicked her out of their apartment. Both were crashing with Dianna. As soon as I saw them, I knew that any hope of keeping Rendell from finding out that I was buying coke from Dianna without him was gone. My secret was out.

CHAPTER 12

"Hope youse are hungry! I got Chinese food from that place you like, Ma. And I got that extra sauce for Da-" My father's punch stuffed the rest of my words back down my throat. Even if I'd seen it coming, with all his weight behind it like that, my Dad would have put me on my ass. I went down. The dinner I'd been so happy to bring home exploded across the floor. The smell of rice, chicken and egg rolls mixed in my head with the taste of my own blood and the throbbing in my chin and lip.

"I knew you would turn out rotten," my father said. I'd fallen to my hands and knees. My head was still spinning from the blow, but I guess the vulnerable position I was in was too tempting. He kicked me, burying his boot right below my rib. The world went black for a second and spots raced before my eyes. The kick rolled me over on to my back. As I lay there looking up at him and Ma I realized my brother Adam was there too. I hadn't noticed him at first. Not until he'd run to cower in the corner. I'm not sure who I felt worse for, me for taking the beating or him for having to watch.

"I let your mother spoil you. I let her baby you, 'cause God knows the woman been through enough. Even though I knew better."

"Wha.... What'd I do? Why?" I managed. Ma, still standing over me, sobbed and threw something at me. I tried to dodge it and the sudden movement caused a horrible pain to shoot through my side. Whatever my mother tossed landed softly on my chest anyways. Before I looked down at it, I knew what it was. They'd found my drugs, just a little weed I'd been keeping in the house for my own use.

"When your mother agreed to let you get that damn pager, I knew' only drug dealers and doctors wear pagers. I knew you were up to something. But, I let her convince me it was just something you kids were into nowadays. Bullshit. The money. The new clothes. That ain't come from somewhere good. Not from no honest hard work. I knew it. Get up!"

I didn't move. Partially because I couldn't, but mostly because I didn't want to. I knew if I got to my feet it would just be a reason for him to knock me down again. Dad grabbed the collar of my shirt and yanked me off the floor. He slammed me against the wall right next to the front door. I was crying. Ma was crying. And as my father put his hands around my throat, out of the corner of my eye, I saw Adam in the corner hitting his head against the wall and whimpering.

"Look at me!" my Dad ordered. And I did. "Bad enough Scott running in the streets, a damn junkie, you think I'm gonna let you deal drugs out of my house? Under my roof? Who the fuck do you think you are? You think you're some big man 'cause you're selling dope?"

He squeezed. Even with Ma's help, I couldn't pry those hands off me. I thought he was really going to kill me. But, for some reason, Dad let go on his own and just started slapping me across the face. I tried blocking, but it was like the hits were coming from everywhere. I slid to the floor, which just made him kick me. I respected him too much to fight back and defend myself. And I was afraid that would just make it worse. When he finally got angry enough to get out of his chair, Dad was a storm you just had to endure until it ended. He told me what a worthless piece of shit I was. How I'd broken my mother's heart. My face was covered, but at some point I think between the punches and kicks, Dad spit on me. And when he was done, I heard him walk away and slink down in his chair, click on the TV and flip through channels. His job was done.

Then there was Ma. I heard her knees crack as she sank to the floor and kneeled over me, touching me tenderly on my back.

"I don't understand this, Noah. I just don't." She was still crying. "why would you do this!"

Funny thing, I wasn't dealing, but I already took the beating for it and in the back of my mind I knew that even though I had stopped, I was spending money like water, and it wasn't going to last long. I needed to make money and selling drugs was the only way I knew how.

"You won't sell this stuff and live under our roof, Noah. I won't have it in my house."

I finally took my hands away from my face and looked at my mother. Her eyes were puffy from crying. She looked sad. Maybe even hurt and disappointed. But there was also anger there. She got up and went to join my father in front of the television. I got up and started to clean up the dinner I'd bought my family with the drug money they'd pretended to know nothing about. Then it dawned on me that if they'd found my stash of weed, they must have also found the $200 I'd hidden with it. Funny, how Dad hadn't thrown that at me. Fine. If I couldn't sell drugs while living under their roof, I would move out.

I gave it some time, but had to go back and get the rest of my stuff, so there I was a couple of days later. I stuffed the last of my clothes into a duffel bag Ma stood in the doorway. I refused to look at her, but I could hear her crying and wheezing like she couldn't breathe. All day she had screamed and yelled about how I belonged home and should just stop selling drugs. I got the impression that she didn't believe me when I said I was moving out. She hadn't even believed me when I told her that I had found a place I was going to share with my two new friends, KTU and Shorty. I don't think it hit her until I started packing. Something about seeing an empty space in the closet and dresser drawers where my things had been really pushed her over the edge.

The day before, when I was there packing up the first of my things, Ma pulled stuff out of my hands, tried to unpack my bags, grabbed me, blocked the doors, even screamed after me when I'd gotten in the cab. So, today, when I came back for the rest of it, I was expecting more of the same. More kicking and screaming. But this time, there was only her quiet sobs and troubled breathing. Then she followed me from room to room, daring me to look at her. I was used to pissed off Ma, to the Ma that busted my balls when she found out I'd fucked up. But now she was scared and sad and, for once in my life, seemed fragile and vulnerable.

"How are you gonna eat? Who's gonna take care of you?" I was her baby. She was scared for me. Which really only pushed me faster out the door.

I was not a baby. Soon, I would be 16. And I was not afraid. I was tired of being crammed into this tiny-ass apartment, hiding money that I should be free to spend and missing out on fun and freedom because I lived with my parents. I was tired of watching my parents not have enough money for food and my brother Adam hungry and scared. And I was also tired of having to hide the fact that I could afford to support them.

"How are you gonna support yourself?"

I had known the answer to that since the first time I was in the basement with Rendell and Kathy. Since the first time I did a line. Coke is an amazing high. I'd gone through almost all the $20,000 I had saved, just using coke. I figured that if I got just a few clients who used like I used, I would make crazy money. More money than I made selling weed. That was my plan. More than anything, that was why I was moving. What was even worse than leaving Ma, was what came next: a gentle knock on the door. It was my brother Adam.

"Hey Noah take me with you." He was wearing his book bag and had his suitcase in his hand as if he were ready to go. I wanted to take him with me. I really did. But how could I?

"Sorry Adam ..."

Before I could get the words out he stomped away down the hall, crying and screaming and punching holes in the walls, bloodying his hands. He had a very violent temper. And I'd seen him bang and yell, but never like that. I was actually scared. The thought of leaving at that moment made me want to cry. But I had to go. I had a plan and, if all went well, it would help all of them more than me staying. I had to get myself out of this dump first, before I could rescue them.

I threw the duffel bag over my shoulder and pushed by Ma. Dad was, as usual on the couch watching TV. He didn't move, didn't look in my direction and didn't say a word. And, he wouldn't say a word anyways, unless Ma made him.

As I walked down the hall Ma grabbed Adam to stop him from following me. Her quiet weeping turned into a wail when I opened the door. Adam screamed my name. But I didn't look back.

"I'll call you," I said. "I love you."

I closed the door and walked down those dingy, rickety steps with my pit bull Dutchy behind me. Out onto the hot summer streets. Sad isn't close to the word that described what I felt, but ironically, I had never felt so goddamn free.

CHAPTER 13

It was not an exaggeration. I had snorted almost $20,000 worth of coke in less than a year. By the time I moved in with Tash and KTU, I only had about $2,500 left of the money I'd saved up. That was enough to pay my share of the first month's rent buy some groceries, food for Dutchy and of course pot. But now that I was on my own and with a whole bunch of new expenses, I needed to make money and fast. Before my first week living away from my parents was over, I went back to Crown Heights and picked up a pound of weed. Selling 16 ounces was a sure thing for me, not a gamble. My old dealers and my old customers, all of them, were still around. The kids that sold for me were eager to work for me again. Getting back into dealing was simple. I thought it was a mistake for me to ever have stopped. This was exactly what I was meant to do.

It took me a couple of days to make the right calls and spread the word, but pretty soon my weed business was up-and-running. And with guys hustling for me on the street, I had time to concentrate on branching out into selling cocaine. I didn't know who my clients were going to be. Or, where I could get large amounts of coke. But, I knew Dianna. And I knew who Dianna knew. There was a guy named James, who was her dealer. I figured he would be a good place to start.

Once again, I had Rendell take me to meet a drug connect. When we got to James' block, a tree lined middle class neighborhood filled with brownstones, just three streets away from my new apartment, Rendell told me to wait on the corner. It was early in the evening, but it was autumn so still late enough to be dark already. The streetlights were on. From where I stood, feeling kind of stupid for waiting on a corner by myself, I could still see Rendell. He went into a run-down, two-story house that had a small yard in front and a huge pit-bull on the stoop. Just under ten minutes later Rendell was back by my side. He flashed me the coke in his hand, stuffed it in his pocket and we were off to Dianna's house. Rendell was walking so fast I thought there must be some need for a quick getaway. Once we'd gone a few blocks and turned a corner, the excitement was too much.

"Give me my shit!" I said, nervous but laughing. My hand was shaking from the adrenaline rush, when I reached out to take the Coke.

It was heavier than I expected. Hard and white. I got excited just holding it. Things were about to change. I just knew it. When we got to Dianna's house, I showed her what I had and told her there would be some in it for her if she helped me move it. Dianna chuckled, got right on the phone, and in less than ten minutes she had my first three customers on their way.

"You got to bag that up, honey," she said.

I had gotten an eight-ball, which was 3.5 grams of coke for $125. If I made twelve 20's of coke out of it, I could expect to make $240 when it was all sold. Almost double my money.

But I hadn't even thought about bagging. I didn't know how to bag coke. Reading the inexperience on my face, Dianna gave me a name to ask for at a sex shop down the street on Coney Island Avenue. I did exactly as she said. I walked into the store, went up to counter, and asked for Lyman. The old guy behind the counter didn't even look up from his magazine as if he didn't hear me. I asked for Lyman again, this time adding that I was a friend of Dianna's. I guess those were the magic words because he gave me what I needed, and soon I was back at her house bagging up my first 20s of coke.

If, as I expected, my soon-to-be clientele used as much as me, Rendell and Kathy, I would be going back for more and more and more. In no time, it was clear that I was right. About an hour after the first three customers Dianna called came and went, I was almost sold out. While in mid-sale with the last customer, he asked Dianna, "Is this shit good? Will it come back?"

"Yeah," she replied without missing a beat." You can use my stove to cook it. But, I want a hit."

I had no idea what they were saying, but I didn't interrupt to ask. I watched and learned. The man put the coke, some baking soda and water in a tube and held it over a flame on the stove. Whatever he saw it do put a huge smile on his face.

"Run the cold water, this shit's done already! It looks like the whole thing came back too!" The excitement on his face made me excited. Apparently, I had copped some good shit, meaning it was pure – as pure as it could get. I kept watching as the man pulled out a glass pipe and stuffed the rock he'd just made into it. He put a lighter to one end, his lips to the other and inhaled. It made a crackling sound that reminded me of Rice Krispies in milk. The guy held his breath for what seemed like minutes before letting go. And when he exhaled, his eyes were different. It was like he couldn't really see or focus on anything in the room. His jaw began to move from side to side. And he mumbled,

"I need more. Gimme some more! Now!"

He passed the pipe to Dianna. One hit and she had the same glassy, faraway look in her eye. "Honey, I want more, too," Dianna whispered. They both finished their shit faster then I'd seen anyone finish a bag of coke before. This was going to be a breeze. I knew that I had found my destiny; a way to make tons of money so I could take care of my family and those I loved. Now I could live my life independently and on my own terms. Or so I thought.

One of the best things about not living with my parents and having my own apartment was that I was free to have sex whenever I wanted. I could have Kathy come over every day. Most days, since her parents didn't give a shit, she didn't even leave my apartment. Being able to have sex with my girl, in my bed, in my apartment whenever I wanted definitely made me feel like The Man. As far as I was concerned, I was an adult who could do whatever I wanted. And what I wanted was to make money and be with Kathy as much as possible.

Even more than selling weed, selling coke actually left me with a lot of time on my hands in the beginning. The stuff sold itself. People came to get it. And there was really no reason for me, or any of my people, to leave a spot to go anywhere unless we had to re-up or make a quick run. ☐ So, when I wasn't handling business, I was all about Kathy. And, with her, things were perfect. Well, almost perfect. "Chaz will be home from jail in a few days, babe," It's my guess that girls that liked bad boys were attracted to me because this wasn't the first girl I was with that had a man that was jail. Kathy reminded me one morning while we were still in bed. I was annoyed that she would even mention her ex-man's name after we'd fucked. But, what pissed me off even more was that she sounded worried. Like, she was afraid I wasn't man enough to handle whatever Chaz did when he hit the streets. "Why do you keep saying that to me? I don't care about him. You wit' me now. I'm not worried about Chaz."

I was partly lying. I definitely cared. Kathy loved me. There wasn't a doubt in my mind that she wanted to be with me. Not a single part of me even considered the idea that she would want to go back to him when he got out. What I cared about was the story on the street. On the street, I was a kid who took Chaz's girl while he was away. And now, I'd made a name for myself in the game. Chaz had a name in the streets too. And when he came out, if he wanted to keep that name, he would have to deal with me or look like a punk. You couldn't be taken seriously as a man in our circles if a 15 year old stole your lady with no retaliation.

I understood that. Respected it. Of course, I had something at stake too. I'd carved out a pretty sweet drug business for myself. Even though Chaz would be coming at me about a girl, it would be the first chance anyone watching would see how I dealt with someone trying to take what was mine. How I handled Chaz would essentially solidify my reputation. I definitely had something planned. Something that would send a message to anyone thinking I was soft; that I handled any and all challenges quickly and permanently. And when you're a Jewish kid selling coke in Brooklyn, there's not a more important message to send.

"What are you thinking, Noah?" Kathy asked. I could see the worry on her face. "Are you planning something?"

"Don't ask questions you don't want the answers to. Don't make me lie to you," I said. How does it go? 'Some things are better left unsaid.' And this was definitely one of those things.

CHAPTER 14

Business was booming. Moving out really did help my success. I could do business from my own place without having to trek out to see people. My employees could come to see me. A couple of times a week, Rendell would come by and take me to James' house. Every time, I would wait on the corner while Rendell went in and bought the cocaine. Then we would spend the next couple of days using and selling. Rendell practically lived at my apartment. He was there almost as much as Kathy.

One night, less than a month after I'd been selling coke and was out of inventory again, Rendell came out of James' spot with a worried look on his face.

"What's wrong?" I asked.

"Tomorrow, James wants to talk to you. He wants to meet you at three o'clock." Panic fluttered through my chest. But just for a second. I knew I couldn't have done anything wrong. Not a chance. I had been bringing in money and watching my back to avoid any heat. I'd been here before, I told myself. This is exactly what happened when I sold weed. I was a top-seller. It made sense that James would want to meet me.

The next morning I got up and went to the corner store to buy breakfast. I took Dutchy my Pitbull with me as usual. I would take my dog everywhere I could. Dutchy was a beautiful pit bull that someone who owed me money had gotten and couldn't pay me, so he gave me the dog.

I trained him to attack on command, and he did so whenever I ran into people who owed me money: it would scare them so much that they would get the money, or I would never see them again. I found it hilarious when I saw him attack the crack heads that owed me.

Before I left the house, three customers paged me looking to buy coke. I had them all meet me on my way to the store. I got breakfast for Kathy and me – two bacon, egg, and cheese sandwiches on a roll, a carton of orange juice, and two coffees. We ate and spent the morning fooling around in bed until Rendell came over in the early afternoon. I went back to the corner store to get the three of us turkey sandwiches, chips and soda for lunch. After we ate, I kissed Kathy goodbye and gave her money to go out. Rendell and me left to meet James.

"When we get inside, let me do the talking," Rendell said once we stepped out onto the sidewalk.

"What do you think? I'm an idiot?" This wasn't my first time at the rodeo. I knew how these meetings went down. "Don't forget, though, he wants to talk to me. That's what this meeting is about. So, once me and him start talking, you be quiet."

Almost as soon as we got in the cab, Rendell asked if I could hit him off with some coke. I thought to myself that it wasn't even 3 o'clock and he already wanted to get high. Damn. I couldn't say anything, though. He was my boy.

"I got you, bro," I said. "You pluggin' me in with this connect. That's a big deal and I owe you." He did a couple of bumps before we arrived at the house. I wasn't in the mood to get high right then and there. I wanted to focus on the meeting. In front of the house, as usual, was the huge pit bull pacing behind the gate. As we approached, he was barking his head off. As if that were the doorbell, a guy came out of the house. He was a dark-skinned white guy, maybe Italian, short, stocky and looked to be in his early twenties. He had a head full of wavy black hair that was gelled to the point of being bullet proof. His only job in the world must have been working out every day. That's how built he was. He put a leash through the dog's motorcycle-chain-collar.

"Follow me," the stocky dude said. He led us up the stairs, ducked inside the house and immediately tied the pit bull to a radiator. He waived for us to enter the house and we stepped into an almost empty living room. Other than an old couch, I don't remember much of what that place looked like. I was too busy imagining that the pit bull – who at this point was barking like crazy and foaming at the mouth – could pull the radiator from the wall and attack us all.

"Quiet!" the stocky dude yelled. And just like that, the dog was silent. I looked at them both for a moment and couldn't decide who was scarier. And it finally dawned on me that this short stack of frightening muscles was James, The Connect.

"So you're Noah," he said, turning from the pit bull and plopping down on the old couch. He looked me up and down.

"Rendell has told me a lot of good things about you."

"He hasn't told me much about you at all." I said so James would know that Rendell hadn't spilled any details about James' business to me. I wanted him to know that Rendell was loyal. James gave Rendell just the slightest of nods. And then got down to business.

"Here's the deal, kid. You're doing a good job of moving this blow for me," James said, "and even though we're in the same area, your business is not interfering with my business. You're not selling to my customers. All that is good." He let out a sigh. "But, here's my problem; you have Rendell coming here too often. He is at my door three and four times a week. Sometimes, more."

"Wait. That's a problem?" I said. "That's a good thing, right? If he is coming here, it means we're making money. If we make money, you make money."

James looked from me to Rendell and smiled. He pointed at me and laughed as if he wanted to make sure Rendell heard this cute, funny thing I'd said. Then he turned his attention back to me and the smile was gone.

"In this game you don't want to get hot. Having your boy at my door all the time is going to make me hot and fuck shit up for all of us. So, here's my solution: I'm going to give you some weight on the arm. You will pay me when you make the money. I always get mine off the top. You take your profit after I get my cut. That way, you will never be in the hole."

"And, I have to tell you this because I tell everyone this. I would tell my own mother this if I was doing business with her: Don't fuck with my money. Ever. Whether I like you or not, I have no heart for people who fuck with my money."

Even with this warning, I immediately agreed to the terms. Not only was James giving me more coke, but he was giving it to me at a lower price. Before, I had been paying $30 for a gram of coke; now I was paying $25. And since I was getting a gram for less than other dealers in the area, I could start selling to them as well as to the coke fiends and crack heads.

James stepped out of the room while all these plans were dancing through my head. When he came back, he threw me 62 grams of cocaine and said, "Go do your thing."

That was all I needed to hear.

CHAPTER 15

I picked up the phone as it rang. It was Dianna calling to tell me she had a "Big Fish", a code name we used in case our phones were tapped. It meant we had a new customer with big bucks and to come right away! I said I would be there in 5 minutes.

I had other customers to meet, but none that couldn't wait. When I pulled up to the building, Dianna was on the stoop with her cordless phone in hand.

"Hey baby," she greeted me with a wide eyed look I'd seen before and, although she was always happy to see me, I knew that look of excitement wasn't for me, it was for the crack rocks she knew I had.

"Hey Dianna, what's the deal with you being outside on the stoop?" I said looking around nervously.

"I wanted to talk to you before you went in," she whispered. "The guy inside is a stock broker who hits me up from time to time when his regular dealer is out. His name is Martin, and Martin has a lot of money, crazy money, and he wants to meet you." I nodded, "So treat him good, and he could become a good customer of yours. I'm talking BIG!"

"No problem. Now can we get off this stoop, there's a lot of cops out tonight!" When we walked inside, Martin was literally at the edge of his seat. He jumped up so quickly you would have thought his ass was on fire.

"Hey, I'm Martin"

"I'm Jeremy." Before the words left my lips I realized that along with his handshake, the money was already in my palm. I counted out ten brand new one hundred-dollar bills and then went into the stash in my underwear to get what they were so anxiously waiting for. I counted out 20 fifty-dollar pieces on the table and then gave both Dianna and Marty 2 extra ones.

"Hey get back in your room Kevin." Diana screamed at her son, as he peeked his head out in curiosity. Dianna was in no mood to play. With the crack pipe loaded in hand, she just wanted to smoke. I watched the both of them light up simultaneously, as if it was a race as to who can get it smoked first. I couldn't help but wonder; how did this guy start smoking crack? I mean he was tall and handsome, kind of looked like Tom Cruise. You could tell by how fitted his pin striped suit was and the initials on the sleeves of his shirt, that his clothes cost a lot of money. And if that wasn't enough of a tip off that he was rich, the Rolex he was wearing and the Mercedes Benz parked outside were sure signs.

"Hey Noah, you look like you would fill out a suit nicely. How old are you?"

What the fuck was he talking about? I looked at Martin as if he were crazy. "Sixteen," I said. The crack was definitely kicking in, was all I could think.

"Wow I'm impressed" Martin smiled. "What I mean is, how would you like to get paid to sell coke and crack during the day at my office?"

Now I really thought he's was crazy.

"Instead of my brokers at work calling drug dealers over and running in and out of the office all day, you can just stay there, and I'll pay you like we do all of our cold callers: $250 cash a week, and these guys will be spending hundreds if not thousands a day."

I didn't have a clue what a cold caller was, but getting paid to sell drugs to a bunch of rich guys 9 to 5 sounded good to me.

"I'm in, where and when?"

Flipping me his card and barely able to talk he said, "Tomorrow morning 9 am, One World Trade, 55th floor, and bring ID or you can't get a pass to come up. Make sure you wear a suit, bring plenty of coke and definitely crack for me." Then he left. But not before looking out of the venetian blinds. Checking both ways as he walked out the door.

After seeing the rest of that day's customers and making arrangements to have some of my boys take over dealing for me in the following days, I bought a new suit, shirt and tie at a discount clothing store, a few blocks from where I lived. And went home to get some sleep. I had to be up early and didn't want to be tired all day. I was excited about my new job even though it wasn't a 'real' job. I had never had a job before.

Tomorrow came fast. Getting dressed up that morning made me feel important, and I liked the way it felt. I took the train into the city and got off on Center Street, the train was crowded and so was the city. I never realized how many people worked for a living. The thought never even crossed my mind. People were traveling in both directions in masses as if they were all going to the same place. It was strange to me, probably because when all these people were getting up in the morning, I was just finishing up collecting money or selling drugs to someone and hitting the sack. When I got into the building, I couldn't help but be a little paranoid because there were police everywhere. I walked right up to the desk and told the guard, "I'm going up to Solomon & Gorstein Securities, Martin is expecting me."

The guard asked for my ID and immediately started writing my name on a sticker that I was told to wear on my chest. Then he pointed me in the direction of the elevator.

I never could have imagined seeing what I saw when I got off the elevator. There were men screaming and hollering and hot luscious women running papers from one office to another. One guy was even standing on his chair, screaming at what I thought must have been a client about missing some great opportunity.

Martin greeted me with that hungry look in his eyes. He also saw a look of intrigue in my eyes. I must admit there was something exciting about all this. Martin immediately escorted me into his office at the end of the hall. It was bigger than any office I'd ever seen. There were big leather couches and a bar, two big screen TVs, one of which had numbers and letters that I later found out was a Quotron, a way to monitor the stocks and their activities in real time. As soon as the door was closed, the question was asked:

"Did you bring the stuff?" I hadn't noticed until the second he asked that he was already holding his crack pipe.

"Yes, I brought the stuff," I said.

"Good, I'll take $500 worth to start, then I'll introduce you to the boys.

He was like a starving child when he gets his hands on some food. The pipe was lit before I even saw how the rock got in there. After a few seconds of Martin holding in the smoke, he let his smokeless breath out.

"That was a good one" he said, "now let's rock and roll. I'll show you how the money gets made around here."

CHAPTER 16

"Hey, KTU, here's an eight ball. You and Shorty can split it. Then you guys will just owe me like a hundred bucks. So, like, just hold that hundred and put it towards my portion of the rent."

KTU looked at the big rock in a bag I had tossed on the kitchen table where we were sitting. For a second, the expression on her face made me think she wasn't going to take it. I knew she liked to party, but maybe the thought of owing me more money was too much for her. Then suddenly, as if some debate in her head had just resolved itself, KTU nodded, smiled, and scooped up the eight ball. She was in her pajamas but it was late, well past the time she should have been asleep to get up for her 9 to 5 job in the morning. I watched KTU pad away in the cute, fuzzy bunny slippers she wore around the house, to find Shorty.

That's pretty much how the real partying started. KTU and Shorty Tash were inseparable. They shared everything. Including drugs. I had more drugs coming in now than we fucking knew what to do with. And yeah, sometimes I paid my part of the rent in coke. KTU and Shorty would stay up all night, drinking and doing drugs. Then, of course, they needed some coke in the morning to help them get through the day. Me, I would sleep on the train during the trip into the city, if I did party with them the night before.

KTU got so used to doing bumps on the train during her morning commute that she started traveling with this tiny bag with a straw in it.

KTU would hide the bag in her hand, put it to her nose and take a snort, but make it look like she was just clearing her sinuses or her throat or something. It was smooth. I was impressed the first time I saw her do it. She told me that in order to make it through the day, working at Macy's as a sales clerk, she would have to go to the bathroom a few times a day and do more bumps.

Shorty didn't work. She was collecting government checks, which weren't much, but helped. She slept during the day and would wake up about the time KTU came home from work. Then they would do it all over again. And to support their habits they would commit occasional robberies on unsuspecting people walking through the neighborhood. Did I think their drug use was getting out of hand? Maybe, but who was I to judge? I was doing a shit load myself and selling it to them, so I wasn't gonna complain.

Staring at the bags of coke on the table, I started to feel a little tired. Should I or shouldn't I? 'No!' a little voice sounded in my head. So I got up from the table to head to my room. I wanted to take a little nap. I never slept through the entire night now because my pager was always going off. Business was good. But as soon as I climbed into my bed I heard my damn dog barking like crazy from the back of the apartment. "

"Dutchy, get in here!" I yelled, annoyed because I knew I would have to listen to some complaints from the girls and our neighbors in the morning if he didn't shut the fuck up.

Dutchy didn't come. In fact, he was still growling and it sounded like he was tearing something up in that back room. I called him again, but he paid me no mind. The damn dog was growling like he really had a hold of something back there. I threw off my blanket and stomped down the hall, passed the kitchen into the little room that led to our back porch.

"What the fuck?" were the only words that would come out of my mouth when I saw what Dutchy was up to. He had one of the Mexican dudes who lived upstairs by the leg. The guys from that apartment had gotten in the habit of using the back fire escape for some stupid reason. The ladder from the fire escape led down to our back porch, which was right in front of our window. If that window was open and Dutchy wasn't tied up, which he never was when we were home, anyone climbing down in front of that window would definitely set him off.

Suddenly I realized that Dutchy had the guy's leg inside our apartment. And the guy was trying to climb out. If Dutchy had attacked him while he was coming down the fire escape, Dutchy would have to have gone through the window to the outside. This motherfucker had to have come through the window on his own and tried to run when Dutchy caught his ass. I ran back to my room and went directly to the closet for one of my guns. Should I grab the AK47? The AR15? I chose the 9mm Beretta, by then I had acquired quite the collection. When I returned to our back room, the guy was screaming – more like crying. Dutchy wouldn't turn him loose. Blood had soaked through the leg of his jeans.

"Dutchy, off!" I commanded and pulled him by his collar. He let the fucker go. I put my Beretta to the guy's head. "You trying to rob me, mother fucker?"

The guy's eyes got as wide as saucers. He shook his head back and forth and started crying even more. His words were in some language I didn't understand, Arabic, I think. Definitely not Spanish, so he wasn't one of the guys who lived upstairs. Whatever language he spoke, I am sure my gun to his head was a message he understood loud and clear. As soon as I took my gun away and backed up a couple of steps, he stumbled his way out the window. There was blood everywhere. I went to get Dutchy a steak as a reward and to tell the girls what had just happened. They were probably already high and would think it was funny, and I thought maybe I could convince them to clean up the blood.

CHAPTER 17

The next morning, a little shaken from the break-in, I found myself back in the Wall Street war room. I never would have imagined three weeks ago that I would be wearing a suit and tie, gunning for a cash prize. For some reason Martin thought I had it in me to be a broker and started training me. So, when he dangled five, one-hundred dollar bills in front of the room, a prize for the first person to open a new account, I knew they were definitely going to be mine!

I had been encouraged to get on the phones and read from a script. Within the week I had thrown it away and was cold calling with my own spiel. The task was basically prepping potential customers to talk to a licensed stock-broker, getting them interested in buying some "hot stock" the whole office was selling. After the first week and the way I was able to get these potential buyers interested, Martin and the other guys in the office felt I was a natural.

Turns out I was so good, they moved me into what they called the "boiler room". It was a real shit hole, nothing but desks and chairs and a few Quotrons, but it was where the real action was. I was instructed to learn a licensed broker's name and personal information, so I could sell stocks under his identity. In the event a client, I was trying to pitch a stock to, asked me questions about the broker I was playing, I would be able to answer them. Even though I had never met him. My new name was Jack Adams, and I wore it well. I instantly started selling and opening new accounts.

Within two weeks I was known to everyone in the office as 'The Natural'.

"Hi good morning, is this Sahara? Wonderful, this is Jack Adams with Solomon and Gorstein securities, how are you?"

A soft-spoken woman replied and I could tell by the sound of her tired voice that she was definitely not a young lady.

"I'm doing well, thanks for asking," she replied.

"The reason for my call ma'am is I have an exciting business opportunity for you. It's called an initial public offering, and only my company has access to it. I'd like to help share the wealth on an already fast growing investment. I put several of my clients into this stock, and they are already very pleased. Now I cannot make you any promises, but I can say this, no one thus far has done anything but make money with this."

Truth was I had no clue whether or not anyone made money with it. All I knew was I wanted to make money off of this woman, and I would say anything short of promising her a return on her money, because if she was recording or the F.C.C. was listening that would be illegal.

"Well, Jack I have my money tied up in CDs and 401Ks so I'm not liquid, which I would need to be in order to invest it this stock... although it does sound enticing."

"Sahara, listen, CDs are about as slow at making you money as snails are at racing. This is a real investment, this is the excitement your life needs right now, not to mention your portfolio. I'll tell you what, I'll waive my commission on this trade completely if you break 10,000 dollars' worth of your CDs, a small investment in our what I will call a long lasting and fruitful business relationship, and when I do make you a bunch of money the next time we speak, we get you out of all those CDs, and I get my commission on those new winners I put you in. What do you say?"

She wasn't saying anything, but I could tell from the green light on my phone that she was still there. This was it: the moment of silence and the first one to speak loses.

"Um, well, why not? Let's do it," she said.

With my hand over the mouth-piece of the phone I was jumping for joy. I forced myself to calm down and get back to her.

"Sahara you made a wise decision, I'm going to put you on the phone with my secretary, and she will take all your information and begin this trade, welcome aboard!"

By day's end those five 100-dollar bills were mine and before we got off work, Martin asked me to meet him in his private office. I already knew what he wanted. He had probably already blown through the 500 dollars in crack that he bought from me that morning and needed more for the upcoming weekend. He and about 5 other guys from the office in the Trade

Center had come to see me, and I must have sold about 25,000 dollars' worth before lunch; things were going great!

I stood in the doorway and knocked lightly on the trim.

"Who is it?" Martin asked, as he filed his nails.

"It's me, Noah."

"Come in, close the door behind you," Martin said as he took his feet out of his shoes and rested them on the desk. You're doing a great job and I want to show my appreciation. We make a shit load of money on the IPOs and penny stock that you're selling for us. And you should look the part of a successful broker, not like a Bridge and Tunnel guy -- in a cheap suit. I've got a limo outside -- and we're going shopping."

When we pulled up in Martin's stretch limo to Giorgio Armani on Madison Avenue, it was a total surprise and not where I expected to have been taken. As soon as we walked in the store, the gentleman (obviously gay) greeted us.

"Hello Mr. Gorstein how are you?"

"Show my friend here something nice, he works with us downtown and has to start to look like one of us."

Before I knew it we were checking out with what looked like five new suits for Martin, two he had sized for me (probably the nicest suits I'd ever seen) and a pile of shirts, ties and shoes for us both.

"That will be 13,854 dollars and 26 cents."

I looked at the salesman as if he was crazy. Either I heard wrong or he added wrong, I was sure of it.

Martin pulled out a silvery looking credit card and threw it on the counter. I didn't want to seem stupid, but I had never seen one like that before.

"What's that card?"

"It's my Platinum American Express card, here look", It was definitely the coolest credit card I'd ever seen. "Ok Noah, time to go, I have business to attend to so I'll have the limo drop you off, and I'll see you Monday -- 10am sharp," Martin barked, "Keep up the good work and we could sponsor you for your series 7 and make you a licensed broker one day. Now go home and get some rest. We have fuckin' money to make!"

On my ride home I could not help but think that this was a life I could get used to. I swore to do my best to learn as much as I could about trading stocks and to become very successful doing it.

CHAPTER 18

Beep Beep Beep Beep.

The sound of my pager going off meant money. It meant some customer was trying to reach me to score. And, it was a sound I heard all the time. As much as I loved money and the hustle of it all, I am not gonna lie. Sometimes, I hated it and wished my job at Solomon & Gorstein was the only job I had. Like, when that damn pager woke me up, and I'd barely had any sleep between the brokerage firm business and the street business.

It was Saturday morning. I looked over at the table by my bed, and I saw I had 24 missed pages. I pressed the button. All the missed pages were from about 9 different numbers. One of those numbers was James, my supplier. I wanted to see what he wanted first, so I threw some clothes on, grabbed the dog's leash, whistled for Dutchy and walked out the door. I headed to the corner store and called James from the pay phone.

"You need to come by today. ASAP," he said as soon as he heard my voice. I knew better than to ask him to discuss business details over the phone – you never knew who was listening. So, I agreed to swing by at five that evening.

That settled, I returned the calls to the other eight people looking for me. After 15 minutes, I had sales set up for the morning. Before going back home, I went to the corner store to get Kathy, Rendell and me our usual breakfasts. The eight customers I'd called back were waiting for me outside the apartment by the time I got back with our sandwiches and coffee. But, by the time I had them all squared away, my pager went off four more times.

"Yo, ya'll get up! Here's breakfast you two. I'm on my way out. I got business to handle. I called a cab already, and it will be picking me up in a few." I said as I laid out breakfast on the kitchen table. Kathy kissed me deeply on the lips as she sat down at the table. She ran her hand down my back and I felt my dick starting to rise in my jeans. But, there wasn't any time to do anything about it.

I grabbed my drugs for the trip I was about to make and a little .25 Beretta. I loved that gun because it was small enough to fit inside my Timberland boots. It was also in really good condition considering what I paid for it, which was next to nothing. I never had to worry about shooting my foot off.

Nothing in particular crossed my mind on the ride to Coney Island Ave and Dianna's house. I knew I was going to do my usual Saturday morning thing. Dianna would have customers lined up for me, basically piled up on her stoop. And for most of the morning, I would deal to them. Some of them I would sell to two or three times before the day was over.

When the driver pulled up to Dianna's apartment, I don't know if it was something about how the bright summer sun that morning lit up all the customers waiting around Dianna's apartment or my mood, but I was struck with how obvious it was that her place was a drug spot. The people waiting outside, coming and going had vacant, hungry looks about them – like zombies. I decided then that I would have to change this up. I would need different spots. Having people gather like that would attract the cops. I finally understood what James and my weed connect had been saying. This would be my last time doing it like this from Dianna's place. ☐

After a couple of hours on Dianna's stoop, the last customer of the morning came up to me with a VCR in his hands. He begged me to give him, even just a little crack for it. I gave him a ten-dollar rock and told him if the damn VCR didn't work, the next time I saw him, I would bust him over the head with it. Before leaving, I popped into Dianna's apartment and gave her kids some money and Dianna some rock.

"Why don't you guys go to the movies tonight, around seven? It's the weekend, go have some fun," I said to the kids. "And then after that go grab some food." I was sure by now even Kevin knew that when I gave him and Ariela movie and dinner money, it meant that I needed them out of the apartment while I did some bagging. They were smart kids and had already seen too much. I hung with them for a bit and then was off in a cab to James' house. I had already made over $4,000 and it wasn't even dinnertime.

"What's good, Little Man?" James asked when I came inside, giving me a hug.

"Nada," I said. I liked that he seemed happy to see me. James could be a moody fuck sometimes. "I just been getting' this money." I handed him $2,000. I figured since I was coming over, I might as well give him part of his cut.

"My man!" he said, counting the dough and smiling even wider than he had when I arrived.

"OK, listen, you're doing great. Really great, man. These last few months you've made me a lot of money. But you're selling too fast. There's too much traffic back and forth. I don't like that. I wanna give you 250 grams. That's a quarter of a kilo. I'm gonna give it to you at 23 a gram. Let's see how long it takes for you to get it off and get back to me. But, be careful it's a lot of weight, and a lot of money. You a little dude." He joked.

"You right," I said. In some ways I was still a puny kid. I still had to earn respect. I knew that. "But, I'm not exactly the stupidest fool in the game either." I pulled out my gun and showed it to him. I wasn't trying to show off, but I needed to let James know that I understood that anything could happen in the game we were in, and I was prepared to go all the way to protect what I had.

James smiled at me. Nodded. He never broke eye contact with me, even when he had his boy hand over a quarter of a kilo of his drugs to me.

"Now make me proud," he said as he opened the door to let me out.

As I walked away that evening with the largest amount of drugs I'd ever had, I was struck by how much James trusted me. James was becoming like a brother. I really looked up to him. I admired the way he handled his business and the way he carried himself. People respected him. Some even feared him. And, I wanted that.

In the car, on my way back to Dianna's, I thought about all the things I'd have to do to be more like James. Tighten up my business a little. Think bigger. And no more of this puny kid shit. I needed to start lifting weights so people would look at me and know I wasn't to be fucked with. I was going to do my best to make James proud. Just like I was doing my best to make Martin proud.

At Solomon & Gorstein, I was rocking. The days flew by, and the money was rolling in. Marty was definitely happy with my performance. He was always inviting me out to dinners with some of the other brokers and clients at restaurants with names I couldn't even pronounce, like Le Bernardin, La Grenouille and Le Cirque. The Champagne was flowing and, of course, the drugs were never ending. Life was great!

I met all kinds of people with crazy stories. Charlie was an 18 year old who had been busted for heroin and crack possession and was court mandated to work at the brokerage firm as part of his rehabilitation. How loony was that? The very place that was supposed to straighten him out was a haven for smoking crack.

Even though Gorstein was married, he was banging the head secretary. It got so wild in his private office at times that the walls would shake and the screams would get really loud and scary. We would laugh, but it was really fucking annoying, especially when you were on a call with a potential client and you would start to laugh so hard your train of thought would be blown.

Several months into my job at Solomon & Gorstein, I got stuck on the D train and was late for the morning bell. The second I got off the elevator I knew something was off. I didn't hear a sound. In the morning, you could always hear the guys roaring before you got to the floor. But that morning, it was silent. As I stepped into the waiting area, I saw there was police tape and chains on the door. There were signs everywhere: "Do not enter by order of police." I could see through the glass doors that the office had been ransacked.

I guess I knew deep down that what we were doing was wrong, because Martin told me if anyone asked, I was to say that I was just a cold caller, setting up potential clients for a broker to talk to, But I never really took it seriously until that moment. My heart was beating so hard that I think I could actually hear it. It didn't take a genius to see what had happened here. Then it struck me that law enforcement could still be there or on their way back, and I had a ton of coke on me not to mention they might nab me for working there and put me away. I ran back to the elevator and decided that if anyone stopped me, I would say I got off on the wrong floor.

I pressed the button and waited for what seems like an hour but was probably only about a minute. As I got on the elevator, all I could think was, easy come, easy go. A few minutes later, I left One World Trade and raced for the subway. Back to Brooklyn and back to business as usual. I never saw Martin again, but I heard from another broker I later ran into, that he was hauled off to jail and took the entire rap.

A few days later I was sitting in front of my apartment thinking about how lucky I was not to have been at Solomon Gorstein when the place was raided. And a crack head ran from across the street with his hands flailing.

"Yo! Stop waving me down like that, man!" I said, "Are you nuts? The fucking cops are going to see you and start watching us if they ain't already! The drugs are making you stupid. If you didn't have a hundred dollars to spend, I never would have come out this early for yo' dumb ass."

Perched on my stoop like it was a throne, I handed the crack head what he came for and shooed him away. Crack heads were the fucking worst part of dealing. On the one hand, they would spend all they had and everything they could steal on what I was selling, putting lots of loot in my pocket. On the other hand, their need for the rock made them desperate and dumb. I used to say to myself that if I didn't sell it to them, someone else would

They made shit obvious, which always brought the cops. After a few weeks of dealing cocaine and crack, I was always hearing stories of people getting caught out there. Dealing to undercover cops, getting snitched on by dudes in their crew, and catching crazy time for it. And it all started with people getting sloppy. With the cops watching them because some stupid crack head couldn't be more nonchalant.

It was 10 am on a day in mid-August. It was already pretty warm out, so I wasn't wearing a shirt. As the crack head shuffled his way down the block, I noticed two hot girls coming towards me. They were both short, one with dark brown hair, the other a strawberry blonde. The one with dark hair was also tan and thick the way I liked. The blonde was pretty, but skinny -- still hot though. Each of them was carrying a towel and wearing a swimsuit top, clearly heading to the beach. I guess I caught their eye because they were staring at me and smiling. When they got in front of my building, they stopped.

"Hi," the brunette said and waved. Her friend started to giggle and act like she was embarrassed. Without skipping a beat, I said hi back and struck up a conversation. Before long, I was putting the brunette's number in my pocket. I also gave her my pager number.

We finished up our flirting with a promise to hook up that weekend. Just as the ladies began walking away, I saw my next customer making his way toward me from the other end of the block. Christy, the brunette, kept turning back to look at me until she and Blondie (Tiffany), turned the corner. So I didn't even acknowledge the customer trying to buy crack until the girls were out of sight.

As soon as I broke him off, my pager went off again, which reminded me for the hundredth time that I needed to get myself a cell phone. I hated making the walk to the corner store to use the pay-phone. It was ridiculous since I was making about two grand a week by this point, that I shouldn't have a cell phone. But I was spending about $150 a day on cab fare, buying brand named clothes and jewelry for myself and Kathy, gifting whatever girl I was fucking on the side, helping support my parents, and I loved taking all my friends out eating and drinking. I was the man.

Before the first ring was done, my boy, Willy picked up. He was calling because he had a solution to my problem: My block was getting too hot. I needed to separate my customers from the block. I also needed to separate myself from this pager number. Willy said he had a friend I could trust that could work for me. He wanted to set up a meeting to introduce us. I hung up after telling him to come over for some lunch. As soon as I put the pay-phone back on its hook, more customers were coming right up to me. Right on the street. Right in broad daylight. Yeah. I definitely needed to lower my profile before I got picked up.

I served them, then ducked over to Dianna's house to get off the street. After a couple of hours lying low, from Dianna's I headed over to the pizzeria where I had a charge account. These days, I had a charge account at most stores in the area. Everyone knew me and knew that I had money. When I arrived at the pizzeria, Willy was already there with a tall, skinny Puerto Rican guy who I would have guessed was about 19.

"Yo, Noah, this is José," Willy said, introducing us as I sat down in the booth they'd chosen.

"Nice, to meet you, bro," I said, reaching across the table to shake his hand.

I was still shirtless and thought I noticed José checking out my body. That wasn't unusual. Since I started working out, people had been noticing. They only thing different about this time was that I liked that José was looking.

Really liked it. And thought, "Damn this kid is sexy as hell!" As soon as the thought danced across my mind, I quickly pushed it away. It had been a long time since I'd had any feeling like that about another guy. Maybe not since I was about 9 or 10 years old when I thought one of my male classmates was cute. Thoughts like that were wrong.

Dirty.

When I was young, I can't even remember how old, my parents, as punishment, made me stand in the back of our living room after kicking the shit out of me, in silence, while they watched TV. I had to just stand there, for hours, without speaking, and watch whatever they watched. The news. MASH. All those boring grown-up shows I didn't understand.

I remembered that one of the shows they were watching was an episode about a boy coming out to his parents about being gay.

Ma said, "If that was my son I would bash his head in." And my dad mumbled his agreement. Once during an argument with my father, I saw her take a lamp and break it over his head. I had little doubt she would bash someone's head in. I didn't totally understand what gay was then, but I vowed to never be it. Later on, once I started having thoughts about guys, I swore I would never tell anyone. And, certainly never act on any of it. Even if they looked at me like José just did. Never. I pushed the thought away and got down to business. I explained that I needed him to sit on the block and serve the customers, while I kept the pager and did deliveries to my dealers. This would also give me a chance to concentrate on expanding. José agreed to do it if he got paid 25 dollars for every hundred dollars he sold.

Perfect.

We shook hands on our deal and arranged for him to shadow me for a couple days to get a sense of how business went in the neighborhood. He'd start the following day. After that, I would leave him to sling drugs on his own and only meet up with him to collect money and give him more product. With the new free time, I would find more clients. And see Christy without Kathy knowing.

CHAPTER 19

"I'll take both of them," I said.

I couldn't stand the pay phone bullshit anymore, so I bought two cell phones off of one of my customers who owned a cell phone store. One phone was legal; cost me $300 for the actual phone and about a $1 a minute for service. The other was $400. On that one, I could only make calls; not receive them, but it would be totally free for about six months before I needed to pay again.

It was a "bootleg" phone, basically a phone whose service was attached to other bills. So some poor schmos who I didn't even know – were getting charged a little bit extra on their bills for my phone, so little, in fact, that they wouldn't even notice. This way, I had one legit phone that everyone could call me on and another phone that I could talk business on, that wasn't linked to me in any way, and that I could get rid of whenever I needed. I paid half the cost of the phones in cash and the other half in crack. I loved buying things with crack, because I got coke so cheaply that I was really getting things 75% cheaper than people thought.

As I left the store, I dialed the number that Christy, the hot girl in the bikini top from the other day, gave me. A woman I assumed to be her mother answered on the first ring. She sounded annoyed after I asked for her daughter, and she had to call Christy to the phone.

"Hello?" said the pretty voice I'd been dying to hear all day.

"What's up girl? D'ya know who this is?" She didn't. Which told me she gave her number to a lot of guys. At first, I was offended and was about to curse her out for being a whore and trying to play me. But, then I remembered that I was in love and in a relationship already. I didn't have time for a girl who was looking for a boyfriend.

I reminded Christy who I was – the guy without a shirt she stopped to talk to with her girlfriend on their way to the beach. She giggled when she remembered me. Then I gave her my cell number and made her repeat it back to me after she wrote it down.

"Meet me for lunch today," I told more than asked her. We agreed to meet near my block at the pizzeria. She promised to call me as soon as she got there.

By the time I got off the phone with Christy, I was almost back on the block. From down the street, I could see someone waiting on my stoop and assumed it was a customer looking to score. As I got closer though, I realized that it wasn't someone looking to score. It was José's sexy ass.

I forgot he was supposed to start working for me that day. He looked sharp in a wife-beater T and a snug pair of jeans. His facial hair was shaped into a tight goatee that made it impossible to ignore his full lips. But I was going to ignore them. I had to. Or at least pretend I didn't notice how good he looked.

But, as I showed him the ropes, what I learned that day was that not only was José handsome, but he had a lot of little habits I found distracting. He licked his lips a lot. And had a way of letting the tip of his tongue rest in the corner of his mouth when he was paying attention. He made the most intense eye contact when he was talking to you and laughed the whole way through a joke, even before he got to the part that was funny.

Most distracting though was the way he was constantly grabbing and adjusting his crotch. It took all of my concentration not to follow his hand down and stare every time he did it. Finally, after a few hours of making sales, I let him go early and planned to meet up with him at Dianna's later that day. I told him it was because I had a date. I had plans with Christy. I let José walk me back to the pizzeria. Christy was waiting out front by the time we arrived. I didn't introduce them. José didn't even give me a chance.

"That's you?" He asked pointing at Christy as we walked up the block. I nodded, and he let out a whistle. Christy was wearing a bikini top and jean shorts. Her hair was up in a loose pony tail. José slapped me on the back. "Enjoy your...uh...lunch," he said before giving me that smile of his and going on his way.

"You're late," Christy said.

"Sorry, sweetie. I was working. You hungry?" I said with a grin.

Christy looked me up and down as if she were seeing me for the first time. I'd never seen a girl look at a guy so openly before.

"I've had lunch. Let's go back to my house."

"Oh, really? What's going to happen at your house?"

Christy moved in. She planted a kiss right on my lips and grabbed my dick through my sweats.

"You're gonna show me yours and I'll show you mine." I felt myself get hard in her hand. My lower half was definitely in agreement with her plan. For some reason, José crossed my mind. I pushed the thought away and couldn't get to Christy's house fast enough for her version of show-and-tell.

As Jose and I sat on the stoop outside of Dianna's later that afternoon, Kathy appeared with her usual big bright smile that lit up her face. She was so sweet and loved me so much. But I had my needs and had to have lots of sex. And if it took more than one or two to satisfy me, so be it.

"Can I have money for my nails?" Kathy asked, giving me that wide-eyed look she'd get when she wanted something.

"Damn, girl! You just got home from school, not even a kiss, I pay for your cab and the first thing you say is 'Can I have money for my nails?'" She laughed, walked up the stairs to where I was sitting on the stoop, slid into my lap and gave me a kiss. Which was exactly what I wanted. The way I looked at it Christy was the main course and Kathy was the dessert.

"Who's this?" she remarked looking at Jose.

"This is my new assistant Jose," I answered, "he's going to help me, so I can have more time to spend with you." She kissed me with a giggle and thanked Jose.

He nodded back and said, "No problem."

"Now, how 'bout you give me some of that ass first. Then you can go get your nails done, and I can get back to work. Oh by the way, this is for you." I said.

She looked at the small box all wrapped up and instantly knew. It was from Cartier. I was making so much money I just wanted to spoil her. She ripped the wrapping paper off so fast she must have done it in a split second.

"Oh my god, the Cartier Love bracelet!" She screamed, as she hugged me with all her strength and it made me feel so good.

"While I was out I also got a little something for myself." From under my shirt I pulled out a 125 gram gold chain, made by Baraka and a Jewish star that had 3 carats of baguettes. She couldn't believe how big it was.

"How much did that cost"?

"The jeweler wanted $8,000 for it, but I paid in cash so I got it for 7. Enough questions, let's get busy!."

We walked up the stairs to Dianna's apartment and right by José who'd also been on the stoop with me. He was still in training to take over dealing in my place.

"We'll be back in a few," I said to him. "If anyone comes, you know what to do."

"I got this," he replied with a cockiness that made me smile. I really liked that dude.

As soon as we were in the darkness of Dianna's house, I ripped off Kathy's stockings from under her Catholic school skirt. I couldn't tell you how many times I'd done that to her. I just loved the way she looked in that skirt.

No one was home because I'd already sent the kids out for pizza while I dealt from their stoop for a couple of hours. So, Kathy and I kissed and fondled our way to the kids' rooms. Before I could climb into the bed, Kathy turned around, hiked up her skirt, and bent herself over the bed. I dropped to my knees and started to work my tongue across her pussy lips and up to her tight asshole. She moaned my name, which got me crazy hard. I stood up and grabbed her hair with force. She tilted her head back into my grip. I bent over her from behind and softly, but firmly bit her neck as I slide the tip of my cock into her.

"Put it in, daddy. Put it all the way in!"

I got high off her begging me to fuck her like that. I wanted her to beg me even more. I slammed myself into her as hard, as fast, and as far as I could. I felt my balls slap against her, I was in so deep.

"Harder, daddy! Harder, daddy!" I took one of her breasts into my left hand and with the right, reached underneath to massage her clit. A wordless hiss and then a series of moans let me know she was cumming. That was all I needed to hear to let myself go. I buried my face into the side of her neck, kissing her, grabbing her, pinning her to the bed with my thrusts as I emptied myself into her. Still on top of her, we collapsed into a sweaty pile of arms and damp clothes. My dick was still hard, but growing soft inside her. I didn't want to move.

Kathy laughed and mumbled, "We didn't even take off our clothes."

I still couldn't talk, but chuckled at how carried away we got. My pants and boxers were around my ankles. The boots were still on my feet. And, except for her stockings that were somewhere in Dianna's living room, Kathy still wore her Catholic school uniform.

"Love you," she said. And I kissed her right behind her ear. We snoozed for a bit, then got up and fixed our clothes in silence. I took her hand as we walked to the door, and I slipped her some money. "Go get food and your nails done."

Kathy counted what I gave her and then looked up at me.

"I wanted to take Tammie with me, but she has no money" Kathy knew she got whatever she wanted from me and so did her friends. She had more jewelry then any of her friends, money in her pocket every day, even a driver from a cab company on a regular basis to take her and her friends all over the place. I took back the $50 and gave her a hundred dollar bill.

"Tell Tammie that her man needs to come see me and start working for me so he can pay for her damn nails." Kathy kissed me on the cheek and laughed that laugh that I would do just about anything to keep hearing for the rest of my life.

"I love you," she called over her shoulder as she hurried down the stoop and onto the sidewalk. She did love me. I loved her too. I really did. But even though I had just had amazing sex with Kathy – and she had my heart – I watched her walk away and still couldn't help but think about Christy who I'd just fucked the a few hours before. I was an animal, and I loved it.

CHAPTER 20

I knew I was dreaming. But I didn't care. I liked the dream. In it, I was getting my dick sucked just the way I liked. All warm and wet and deep. It was dark in my dream. And I was moaning. The bed I was in, my bed I guess, was creaking as I thrust my hips to force my dick deeper. There was something hot about the rhythm of the creaking. But, then I noticed the creaking changed. But I couldn't hear it anymore because there was this buzzing. The more I tried to focus on the creaking and my thrusting and the mouth on my dick, the more annoying the buzzing became. The mouth pulled away from my dick, making me look down. It was Jose.

"Answer your phone," he said.

"What the fuck?" I yelled. And then I was suddenly awake, in my bed, alone, in my room. On the nightstand next to me, my pagers and cell phone were all buzzing and ringing, telling me there was business being neglected. I scooped them all up, pushing the dream and what it meant from my mind.

Missed calls and pages from Ma, as usual. José had called, Dog had called; who I hadn't heard from in a while. And there was also a call from James. The rest of the missed calls were from customers. I heard Shorty and KTU in the next room. It was early on a Saturday morning, maybe around 8. Obviously, they were still up from the night before. They must have heard me yell or my moving around, because KTU burst through my door.

"Hey, Noah! Glad you're awake. We need more shit," she said. She was speaking fast, and her eyes were intense. I knew she was in a middle of a good high and wanted to keep it going. Avoid the come down for as long as possible was the rule of any good user.

"Are you guys ever going to sleep? "I asked. Maybe in the back of my mind I was worried about them. Worried about the amount of blow we all were doing. If I focused on their use, I didn't have to confront my own.

"Yes," she said in a serious tone. "We will sleep on Sunday." And then, just as serious as she'd been a second ago, KTU started laughing. And that made me laugh. I was still sitting on the edge of my bed; so I just reached into the bottom drawer of my night stand to get what she was looking for.

"Here you go," I said and threw KTU another 8-ball. She caught it, mumbled a thank you and was gone. With my pagers and phone, I went out onto the porch to start my day. I called back all the missed calls, starting with Ma. My calls with her, by the end of that summer were all the same. I told her that I was fine and yes, I was eating enough. And then she asked me for money, and I promised to bring over a couple of hundred later in the day: on one hand she didn't want me selling, but on the other she would ask me for money knowing where it came from.

I called José back and asked him questions about how business was going, even though I already knew. To keep track of him, I had a duplicate pager made, which he didn't know about, so I could see who beeped him and how often. That way, I knew how long it took him to get back to people and if he was really handling things. José, to his credit, always kept it real. But other dealers that worked for me weren't always so real, and I would catch them after they fucked up. Much to their sorry-ass surprise.

José told me it was busy, and I told him I would come through to relieve him. I hit up a few customers to let them know where I was going to be once I relieved José so they could come to score.

Finally, I called back Dog who just wanted to make sure I came through because he had more guns to show me. He was the one who sold me my first gun and a few others over the last few years. Of everything I heard in my twenty minutes of phone calls, that bit of information, got me the most excited. I went back inside, back to my room to get clothes and a towel for a shower. As I was looking through my closet for some shorts to wear, I heard something move behind me, and spun around ready to fight.

"Where you going?" a soft voice asked from underneath the tangle of sheets and blankets on my bed. Kathy. Shit. I forgot she was there.

"I'm going to work, babe." And I grabbed my clothes and my towel and hit the shower. I got dressed and rushed back into my room just long enough to drop $20 on the night-stand for Kathy and Rendell's breakfast. Then I ran out the door to start my day...and forget my dream.

I stood in front of a pizzeria on Flatbush Ave, with a cardboard sign outside that read; Schlomo's: 2 slices and a coke $2.25. This one was a typical Jewish pizzeria, with shoddy, stained furniture. I preferred the Italian pizza places because they were clean, bright and cheery with neon signs that lit up the streets, but I wasn't here to eat.

Dog had taken me here to this Jewish/Kosher pizzeria in the neighborhood. Never in a million years would I have thought that a rabbi would be dealing guns out of that place. I learned that the Rabbi Ben-Abraham, short, fat with a white beard and very serious, had a guy that brought the guns up from North Carolina every month to fill specific orders and sell any leftovers to guys like me.

On this particular day, the Rabbi let us in the pizzeria early in the morning before it opened and then disappeared somewhere in the store. Dog, with his evil face and big-ass Medicaid glasses, led me to the back where the guy who delivered the guns (I never learned his name and I'm sure he wanted it that way) had them spread out on a tall metal table.

"These are fucking nice!" I had never seen so many guns in one place. To say I felt like a kid in a candy store would be an understatement. I loved guns because they gave me the feeling of power, and they made my enemies as much as my friends fear and respect me. I was a bad ass. No one was going to fuck with me!

"So, which one you want, kid? The Uzi? The tech-nine? The 9mm Berretta?" Dog asked as he picked up each gun he mentioned and showed it to me. The deliveryman just stood off to the side, kind of quiet. He was a short, skinny guy with longish dark hair.

I couldn't decide which gun I wanted. Truth be told, I'd already bought about 10 guns over the past two years. But, in my line of work, I didn't think a person could have enough.

"I'll take 'em all." I finally said. I took the ones Dog showed me, and several others on the table, about 15 guns in all.

"That'll be $4,500," the deliveryman finally spoke. I was surprised, given how tiny he was, at what a deep voice he had. "I'll have the guns cleaned and ready for you when you come back with the money."

"Come back?" I asked. "I have the money right now. All of it."

Both Dog and the delivery-man looked at me strangely. Was it crazy to walk around with that much money? I never figured out what surprised them or what their problem was. But I took my guns from the pizzeria that morning. Then, I stashed them in various places close to the areas where I did business. I left some at Alyssa Russo's house, in my mom's basement, at Dianna's, at Kathy's. Gave a couple to José to hold and even left a few at Rendell's place.

I went to James' place to show my appreciation for all the trust he'd place in me. I gave him a 357, 2-shot Derringer. It was the cutest gun I'd ever seen. I hated to part with it. But, it was good business to let James know how much our business relationship meant to me. Looking back, I guess it seems funny for one drug dealer to give another drug dealer a gun as a gift. But it's not like I ever thought a day would come where James and I would ever think about shooting each other.

After all the guns were safely tucked away, I met up with José back on the block so I could watch my money get made. It was a great day and life was good. I would sleep well that night.

When I opened my eyes the next morning to see KTU standing over me with Shorty, Tash right behind her I was startled.

"Noah! Just one more eight-ball. Pleeeease!" KTU pleaded. My mind was fuzzy because it was really early in the fucking morning. But, my first thought was to wonder how the hell they had gotten into my room when I was sure I'd locked my door before Kathy and me had gone to sleep just to avoid this very moment.

I felt Kathy's arm around me tighten underneath our blanket, and she moved even closer to me. I closed my eyes, telling them I wanted to go back to sleep without saying it. But, what I did say was, "The rent's due. Are you sure you guys can afford it? I don't want you to say you don't have it again."

"Don't worry about it," they said at the same time. Even with my eyes closed, I could feel them staring down at me. I reached down into the nightstand and tossed KTU another eight-ball just to get rid of them. I didn't believe they had the rent covered.

As soon as they closed my bedroom door behind them, I heard Kathy's whisper, "I'm tired of all the ins and outs. All these people coming and going all night long is bullshit. We don't have any privacy."

My answer was to get out of bed and get dressed to start my day. I didn't look at her as I moved around the room, pulling on my jeans, throwing on a t-shirt and my gold chain. Then I scooped up my cell, my pagers and my .25 automatic and shoved it into my Timberland boot.

When she realized I wasn't going to respond, Kathy went on and on about how her grandmother had moved to an old folks' home, and her parents now had an empty apartment upstairs that they wanted to rent out. If we took it, they would give it to us for half what they would charge anyone else. And, I could probably get an even better deal if I hooked them up with drugs. Kathy said all of this from bed with a sheet wrapped around her. I walked over, bent down and kissed her lips.

"Let me think about it," I said, pulling a knot of cash out of my pocket, peeling off two twenties and leaving it on the night stand for her. I stuffed the cash back in my pocket and left her there. As I stepped onto my stoop into the heat of a late summer day in Brooklyn, I knew two things: Kathy was right. I'd lived with KTU and Shorty for over a year now. And honestly, I was tired of it. I needed to move so that I could have some privacy. But, the truth was, Kathy was one of the people I needed privacy from.

CHAPTER 21

"My man! What's up Dog? What you doing out here so early?" I asked as I approached Dianna's stoop. In reality, it was late in the afternoon, not early at all. But for the people I'd come to hang out with, the day didn't usually start until the sun was going down. Especially when it came to hanging out at Dianna's. Her apartment had always been the after-hours spot to get some weed or some coke. But, after I started dealing there, it became a non-stop party. People came over to smoke blunts, drop acid, do ecstasy and all kinds of other shit.

That summer at Dianna's, I tried everything except heroin, crack and meth. I was too afraid of what that shit did to people. But you could see it all at Dianna's. Wild stuff went down there at night. Like people just sitting around with blank stares, or trying to talk some incoherent gibberish. Sometimes there would be so many bodies passed out on the floor you'd have to step over them. Things stayed pretty tame during the day. Which is why I was surprised to see Dog hanging around.

When I asked what was up, Dog smiled at me and pointed to a duffel bag by his feet. He said that he was on his way to do a robbery. Some fool was going to meet him somewhere to buy what was supposed to be $50,000 worth of ecstasy, but was really Sudafed.

"You should come with me, man. We can split this money and then go get some pussy and party! $50,000!"

I couldn't even imagine getting that much money at one time. But, I had a lot going on with all the drugs I was selling at that point. I was flipping half a key of coke every week and over 20 pounds of weed. I didn't see the need for me to rob somebody or sell fake drugs.

"I'm good, Dog," I said as I gave him a pound and went into Dianna's.

Two hours later, Dog hit me up and asked me to meet him at another spot in the neighborhood. To be honest, I don't remember what the fuck he said to me when I got there. I just remember looking at a mountain of money piled on a kitchen table as Dog sat there counting it. He must have made in five minutes what I hadn't even managed to save up in all the time I had been dealing. Half of which could have been mine if I'd just gone with him. I'd missed out. Big time. But, I promised myself I would never miss out again. I'd never let myself be too cautious or afraid to make money.

When he'd finished counting his loot and had it back in the duffel bag, Dog told me to call a limo.

"We going shopping," he said. I'd never seen him smile so big before. It took some time for the limo to come. But, when it did, it was worth the wait. It was a beautiful sight watching that classy, black limo cruise down the block for us. I loved the feeling of walking out of that apartment with Dog and climbing into that car knowing that we had all this money to blow on whatever we wanted. I loved seeing people on their porches and walking down the sidewalk stop to stare at us as we drove off.

When I settled into my seat I heard Dog telling the driver to go to kings plaza Mall, "were going clothes shopping." I remembered another time Dog had hooked me up. I'd ruined a new pair of cheap sneakers while riding a bike that wasn't mine. I might have been like 8 or 9 years old. I was scared that Ma was going to whip my ass. Dog bought me a new pair just so she wouldn't find out. Here he was, hooking me up again in a much bigger way. I always took good care of Dog, giving him drugs cheaper than I did most people so he could make money and if he was partying I wouldn't charge him for the drugs at all. When I was kid I couldn't wait for the day to come when I could do something for him just like he always did for me.

"I'm home! Where is everyone?" I called as soon as I walked into the apartment. I was a little surprised that no one is in the living room or kitchen waiting for me. KTU and Shorty called me an hour ago asking me to hurry home. They said they needed to talk to me about something. I hurried. At first, I was pissed because I didn't think anyone was there. But, as I walked further into the apartment and down the hall, I could hear them in their bedroom whispering. It took me a second to realize that they didn't know I was home. They are too busy trying to figure out how to tell me that they can't make rent. Again.

And that they still want more blow.

After a few more minutes of eavesdropping, I noisily entered the room, pretending like I hadn't heard a thing.

"Hey, what was the emergency?" I said. They both give nervous laughs and looked at me with big eyes. "No emergency," Shorty says. "We just needed another eight ball." I didn't mention all the money they already owed. There wasn't any reason to bring it up or fight about it. I knew what to do. I tossed them one of the two eight balls I had on me and told them that I will see them later and walked back outside my apartment without another word. Kathy and my next oldest brother, David, were waiting for me.

He had just started crashing on my sofa partly to get out of the drama at home and partly because Ma convinced him to be her spy and look after me.

"Is your mom still willing to give you that apartment?" I asked Kathy.

"Sure!" she said. "I just have to let her know. Why?"

"Because we are moving in. Just don't tell anyone."

CHAPTER 22

"Wow!" I said as I finished counting the money. I wasn't even noon yet and José had already brought in well over $1500. "Today is gonna be a really great day." José smiled and gave me a handshake.

"I've been at it all morning, Jeremy, and the day isn't nearly over." It was obvious, that he was proud of himself. I pulled a few bills off the stack I'd just counted and handed him his cut, put some in my pocket, and then took the rest to put with my stash inside Dianna's. I came back out and sat next to José on the steps.

I made a mental note that the next time I saw James, I'd have to tell him that I needed half a kilo. 500 grams. People selling for me were moving our product faster than I was able to handle with what he'd been giving to me. I was running out of stuff for the street too quickly.

Before I could finish my thought about getting more product from James, something at Dianna's gate caught my attention. I looked up just in time to see Dog pushing a red motor scooter into the yard and behind the garbage can. He didn't speak or even look at me or José.

"What's up, Dog?" I asked. "Where'd you get that?" He gave me a fuck you look.

"DON'T RIDE IT!" he growled as he ran inside. What the hell was his problem, I wondered. Then, I looked over at the scooter. Dog had left the keys in it.

"Fuck it!" I screamed as I jumped on its back.

José shook his head at me as I rode down Coney Island Avenue. When I got to the corner, I turned towards East 12th Street. As I approached my turn, I heard sirens, looked behind me, and saw a cop car. I figured they were on their way to some emergency. I turned on to East 12th Street. Down the block, on the corner, I saw another cop car; this one also had its sirens and flashing lights on. It was like the car had been waiting for me. Over a loud speaker, I heard an officer tell me to pull over.

I turned around and hauled ass back down the opposite way. I thought that the cop wouldn't go against traffic. I thought wrong. He caught up to me and bumped my tire. The scooter skid and I hit the ground. The world went black for I don't know how long. I felt myself being pulled up by the back of my shirt. Four cops were standing around me, cursing me out, calling me names.

"You stupid little fuck! Why'd you make us chase you like that?"

"What did I do? What you arresting me for?" I asked when one cop snapped cuffs on me.

"For being young and stupid, punk."

I admit I was young, I was 16, but I was no punk. He answered and started going through my pockets. Shit. I remembered that I had a pocket-knife and a quarter ounce of weed, that day's smoke.

"You're stupider than I thought," the cop said as he pulled the knife out of my pocket. I knew then that I was going to jail. But for what? Did someone snitch again? Had José sold to an undercover or some shit?

At the precinct, an officer I hadn't seen on East 12th Street told me that I was going to be in a lineup.

"For what?" I asked.

The officer laughed at me. "For the Chinese food delivery guy you robbed for the scooter we caught you riding, his money and some food."

I was put in a line-up of guys that didn't look anything like me. Out of the six of us standing there facing that one-way mirror, I was clearly the youngest. I was also the whitest.

I swear we stood there for what seemed like hours, just waiting. My heart was thumping so loudly I was sure the guys on either side of me could hear it. Nervous sweat gathered in my armpits and trickled down my sides. I knew that I must've looked scared which meant I looked guilty. What if the guy hadn't really seen who robbed him? What if the cops told him they caught me with his scooter? Even in my own head, the story that someone robbed him ran, and minutes later a different kid was caught riding the same scooter sounded lame.

I knew I was fucked.

But, as time dragged on, nothing happened. It wasn't like it was on TV where they ask dudes to step forward and turn to the left and to the right or say something, at least not in this lineup. We just stood there. I was afraid to hope, but figured that if I'd been chosen, the cops would have pulled me out of the lineup right away.

Instead, after a few more very long minutes of standing there, we were led out of the room and back to our holding cells. I was fucking relieved and thought I'd be let go soon. No such luck. I spent the next few hours watching drug addicts, no different than some of my customers, come into the holding. As much as I'd been selling, those hours in that cell was the first time I'd seen crack and heroin addicts go through withdrawal. I hadn't really understood that when they couldn't get their next hit, they got sick like that. Some of them looked like they might die.

"Come on, Braverman!" someone shouted from outside the bars. Finally, I thought, I can get the fuck out of here. Other names were called and grumpy, dirty, stinky men who'd also spent hours waiting were put in a line. Then we were shackled to each other. I realized, I wasn't being let go. I was being put with the guys being sent from the precinct to central booking. That meant I was being charged! I'd have to wait for God knew how many hours more just to see a judge and find out what was going to happen to me. "What the fuck am I going to the bookings for?" I yelled at the officer, panic getting the best of me. I was about to lose it. I hadn't been picked out of the line-up. I didn't rob and beat that guy! But I was, the officer said, still caught riding a stolen vehicle, in possession of a weapon, and with weed on me. I was in some trouble.

My mind was crowding up with questions. What was jail like? What would happen to my jewelry, phone, all my stuff? And out of nowhere, I thought, "I miss my ma."

If and when Ma found out about this, she'd lose it. I knew that. But, I was scared. Really scared. Thinking of her comforted me though.

"Everybody off! When you hear your name, give me the last four digits of your social and step down!"

We pulled into a garage across the street from the Brooklyn House of Detention. It was no ordinary car garage. It was attached to the back Brooklyn Criminal Court. One of the guys on the bus, who'd been through the system a few times, told me that we would be rushed in, fingerprinted and then sent up to see the judge after a few hours – or days – depending on how many people were there. The first thing I noticed was that corrections officers never spoke. Everything was yelled. Even though there were less than a dozen of us being taken in at that moment, we were getting screamed at like we were a rowdy crowd. We were led inside, and were each told in a yell to stand against the wall while they took our pictures and fingerprints.

We were then moved upstairs, to the second floor to see "The Medic." I am not sure if The Medic was a real doctor or what. He was a guy in his 40s who looked like he was bored and hadn't slept in a day or two. He asked me if anything was wrong in a way that let me know he really hoped that nothing was wrong, so he wouldn't have to deal with me.

"I'm fine," I said. Because physically I was alright. I mean I hadn't shit my pants or anything. I was just scared as hell. Then I was sent to be searched and, finally, off to a cell. After being cuffed behind my back on the ride over, I was relieved to have my hands free. The cell smelled like bleach. In fact, the entire place reeked of bleach, like they were trying to cover up the odor of something worse. And it was freezing, especially since I was just wearing shorts and a tank top.

The place was filled with drug addicts, lying semi-conscious on the floor and gang members giving each other gang handshakes as they were piled into the cell one by one. As I walked into the cell, no one gave me more than a passing glance. I saw a payphone in a corner not being used. For the first time all day, I smiled. I had to call Ma. Without hesitation when the operator for the collect call said my name, Ma accepted the charges and we were connected.

"Noah, are you ok?"

"Yeah, Ma. I'm in central booking."

"I know all about it. Your friend Kim from Dianna's block came running here to tell me as soon as it happened. And by the way she's a very nice girl! I gave her my number and told her to call me any time you or she needs me for anything." That was typical of my mother. She always wanted to be involved and be there for the world. She started to bawl and in between sobs, asked me if I would be ok. Shit. I hated upsetting her. I really did. I knew I was disappointing her.

"I'mma be fine, Ma. Don't cry," I said, holding back some tears of my own. "One of the guys on the ride over told me this was no big deal. He said Legal Aid would get me some community service or something. I'm not going away or nothing. I'm young and it's my first time in trouble."

By the time we got off the phone, Ma seemed better. Still worried, but not crying. I told her that I loved her. Walking away from the phone, I realized how tired I was. Trying not to make eye contact with anyone, I made my way over to an empty corner and sat down.

"Braverman!" A lady screaming my name yanked me out of sleep. To me, it felt like I did little more than close my eyes for a second, but I must've drifted off for a while because the cell was a lot emptier than it was when I closed my eyes. And my butt and legs were numb from being in the same position for too long. The lady officer escorted me up to a courtroom. I was told to stand by a man I guess was my Legal Aid attorney. He and the prosecutor went back and forth for a minute or two using words I didn't understand. The judge didn't even look in my direction, but after 5 minutes, I saw that what the guy told me on the bus ride over was true. I was set free after promising to do some community service. As I walked out of court, I was only thinking two things: 1) Getting arrested was some inconvenient bullshit, but nothing to be afraid of; and 2) From what I saw of those addicts going through withdrawal in holding, crack heads and dope fiends didn't just want drugs, they needed drugs. And with my new education, I was back to work because I had money to make.

CHAPTER 23

I was happy to leave the apartment. Splitting with KTU and Shorty was a long time coming.

"Is that the last of our stuff?"

"Yea, baby. Call your mom and tell her to have the door open so we can move right in and start unpacking as soon as we get there." We were standing in the living room. A town car filled with our stuff was waiting to take us to our new home.

Shorty and KTU stood silently in the hallway and looked sad to see me go. But I wasn't the only one who had to leave. Just like I'd thought, they hadn't been paying the rent to the landlord for I don't know how long. So, they were going to get kicked out as well. Our splitting up was inevitable.

"We gonna head out. I'll call you later,"

I said to Shorty and KTU as I grabbed them both up in a tight hug. By the time I let them go, Kathy was already halfway out the door.

Kathy's parent's house was a two-family home with separate entrances. So, privacy wasn't going to be an issue. Her mom and step dad were two of my most consistent customers, and they loved me dating their daughter. This combined to give me an unspoken discount. An apartment that would usually be rented for $1000 a month was ours for only $600. And that $600 would most likely be paid in drugs.

Something that was both good and bad about our new place was that it was close to my family's apartment. Good because I could pop over and see them whenever I wanted and give them anything they needed. Bad because Ma could pop over and check on me whenever she wanted.

But, the best thing about having a place of my own was when Kathy was out, it gave me a place to hang out with my boys, get high and conduct my business. I especially enjoyed spending time with José. He was smart and we would brainstorm about ways to expand my drug business and make more money. And he would always kept me aware of how much inventory we had.

"We're out," José said to me as we met up on Dianna's stoop. "We don't have any more."

"Damn," I replied. "Already?"

Again, we had sold out of product more quickly than I'd anticipated. I didn't even have any weight left at the house that I could cook or bag up. Just the day before, James and I had discussed him selling me my first brick – an entire kilo. A thousand grams of cocaine, which is the same size as a brownstone's building brick. It is then wrapped in cellophane, then dipped in either alcohol, mustard or motor oil, so dogs can't smell the drug and sealed with duct tape.

Buying that much at a time meant that I would be getting it even cheaper -- $20 a gram – an unheard of price for anyone else at the time. People literally would have killed for that price. Literally.

I was already selling drugs at a lower price than anyone in my neighborhood. In fact, I had a better price than the Dominicans uptown. If someone bought more than 100 grams and they paid in cash, I would sell it for $34 a gram. But, if they bought that much on a regular basis, I sold it for anywhere between $27 and $30 a gram to my weight customers. Running out so quickly and not having when people needed, bothered me. There was little I hated more than losing money.

"I'll go see my connect tomorrow and get more weight" I said.

"Then it's a wrap for the night," José said. As we were sitting on the stairs he stood up, stretched out his arms, and gave a little yawn. "I don't feel like going home. Let me crash by you?"

"Yeah, that's cool. You can stay with me and Kathy," I told him as if I really didn't care where he slept. I acted like it was no big deal. "We just have to stop by my mom's first. I told her I would drop off some money…" But, even as I was saying it, the thought of José coming home with me for the night made my dick stir. And this was not the first time I'd been aroused just talking or thinking about him. In fact, it was starting to happen all the time.

In some ways, I was more turned on with the idea of fucking José than I had ever been during actual sex with any of the many, girls I'd been with. Maybe because it was forbidden. Or new. The thoughts made me uncomfortable because they went against everything I knew was right. I was usually in control but this was something else, something I didn't know how to handle. I knew he was straight because he would bring the occasional girlfriend around, or I would hear him making plans on the phone with them, but the girls didn't bother me.

As we left Dianna's porch, José walked in front of me. I noticed, for the hundredth time, the fit of his tank top that exposed his shoulders and curved around the muscles in his back and how those red basketball shorts he loved to wear hung off his ass and revealed the top of his boxers.

I wanted to be close to him but how did he feel about it?

CHAPTER 24

"Yo! Noah! Noooah!" Someone was calling my name from a block away. I didn't recognize the voice, but as the person got closer he seemed familiar. It took a second, but then I realized it was this random crack-head, George I'd seen outside a bar two blocks from Ma's apartment. He wasn't a customer of mine. This guy usually bought from James.

"What's up?" I asked as soon he got close enough to speak without yelling.

"I wanted to cop from you. James is out."

"What you mean James is out?"

"He ain't got nothin' I just went to buy from him." I was surprised to hear that James was out of product. He'd just given me my first brick. But, since he was out, I figured it wouldn't be a problem to sell to one of his customers. The money would be going back to him either way.

"How much stuff do you need?" I asked.

"A lot. You should come with me to Ray's Bar. Bring about a thousand dollars' worth, in twenty and fifty dollar bags," George said. "I have a bunch of people waiting there and they all need."

"You go on ahead, and I'll meet you there." I didn't want to be seen on the street with him by anyone, especially the cops. I also didn't want him to know where I kept my supply. And, if I was going to do business myself with that much money involved, I wanted to pick up a gun just in case things got crazy.

When I walked into Ray's, the first thing I realized was that I knew most of the people from the neighborhood. But before I could get five steps in the place, the bartender stopped me, "Kid, I know you're not 21"

"No shit, Sherlock," I said to him as I stepped up to the bar. "And, I know that you know exactly who I am so that don't matter." I tossed a $100 bill onto the bar. "Let me get a Hennessy and coke and keep the change." And I guess it didn't matter. Sipping my drink, I noticed George, the crack-head across the bar at a table with some other guys. He motioned for me to meet him in the bathroom, which was at the end of the bar. It was a typical dive bar bathroom that was dirty and smelled like years of piss and God knew what else. Without a word, George handed me $500 to fill orders he'd gotten from about ten people. I gave him what he purchased.

"You think you can break me off something for helping you get rid of all this for you?" I hit him off with a 50 dollar bag, about the size of a nickel and told him,

"There's more where that came from if you keep business coming."

"In that case, you should stay because this shit goes on all night," he said. That set the wheels in my head rolling. If I could set up action in the bar like I did at the brokerage house it would be a fucking gold mine. But before I made that move, I would have to talk to James. Again, the money would be coming his way in the end, but it was all about respect. And, I definitely respected the man.

CHAPTER 25

"Let's go get a drink. And while we're at it, you take about a thousand dollars' worth of product with you. I want the bartender to get used to you."

Without a word, José obediently went inside to get the shit. I picked up my cell and called Kathy. It was after midnight, and I wanted to let her know I probably wouldn't be home until tomorrow morning.

Dealing out of the bar until 5 am gave me the perfect excuse not to come home. Instead, for the last week since George took me to the spot, I'd been crashing at my mom's house a couple of blocks away with José. We slept in my brother's old room, which was really a closet, but it fit one twin bed inside. Most nights, he fell asleep before me and I watched him, trying to figure out if there was any way he knew what I was feeling and if he felt the same. I knew he had girls he was fucking, but so was I. Were these normal feelings? Would they pass?

Jose and I walked into Ray's like we owned the place. As usual, it was crowded. I gave José a hundred dollar bill and told him to order two drinks and let the bartender keep the change. Then, I went to the bathroom where people had already started to gather as soon as they saw me walk through the door. A few of them gave me the signal to follow them. This was going to be a good night. Ten minutes later, I left the bathroom with half the amount of product I came in with. At the bar, José had finished his drink. I grabbed mine off the bar and downed it.

"Let me get two more and start me a tab!" I was feeling good, and not because of the Jack and coke. I asked the bartender to give me $10 dollars in quarters so José and I could play some pool. Halfway through the first game, more customers started signaling for me to go back to the bathroom. By 3:30, José and I were drunk and completely sold out of product.

"You want me to run back and get some more?" José asked. I noticed his words were a bit slurred and thought it was cute.

"Nah. By the time you got back, it would be time for the bar to close. Let's just go to my mom's and knock out." I slurred. "We can get an early start tomorrow." On the walk home we passed two guys that were obviously drunk, one bigger than the other and both pretty big. I was so drunk that I honestly couldn't make out their faces.

"What the fuck you looking at?" The words hit me like a ton of bricks. And before I knew what I was saying, "You, pussy" left my lips. The next thing I knew one, or both, I don't recall, were throwing punches at me, and I was so drunk all I could do was swing wildly. Before I knew it I was on the ground, but no one was hitting me anymore.

"You okay Noah"?

" I think so. What happened?"

"You got fucked up." José smiled and helped me up.

"You are way too drunk and those mother fuckers started hitting you. Luckily for you, but not so lucky for them, there was a long piece of wood right there by the garbage. I grabbed it and fucked them up."

"Thanks, man." I said.

"I will never let anyone hurt you. Never." José said with sincerity.

Those words made me smile and smiling at the moment hurt. Could he have felt the same way I did? One thing's for sure, he cared about me.

"Let's go home and get some sleep. I'm sure I'm going to feel this more in the morning, but for right now I just want to forget it happened," I slurred.

Walking home wasn't easy. A trip that should have taken five minutes took about twenty. At one point, I stepped off the curb to cross the street and slipped. I threw my arm over José 's shoulder to keep from busting my ass.

"Whoa!" he said as he caught me and helped stand upright. "You wanna chill for a bit."

After the world stopped wobbling before my eyes, I said,

"Nah. Let's get home, handsome." The word was out of my mouth before I could stop myself. My drunken brain tried to come up with some way to play it off and make it a joke. But José just looked at me with those brown eyes and said, "You think I'm as handsome as you are? 'Cause that would be a big compliment."

"Oh," I muttered.

Was he joking? Something about the way he looked right at me with those almond eyes made me bold.

"You should kiss me for giving you a big compliment then." And that ballsy motherfucker did -- right in the middle of the street. With my lips against his, it was like nothing else in the world existed. I didn't care if anyone saw us. I didn't care if anyone we knew found out. I just wanted that kiss to keep going. My dick got hard instantly. Harder than I could ever remember it being. It was throbbing. He broke the kiss first. I don't think I ever would have stopped.

"What do we do now?" he asked. I forced myself to be cool. But being drunk made me bold.

"Let's go to my mom's and go with the flow. But before we leave this spot, give me your mouth again." I demanded.

At Ma's, I followed him up the stairs. His pants were sagging like always, but this time I didn't have to hide the fact that I was looking at his hot ass, with his Calvin Klein boxers, hanging out of his jeans. Tonight I would finally see underneath them.

In that tiny room we needed no words. I closed the door behind me and grabbed his hips in my hands. I kissed his mouth hard, trying to pour weeks of urgent desire into every touch. I slipped my hand under his shirt and found his chest smoother and more muscular than I'd imagined. I stripped off his shirt and ran my hands down his back. I reached inside those boxers and cupped his ass with both my hands.

God. He felt so good to me. I pulled him into me, pressing my hard-on into his crotch and found that he had one of his own. I pulled his boxers and pants down. Just slid them over his narrow hips. José 's huge dick popped free, rock hard, perfect. It had to be at least eight inches long and thick. He pulled my pants down, stroked my dick, and it felt so good to finally have him touch me there. Pre-cum slid from my tip. José went to his knees and took me into his mouth, warm and wet and strong. Watching my boy, this masculine thug, suck me off turned me on like nothing else I'd ever experienced.

Sooner than I wanted I felt myself on the edge of coming. I pulled him back up to his feet and pushed him down on my bed. It was my turn to please him. I sucked him the way I always wanted to be sucked. No hands. Deeply, until the head of his penis brushed the back of my throat. If I relaxed, I could take the whole of him. And I made it wet. If I needed a break, I jerked him smoothly and with a nice grip making sure to really focus on the brim of his head where it was most sensitive.

"I'm gonna cum," he said.

"Me too," I said laying down next to him. He went back to sucking me and I continued sucking him. He went first and exploded right in my mouth. Tasting him, having him throb in my mouth and hearing him moan on my dick sent me over the edge right after. I don't know how long we lay there catching our breaths. But when we were able to move, we kissed each other goodnight. I turned my back to José and was surprised when he wrapped his arms around me.

"I'll probably be gone when you wake up in the morning," I whispered. "I have to go see the connect about taking over the bar." José 's only response was to squeeze me. I felt his breath on the back of my neck. We went to sleep without another word.

CHAPTER 26

When I opened my eyes my bedroom ceiling rocked back and forth as if I were on a ship at sea. Clearly, I was still a little drunk. I crawled out of bed, found my jeans balled up on the floor, and pulled out my cigarettes for a quick smoke. José was still knocked out. Watching him sleep, his slim and muscular body wrapped up in my sheets, I wanted to get inside those full lips. But, business called. I had to go talk to James. I took a quick shower, gulped down a glass of orange juice, got dressed, rolled a blunt and headed out.

"Where you going, Noah?" Ma intercepted me as I was passing through the living room.

"I have shit to do, Ma. Here's fifty dollars. Let José sleep. Don't bother him. When he wakes up tell him to call my cell. I have both beepers so he don't get disturbed."

On the way to meet James, I lit up my blunt and returned the pages José and I had missed. By the time I got to his house, I had fifteen customers lined up for after I was done. The day just started, and I was already looking at making over $1000 plus the money I would collect from people who owed me.

James was outside already playing with his pit bull, Drake. By now the dog loved me and came running up to me as soon as he heard me calling his name. James had a smile on his face. He told me once that he knew he was getting paid when he saw me coming.

"What's up, little bro?" he said as he reached down to pet his dog.

"Chilling. Got some money for you as usual." I said. "I also have to talk to you about something."

"Everything all right?" James asked.

"Yeah. Couldn't be better. I just had an idea I wanted to run by you. You know Ray's that bar you supply on Coney Island Ave? You ran out of work two weeks ago. One of the guys called me up. So, I went over there and made a shit load of money. I figured you wouldn't care because you didn't have any drugs to supply them with." I said, as James continued to pet Drake with a blank look on his face.

"Well here's the thing. I've been going there on a regular basis, pulling more than over 1,000 dollars a day. Before, you were only getting whatever customers George was bringing. But with me setting up shop in there, I'm getting everyone. I figured if you don't mind, I would put someone there permanently. Together, we can get all the money that comes and goes out of the spot. But, of course, only if you approve."

The blank stare was gone. James looked at me with an expression that I knew usually meant danger for whoever was on the receiving end of it. It was a few seconds before he finally spoke.

"If anyone else – ANYONE – were to tell me what you just said, I would have my dog eat their ass right here. And after the dog was done, I would stomp a hole in 'em." I almost shit myself as I looked for any move he would make that meant I would have to defend myself.

"But truth is, with you taking it over, I'm still getting paid. Actually, getting more money. Besides it takes heat off of me because that dude George was coming to my place too much. And, I don't trust him to front him work. You have my blessing, the spot is yours."

It wasn't until James said those last words that I realized I'd been holding my breath. I was relieved that he saw that I meant no disrespect and didn't whip my ass or worse. We shook hands and James started rattling off details about how much product he thought I would need for the bar. I was only half listening. My mind was already calculating the money I'd make. And how bringing in that much money would bring more haters and people trying to take what was mine. I would have to beef up security.

CHAPTER 27

"Who the fuck is this dude?" I asked, eyeing the stranger standing in front of me.

"That's my pops," Laree said. "He wanted to meet you." Laree was this kid I met when I was selling by one of the neighborhood high schools, him and his family moved to my neighborhood when he was kid. Laree loved smoking weed just as much as I did and we hit it off instantly and he started to deal weed for me right away. One day, I gave him a pound to see what he could do with it. He made me money – quickly. So, like everyone else I trusted enough to do business with, I had Laree holding drugs and guns for me. That way, whenever I was on his side of the area, I had product and protection nearby. The guy Laree brought to me, was his pops, but looked young enough to be his brother. When he started speaking – something about his confidence let me know that Pops wasn't a kid or a stranger to the game.

"The blow I sell is 100% raw, and I can do a much better price than anyone you or I know," I said.

"I find that hard to believe. But, if it's true, me and my boys out in Coney Island can pick up hundreds of grams a week. We could come to you instead of going all the way uptown."

I liked how he got straight to business. "Here. Take this," I said as I passed him an eight ball that he immediately shoved into his pocket. "Take that to your people. Cook it up so you can see how pure it is. I promise you, it will come back one hundred percent. Then get back to me if you like it. Tell me how much you want, and I will tell you how much I'll charge. It will be somewhere between twenty-four and twenty-eight per gram, depending on how much you buy."

Pops smiled, "You know, I didn't know what to expect when Laree told me about you. I had doubts about doing business with a kid. But, you're a serious businessman. I'll be in touch".

I shook his hand and said, "Thanks. I am always serious when it comes to my money."

CHAPTER 28

The phone rang and it was Ma, saying the family was hungry and needed some money for food. I was busy and couldn't get over there, so I called Renaldo's, a really fine neighborhood Italian restaurant, and ordered their specials. It made me feel good knowing I was able to send them food without concern for how much it cost.

My parents could now walk into any neighborhood store and buy what they wanted because I had charges at all of them. I was king in the neighborhood. Whatever I needed I had access to. But it came with a price. The drug use, constant paranoia and relentless hours were taking their toll, but there weren't any other options if I wanted to keep up this lifestyle.

It was another late night when I walked into Jimmy's just before midnight, about four hours before the place closed and walked up to José.

"How's it going?" I asked.

"We made about a grand so far," he answered. From the crowd and the pace of people coming and going, I figured we could double that before the night was over.

I waved to the bartender to bring us some drinks. While we waited, I noticed José was fidgeting and staring at someone or something across the room. Before I could ask him what was wrong, he said, "You see that dude over there sitting by himself near the bathrooms? He came here earlier with a bunch of his boys. They were asking me who I worked for and if they could get a free bag. I told them I worked for you. Most of them left after that. But he stayed behind. Been watching me for like an hour. I think they left him behind to start something. I don't trust it."

"Fuck them," I told José just as our Hennessy and Cokes came. I could tell he wasn't satisfied with my dismissing it.

"Fine," I sighed. "I'll go talk to him myself right now." I downed my drink, waved to the bartender to bring me another and headed to the guy's table. Now that I was looking at him, I realized that I knew him. Not by name, I just knew that he hung out with these older cats from the other side of my neighborhood, and I had seen him leaving James's house once. They were petty thieves and small time dealers. Trouble-makers.

As I got closer, I could tell the guy was sizing me up. I didn't like anything about the way he looked with his beady eyes and hair in a ponytail. And I really didn't like the way he was looking at me. I pulled out a chair and sat down,

"My man you were asking about my business?

"Me and my friends was curious to see who's getting money over here," he said.

"Looks like there's a lot of money here to be gotten."

"There is. And, I'm gettin' it. All of it. So why don't you finish your drink and take the fuck off before there's a fucking problem."

We locked eyes. He agreed he would go, but the tone of his voice and the hard stare he gave told me he was weighing his options. And I was weighing mine. I had a 9mm Berretta on me to back up the fact that I was running the game in this bar.

"I'll be seeing you again," he said as he walked by me.

"I'll be right here."

Ignoring the folks that had started to watch the show, I headed back to José and the bar.

"You think they will come back?" José whispered. His eyes told me he was worried. For the first time while working for me, José was scared. His fear bothered me.

"Maybe." That was a lie. They were definitely coming back. They were watching us and knew how much money we were making. They wanted a piece of the action, and the only way that could happen was to get me out of the way and make an example of me. I didn't want to think about that, though. Not at that moment. I didn't want to deal with José 's fear either. Somewhere in the back of my mind, I took his fear to mean that he didn't trust me to protect him. Or maybe he wasn't as tough as I thought he was.

"I have to go," I said. There was a strip club a few blocks away that I wanted to check out. Where there were booze and women, there were dudes with money looking to party. "Stay here," I told José. "I'll be back."

He nodded. I could tell that for me, he was trying to finally hide how worried he was. Maybe I was doing the same damn thing. In this business, with the kind of money we were pulling in, I couldn't show any fear or hesitation. Not for a second.

The next day I started drinking and doing blow early in the afternoon. I wanted to take the edge off and calm my nerves. Just thinking about that asshole trying to take what was mine got me so fucking mad. But the truth was I was scared too.

"Where the fuck were you?" I barked as soon as Kathy came through the door. I was sitting in our apartment on the recliner. I'd been surprised when I'd come home and she wasn't there -- that had been four hours ago. Kathy closed the door and let out an annoyed sigh.

"I was with Mercedes. We went to the mall but didn't see anything we liked."

"It would have been nice if you called me or left a note." I snapped

"I tried to call you this morning but you didn't answer. Your mom said you were sleeping. Why didn't you come home last night?" Kathy began yelling. "Why the fuck are you always out so late and staying at your mother's? Must you get fucked up and not come home every night?"

All her questions were coming so fast, and I only had the usual answers for her.

"We got done late, and I was drunk. Just wanted to sleep," I lied. I had been spending more and more nights sleeping at my mom's house with José. We would go home after work, mess around for hours and then fall asleep in each other's arms. Our attraction for each other had grown to the point where sometimes we wouldn't be able to keep our hands off of each other. Even in the bar we would go into the bathroom and get busy. I guess in some ways, it made me reckless. I was spending more time with José than with Kathy. And fucking loving it.

"Well," I said changing my tone. "I'm glad you're home. I missed you." I didn't want to have another fight about how little I came home. And now that she was standing in front of me, I saw that Kathy looked hot. I stood up, grabbed her by her hair and pulled her face to mine. I devoured her lips with my own, wanting to kiss away any need to have a fight, any doubt about where I'd been and what I'd been doing. With my other hand sliding up her skirt. Slipping my fingers past the thin material of her thong and inside her. A few strokes of my finger and Kathy quickly became warm and wet around my caress. She broke our kiss and let out a moan, pressing herself harder against my thrusting fingers.

I ripped her blouse open and starting kissing and softly biting Kathy along the side of her neck and shoulder. Then I made my way down to her nipples and played my tongue across one then the other until they were both as hard as tiny stones. Kathy ran her palms along the erection still growing in my jeans. "Stick it in, Daddy. Now."

I spun her around and bent her over, making her hands touch the floor. I thrust myself inside her. I quickly realized my dick wasn't fully hard; not the raging boner I usually had when we fucked. It was just barely hard enough to penetrate her. If Kathy noticed anything though, it didn't seem to make a difference. Soon, she was moaning.

"I'm cumming, Daddy. You're making me cum !"

I kept going, trying to make myself come. But it wasn't working. I couldn't bust a nut. So, I faked it.

"I'm about to cum!" I yelled. It sounded false even to me, but I kept it up. I mimicked what I thought I normally did when I came: pounded her hard, beat her pussy with my dick, and moaned one final time.

When I finished my performance, Kathy fell to the floor, her legs were shaking and I knew I'd done well. I'd satisfied her. And fooled her. I left her there on the floor and went to hop in the shower. As I washed our sex off me, I knew that I would tell her I had to go out and work. I knew I'd tell her there were customers I had to serve. And I knew that would be a lie. I was going to find José and fuck him, so I could have the climax I couldn't with my girlfriend. I would find him, take him home to my parent's house and fuck him like I had never fucked him before.

The next morning, the smell of pancakes pulled me out of my sleep. Ma was cooking, and my stomach rumbled its appreciation. With my eyes still closed, I reached across the bed for José. But when my hand found only the mattress, I opened them. Where'd he go? The bathroom? Then, I heard his voice coming from the living room. Ma laughed. I threw on my sweats and went to investigate.

"Good morning, sleepy head," Ma called, poking her head out of the kitchen. "We were about to start without you." José was at our dining table with a plate stacked high with pancakes, hash browns and eggs. He smiled at me. □ "Your mom has been telling me all about you."

"Ma!" I called "Only good stories, right?"

"Sit down Noah, before the food gets cold." She brought out a plate for me and herself. I sat down.

"Mrs. Braverman, thanks for this. It's really good," José managed. He was literally shoveling the food into his mouth. I guess all our nighttime activity had worked up a hearty appetite.

"Got to feed my boys," Ma said. And then, "José, are you seeing anybody? Noah never mentioned you having a girlfriend." I froze, my fork full of eggs halfway between the plate and my mouth.

"No, ma'am. Not right now. I think I met somebody though. Might turn into something serious."

"Oh, good! Either way, you're young. Enjoy it."

"That's the plan, ma'am." And he winked at me. I don't think Ma noticed me blush.

That night Jose and I set up shop in our usual spot at Jimmy's, looking forward to making another killing.

"The bar's about to close, and everyone's talking about going to The Bakery, that after-hours spot again," José said. For the last couple of weeks, each night after Jimmy's closed we'd heard a few patrons talk about keeping the party going at another location nearby. I didn't pay much attention to it at first. Mostly because after Jimmy's closed, I was focused on getting José in bed. But, clearly he wanted to see what all the talk was about.

"Let's go," I said. I caught myself smiling at the thought of chilling with José all night because the delay would just make getting him home that much hotter. And another reason to hit up this after-hours joint was Dianna worked there as a bartender. Through her, I'd recently gotten a message from the wise guy that owned the place, telling me that if I got rid of the guy running the spot, I could run it for a small concession fee.

I wasn't surprised that wise guys from the neighborhood took a liking to me. I was white. And I had a reputation for making and collecting the money. Plus, I didn't let people disrespect me. My guess is that this wise guy wanted me around to see what I could do for him. And I was just as interested in what he could do for me. As much money as I was already pulling in, I knew that there were more customers out there and the possibility to make even more. I knew the guy who ran the after-hours spot – the one the wise guy was trying to get rid of, but I didn't care about him. He was this heavy set, Italian guy named Vito. People weren't respecting him or his business. If he couldn't demand respect, he didn't deserve to keep his business anymore. That's how I saw it. I wanted that money for myself and would do whatever I had to do to get it.

When José and I pulled up to The Bakery it appeared dark inside like it was closed. During the day, the spot was a bakery, which I thought was a great cover. Bakeries have deliveries coming and going through the night. That meant that people moving in and out at all hours wouldn't seem suspicious. But, on top of that – from what I heard – the cops were paid to look the other way. So, it was definitely a good front.

José knocked on the door. Immediately a big, fat Italian guy wearing a blue velour sweat suit peeked through a gap he'd made in the Venetian blinds. After a few seconds of looking us up-and-down, with a not-so-friendly expression on his face, he asked,

"Whaddya want?"

"I'm Dianna's nephew. She works here and told me to come by…" I answered. He let the blinds go, disappearing as they snapped back into place. For a minute or so, nothing happened. Then I heard at least five locks open. The Fat Guy jerked the door up and asked us to raise our hands. He pulled a handheld metal detector out of nowhere and started to scan us. I knew a search for weapons would end badly.

"You don't want to do that," I told him. "Instead, why don't you grab the owner for me?" Right on cue, the Wise Guy who'd sent me the message – Tommy was his name – walked over and waved us through security.

"When you see this guy," Tommy told The Fat Guy and one other security guard nearby, "let him and whoever he's with come through. You search him you might not like what you find. Capisce?"

Tommy gave José and me the grand tour. Just behind the bakery storefront, there was a full bar, a pool table, Joker Poker and Cherry Master slot machines. And in the very back there was a room set up with four tables for professional card games. It was like a small casino. Off to the side of the room with card tables there was a tiny room with nothing in it but a bed.

"This is where the girls work," Tommy said. "If you boys ever want some action, just let me know."

José shot me a devilish smile and then quickly hid it. But it was enough to tell me what he was thinking. Gambling? Prostitution? This was a move into all new territory for our little drug business. But I had the feeling that the money would make it more than worth our while.

"Come. Walk with me to my office," Tommy said. Once there, he settled in behind a huge wooden desk. He didn't speak until José and I sat down as well. "Look, the guy who's got the concession here now, he's a good guy. But, he's careless. Other people come here and do their thing without paying for the right to do business here. In short, if you want the spot, it is yours. But you have to let him know that he cannot do his thing here anymore. Of course, that will not sit right with him, if you know what I mean." I let Tommy's words sink in.

"If I decide to take you up on your offer, let me worry about him. I could take care of that with no problem. And if I ran this spot, you would have no unwanted guests. Ever," I said as Tommy nodded.

"I have heard very good things about the way you handle yourself." He replied. "This is why I am making you an offer."

"But, for me to consider it," I answered, "We would have to negotiate what you expect to receive in rent." I had already done my homework and found out what my soon to be predecessor's take was. And I wanted to cut myself a better deal. Tommy looked at me like I had three heads. And, to be a just turned 17 year-old nobody asking to set new terms with a wise-guy in his own establishment, I might as well have had three heads. It was a crazy thing to do. But, crazy had always worked for me. So I continued. "The way I see it not only am I getting an opportunity to make money for myself, but I am also keeping control over this spot for you. I am keeping out the riffraff that's been coming in here, showing disrespect, and taking money out of your pocket. So, I will be looking out for you as well, helping you make money."

Tommy smiled. "I knew I'd like you...I hope you can do more than talk a good game. Ok. We can set new terms. Tell me what you'd like. But later. Now, let's drink and you check the place out." Tommy stood up and reached across the desk to shake hands. He shook José's first and then he took mine. He gripped my hand tightly and pulled me until I was leaning over the desk, looking him right in the eyes. "I must say, before you commit to doing this, Noah, do not fuck with me."

"You got it, my man," I said. "Now let's drink."

CHAPTER 29

"Wow! It's about fucking time you bought a car! Wait. Do you have your license?" José asked.

"Hell, no," I laughed. "Just got my permit. That's good enough for me. All the cops can do is give me a ticket. Fuck 'em." The car was a brand new, fully loaded, 1995 Mercury Cougar. It had a suede top and came with a booming system and rims.

"Hit the block and go make me some money," I told José. "I'm going to go see Kathy and show her what I bought for us." I ignored the surprised expression that crossed his face as I pulled away from the curb. Maybe I didn't want to admit how deep my feelings were running for Jose. I also didn't want to hurt Kathy because I really loved her. But the truth was, I still wasn't spending much time with, or paying attention to her. We were still fighting like cats and dogs about it. I thought the new car would excite her and that riding around in it all day would stop her from busting my balls.

The drive to our apartment was short, but it was a beautiful day. I had the windows rolled down and blasted the music all the way down Coney Island Avenue. I lit up a blunt and turned the radio even louder as I pulled up in front of our place. I tapped the horn and looked up at our bedroom, expecting to see my girl pop her head out. Instead, I saw a guy I didn't recognize rush by our window. A second after he flashed by, it struck me that he wasn't wearing a shirt. I jumped out of the car.

"Yoooooo!" I yelled even louder than the music playing. The guy I'd just seen popped his head out of the window and called down

"Can I help you?"

Was this motherfucker serious? Was he really half naked in my apartment, with my girl, asking if he could help me?

"Who the fuck are you and what the fuck are you doing with my girl in our house?"

"Your girl? Sorry, my man. This is my girl." Kathy's hands appeared out of nowhere and struggled to pull this guy back inside the window. Then she stuck her head out.

"Leave here, Noah, I'm calling the cops."

What? It was like my mind just refused to understand the words. How could she be saying this to me? Why wasn't she kicking him out? Apologizing for getting caught cheating? She was telling me to leave. Calling the cops on me. Telling me to leave our apartment, where I paid the rent.

"Come the fuck out here and face me like a fucking man!" I screamed. When no one came back to the window, I ran to the door. It was double locked, including the lock I never carried keys for. The idea that she'd locked me out -- her man! -- sent me completely over the edge. I kicked the door and pounded it with my fists until they were bloodied, the door was like a vault and I couldn't get it open.

"The cops are already on their way, so leave Noah," she screamed. Her words crushed me. I didn't know what to say. The only thing that came to mind was, "Fuck you bitch, it's over," I yelled, as I choked back the tears. Neighbors popped their heads out of windows. A few came out on their porches, carrying cordless phones. I knew the cops were coming for sure. I had drugs on me and a gun in the car. I was driving with just a permit. It was beyond time to go.

But, I wouldn't leave without a fight. I found a rock in the yard, a good solid one, and hurled it up at the barricaded door and through its little window. But the crashing sound didn't make me feel any better. By the time I pulled away, I was crying. Probably harder than I had ever cried before. My car's tires screamed as I peeled off. I promised myself that I would get that motherfucker Kathy was with, whoever he was and that I would never be on this side of hurt again. Fuck Kathy, I thought. Fuck that bitch. In fact, fuck all bitches. I went to find José.

CHAPTER 30

"Who's this?" I snarled. I hated when restricted numbers came up on my cell.

"It's Tommy. We need to talk. Sooner than later." I was all fucked up. After leaving Kathy's, I'd picked up José and gone to Dog's apartment. Some of my boys, after hearing Kathy cheated, came through as well. For two days, José, Dog, his three pit bulls and Laree watched me do line after line of coke. Sometimes, they joined me, but none of them kept up with me. They were trying to slow me down, to keep me from completely losing it, but I wasn't having any part of it. I was trying to escape the shit I was facing. I was heartbroken about Kathy, who I loved, and I was totally confused about whether I was straight or gay. I worried about how it would affect my business if it came out. And I resented having to deal drugs all the time with no time to just live my life. I was burnt-out and hadn't done any business since coming to Dog's.

All I could think about was seeing that motherfucker poke his head out of my apartment window and tell me Kathy was his girl. His girl! For two days, I'd ranted about how I should go back over there and kick his ass. But my boys stopped me. It wasn't like with Chaz, her boyfriend who was in jail when she and I first hooked up. This motherfucker was new in her life. Apparently he was some college fool she'd hooked up with. And she'd gone after him. Fucking him up would be bad for business. She wasn't worth it, the boys said. There were other girls. And somewhere in me, I knew I didn't want another girl. I was pretty sure I just wanted José. And that scared me because sooner or later, I would have to come out to everyone. The fear added to my anger. And the anger made me snort more coke.

The phone rang and it was Tommy from The Bakery, after hours club. I had hoped he called to have me take care of a problem so I might have a chance to punch someone out. I was pissed and needed to take it out on someone. I didn't give a fuck who.

"Definitely," I said into my phone. "I'll come to you. "Business was business. I didn't know what Tommy wanted, but I was more than ready to tell the drug dealing fool running the after-hours spot that his time was up. I scooped up my gun off of Dog's coffee table in front of me and slipped on my Timberland boots.

"Let's roll," I told my boys in response to them all giving me the "Wassup?" look. As they gathered their shit, I told them where we were going and tossed Laree my keys.

We got to the club a little bit after 4 a.m., and security waved us through. As we walked back to Tommy's office, I noticed that there weren't many customers. Once we reached Tommy's office, my boys waited outside and I walked right in.

"So, what's up?" I asked. Something about the way Tommy looked me up and down let me know that my two-day binge hadn't left me looking my best. He either didn't care or thought it better not to bring up my appearance.

"Look," he said, "the guy that was doing his thing here ..."

"Where is he? I'll handle him right now," I interrupted.

"Let me finish" Tommy snapped.

"The guy that was doing his thing here before his carelessness caught up to him. He got locked up last night for selling to an undercover NARC. We haven't had anyone here all night. The people are going elsewhere. Some people run in and out of here to just buy shit. That's making me hot and I don't need the heat. So, I need someone to start and start now."

I didn't know whether to be relieved or disappointed that taking over the new spot was going to be so easy. I was really annoyed that I didn't get a chance to work out at least some of the rage I was feeling.

"No problem. I'll have my boys start right now."

"And what about my fee?" Tommy asked.

"You were getting $250 a week before? I will pay $200."

"You Jews love a discount," Tommy laughed and offered me his hand to seal the deal.

That done, I headed out of the office to tell my boys the official news so we could start making the money.

CHAPTER 31

"Your father's having a heart attack! Noah? I've called an ambulance. Noah, I need you to meet me at the hospital. Noah?"

I'd been sleeping off the bottle of Hennessy I'd drunk with José the night before. It took my brain some time to register what Ma was telling me.

"I hear you, Ma. I'll meet you at the hospital. Where they takin' him?"

"Coney Island." I hung up the phone and willed myself to roll out of bed. It felt like the room had rolled with me. José and I had crashed at a cheap hotel in Sheepshead Bay called Windjammer. I knew the place because I often dealt coke to the prostitutes who took their tricks there. It was the perfect place to party it up. I could have stayed in any hotel I wanted in Manhattan. Truth is, I loved my neighborhood. Everyone knew me; it was mine. We had been partying non-stop since my breakup with Kathy. During my clumsy search for my clothes, José woke up and asked me what was going on.

"My dad is having a heart attack and I gotta go."

"I'm going with you," he said, jumping out of bed. José had to be at least as fucked up as I was, but somehow he managed to find his clothes and get dressed while I was still struggling into my jeans.

"Here," he said, handing me my wife-beater, wallet, and car keys. "I'll call a cab." I held up the set of keys he'd just given me.

"We were too drunk to drive last night. You left your car at Tommy's.

"Fuck." I nodded, remembering, and thanked him. It crossed my mind how glad I was to have him with me.

As we went to the front of the hotel to wait for the taxi to come, I felt like I was going to puke my entire insides onto the sidewalk.

"I can't keep doing this."

"Doing what?" José asked. I started to answer him, but realized I wasn't sure what I meant. Getting shit-faced every night? Stressing and hurting over Kathy? Ignoring how serious my feelings for José were getting? For some reason I couldn't say any of those things to José Not yet. So, I said, "Running the business like this. We need more people. Someone posted at the after-hours all night. Someone to take over handling the pager for you, so you can stay at the bar. We gotta keep all the money separate so if we lose one pot, we don't lose it all."

The car pulled up. I settled into the back and closed my eyes. But, I could feel José staring at me.

"What?" I asked, as I opened my eyes and looked at him.

"Nothing. You're just…smart," he said. "And all business. I couldn't think about business if I was going through shit and my dad was in the hospital."

I wanted to tell him how close I was to cracking up, and that most of the time I felt like I was going crazy. I wanted to tell him a lot of things. But the rest of the ride happened in silence. This was my father's third heart attack. He'd already had a pacemaker put in. I figured…or hoped…that if he survived all of that, he could survive this. As the cab pulled into the hospital parking lot, I saw my brother, Scott, smoking a cigarette near the doors to the emergency room. Before I could even get out of the cab, Scott began filling me in. It wasn't a heart attack, but a stroke. Dad was alive. Was going to live. Tests were being run to determine if there'd been any brain damage.

Relief flooded my body as I released a breath I hadn't even realized I was holding. I was uneasy about the thought of Dad having brain damage, but he was alive. In the emergency room waiting area, Ma was with my brothers David, Jared and Adam. "He's having trouble moving around," she said, pulling me into a desperate hug. "They think he might be bedridden for a while. He'll need physical therapy. They want to keep him a few days before sending him home."

I asked if I could see him. Ma nodded. They'd just been in to see him.

It was a shared room. There was a very old man, moaning in the bed next to my father. Which reminded me of why Dad hated hospitals. Dad was sleeping. I almost could not recognize him. It was hard to reconcile the man who used to carry me on his shoulders or let me watch him shave when I was kid with the man in that bed. He looked so small and frail under the blankets. Maybe I'd always known it, but it bubbled to the front of my mind then how much I had resented my Dad for disconnecting from us: for only getting out of his chair when Ma nagged him into beating us. I felt like he'd abandoned us. But seeing him so helpless in a hospital bed made none of that matter. I loved him.

As I moved close to him, the fear of almost losing him again stabbed at me. He was a simple man. Never asked for or expected much. Worked hard for so little. I remembered all the arguments I overheard him and Ma have over money. Arguments about how they were going to feed us kids. The time he sold his wedding ring just to buy two weeks of groceries and refused to let Ma sell hers. I kissed him on the forehead. Even then, with him sick and sleeping, it was awkward. It had been years since I'd been affectionate with Dad.

"You're a good man," I said to my father. "And, I'm gonna be a good son." I'd take care of him and Ma. They'd never worry about money again. Not as long as I was alive. I would do any and everything I could to make sure they had whatever they needed and anything they wanted.

CHAPTER 32

Several months had passed and dad, much to everyone's surprise, had almost fully recovered back to his normal self. Business was great, but I was working my balls off and needed to lighten my load.

"I've got two people waiting to see you" Jose said, as he entered Dianna's apartment. "Roger is this dude from Harlem, I met with some kids that were friends with a girl I used to date". He winked,

"I ran into him at the mall a couple of days ago with his boys, and they are looking to make some money," Jose continued. "And you are always looking to expand, so I figured you might want to talk." I was proud of José for taking the initiative and welcomed his help. "The other is Eddie from Gravesend. You said you needed a driver, and he's got his license. He's waiting up the block at Toni's pizzeria, and Roger is at the bar."

But, as we left Dianna's house after bagging up a half of key of coke, I started thinking that this Roger dude could be a snitch or an undercover cop. I knew Eddie, but who the fuck was Roger?

"Yo José, if this kid Roger is anything but legit...I love you, but it's gonna be your ass, my man."

"I love you too, bro," José said with a smile but then put on a serious face. "I wouldn't bring anyone less than legit around you. It's my job to keep you and this operation safe."

I nodded and held the door for him to enter the pizzeria. When we got inside, Eddie was already sitting at a booth but wasn't eating. He was dressed in black sweats, yellow Timbs and a black hoodie. He had a full, well-trimmed beard and couldn't have been more than 22. Eddie didn't look like a pushover at all. He was taller and definitely looked like he hit the gym.

Eddie stood as I got near the table. We shook hands and slid into our seats. I ordered a large pizza pie for them, grilled chicken on a salad for myself, and a large bottle of diet Pepsi for the table. When the food came, the smell of melted cheese and sauce tempted me and made me want to throw my salad across the room. But, I was heading back to the gym later that day and didn't want the heavy pizza sitting in my stomach. I asked the waiter to put the bill on my tab, passed him a 20-dollar tip and waved him away.

"So, I hear you wanna make some money," I said to Eddie.

"I do. Definitely. And I know with you there is plenty to be made," Eddie said with a wide grin. "Everyone knows who you are. Even from where I live, I could get you more clientele and no one running my area would say shit. I'd be working for you, and no one wants to fuck with you." I listened intently as he continued. "I know you already have a well-established business. José tells me you would need me to run your beeper for you, but I could also bring you customers you don't have that are buying from other dealers. So, I have something to bring to the table too."

I looked him up and down. Sizing him up, I felt good about this guy from the start, but I'll watch him like I do everyone else.

"I think it could be good for us," I said, "I will tell you now if you're in, you're on call. That means when I call, you answer. I don't give a fuck if you're having a wet dream or balls-deep in some pussy, you answer the phone when I call and always get back to whoever pages you."

I paused, waiting for a response, but he just had a vague grin on his face.

"As soon as you leave here, start looking for a car. Something under two thousand and I'll pay for it. I'll also pay for your gas, cell phone and pager." Eddie nodded.

I went on to tell him that for every hundred dollars he made me, he would make forty.

"I expect you to pull in around fourteen hundred dollars a day, which would put four hundred dollars in your pocket and a grand for me," I said. "It could be more, especially if you're saying you can bring in more clients." I took another pause and waited for an answer. He smiled with a nod that said he was in.

"If you have no other questions or anything to add, then we're done here. Welcome to the crew. The only other thing I have to let you know, Eddie, is don't fuck me."

"I understand Jeremy." He said, as we shook hands. "I wouldn't even think of it."

CHAPTER 33

We left the pizzeria and walked a few blocks over to the bar, to meet up with Roger.

"Rendell keeps on calling," José said, clearly annoyed. We were standing outside the bar.

"Okay, okay, I'll call him now. Go inside and tell your boy, Roger, I'll be right in."

As José walked inside, I looked through the little window in the door of the bar to see who this Roger guy was. I had a bad feeling about this kid because I didn't know him, but on second glance, the guy Jose was talking to looked harmless. He was wearing a black Sean John velour sweat suit and Air Jordan's. He was short and skinny but when he turned around, I saw a mean face that didn't look like it belonged on his little body.

I checked my phone and noticed a missed call. It was from Rendell. And I hadn't spoken to him since the shit went down with Kathy. If he asked, I would say it was because he and Kathy were still tight and I wasn't ready to hear about her yet. The other reason was that his freeloading drug use was out of control. But, truth was I missed him. There weren't many people around me from before I started dealing. In fact, there weren't that many people around who still called me Noah.

I liked the name Jeremy and thought it would be smart if new drug connects didn't actually have my real name, and so I started using it in business.

I dialed Rendell's number. He picked up on the first ring. "Hey. What's up? It's Jeremy. Long time, no see, bro."

"You're the one who never answers my calls," Rendell said.

"Yeah. Sorry about that. I've been busy. Let's hang tonight and party. Come by the bar later. We'll get some drinks then crash at my mom's."

It was perfect timing because José's mom had called earlier that day to ask me if I'd send him home. She missed having him around the house, and I'd promised to let him have the night off. So, I was free. Rendell agreed and I hung up the phone.

As I walked into the bar, I approached José and Roger. "This is Roger, Roger this is Jeremy" Jose said.

Since I had other business to attend to, I told the guy to get right to the point. I had to meet my drug connect and I didn't have time to fuck around.

"José says you might be able to help me." Roger said. "I can't afford to buy any coke or weed up front, but I have a whole project building in Harlem that I could be selling to."

"Stop," I said. "So, basically you don't know me and I don't know you. But, you want me to just hand you some work?"

"Well, yeah, I guess that's what I am saying. José knows me, and he knows where I stay."

"Excuse us a minute," I interrupted Roger. I grabbed José by the arm and pulled him a few feet away where Roger couldn't hear over the noise of the bar. "How well do you know this motherfucker?" My face inches from his, José looked more than a little nervous.

"N...Not that well. But, I know where he hangs out and the building he lives in."

"So, what do you think I should do?" I asked Jose, softening my voice but still holding his arm.

"We should give him something small to see what he can do. Then let him work his way up from there."

"Fine. I'll do that. And if he starts making good money, that will become your deal and you can take a percentage off of it." I let go of his arm and we went back to Roger at the bar.

"We'll give you five hundred in twenties of coke. It's all we got on us at the moment anyways. I'll make a call and have someone bring you the same in weed. You bring me back six hundred dollars so you'll make 400 dollars for yourself, because it will be all your own customers, you will get more then I usually would give anyone. If you can move that, when you come back, I'll give you double. From now on, you'll deal strictly with José. And Roger, I don't know you. You don't know me. I'm taking a risk trusting you. I'll only say this once. Don't fuck with my money, and don't try to fuck me. Don't make that mistake." I stared at Roger until he nodded his head.

"I see you have customers waiting, José, so go pick up another package from Dianna's and I'll call you later," I said and left the bar to meet my connect, James.

As usual, when I arrived at James' house, he was outside with his pit bull. I whistled for the dog as I approached the gate. He barked and ran up to me, jumping around playfully. He wasn't the only one happy to see me. James was all smiles as I walked up and gave him a fist pound.

"Let's go inside," I said, looking around. "I have $15,000 on me for you," I said and he smiled. "And I have to get going. There's a lot of customers waiting on me."

"All work and no play today, huh?" James said as we climbed the steps of his porch and went inside. I noticed the smile disappear from his face.

"No play today, man. Sorry," I forced a laugh to bring back a lighter mood.

"Things are really changing with you, Noah. You're becoming a serious business man." James sat down on his couch. I tossed a thick envelope of money onto the coffee table and settled into a recliner across from him.

"I need more coke. A key and a half, to be exact." James looked at me for a second as if he was trying to decide if I was serious.

"I'll be honest with you Noah, I only pick up two keys a week. One for me and one for you. If you do more than a key a week, you're selling more than me."

"Well, that's what I need. Can you make it happen?" I said.

"Sure. Come back when you're almost done with the key you got now and I'll be ready for you."

"Cool," I said, standing up. I was already making a mental list of all the places I had to go after leaving James. "I'll see you later. But next time I come through, I'll stay longer. I promise." We shook hands, but James didn't walk me out.

By the time I got to the bar, everyone was already there. The bar was dark as usual, because the coke-heads there really didn't want to be seen. In the corner booth, made up of an old chipped wooden table and ripped black pleather sofas, Rendell, Laree, and Dog were seated, talking to a group of four girls. The fellas had probably been through a few rounds of drinks, because I had called ahead and picked up the tab. And you could hear them loud and clear over the crowd. I didn't see José, so I figured he was in the bathroom making another sell.

"Jeremy!" Rendell yelled when he saw me. I gave everyone a pound and someone passed me a Hennessy and coke before I even sat down. I noticed that the girls didn't have drinks.

"You guys have no manners. Get these ladies some drinks!" I said, turning to one of the girls, a really cute blonde with beautiful green eyes. "What are you ladies drinking?"

We were all laughing, drinking, and flirting when José emerged from the bathroom after making a sale. Business had been booming. José held down the coke sales at the bar, and Laree was handling my weed trade so well, I just had to collect the money and re-up with my connect to get more drugs. The downside to that was that they worked hard, all hours of the day and night. Laree was still new to working with me. But I could see it was taking a toll on José .

"How much money you got for me so far?" I asked as José sat down and ordered a Corona.

"Eleven hundred," he said. You'd have to be blind to miss how tired he looked.

"Take three hundred and give it to your mom, take another three hundred for yourself and go home for the night. You can take my car."

Reading the questions on his face I told him, "I'll hold down the spot until we close. I'll be here anyway. And I promised your mom you'd be home tonight."

"Thanks, bro," José said. He stood up and leaned towards me. For a second I thought he was going to kiss me, but he gave me a quick pound, said goodbye to the fellas and headed out. He didn't even finish his beer.

A couple of hours and many more drinks into the night, I realized that the blonde was really tall, with huge tits, a small waist and a really big ass. She had not stopped talking to me all night. She was totally hot and was obviously flirting with me. But, I wasn't interested. Not even a little bit. At some point, Dog noticed us talking and whispered in my ear.

"What you gonna do with that? She wants you, bro."

I lied, telling him I wasn't feeling well and that I was going home after the bar closed. As I put my jacket on, Rendell said, "Hey, Jeremy, let me get a few bags. I wanna hang with these girls." I knew Rendell would ask me for some coke before the night was over. I didn't want to, but I slipped him some along with forty dollars.

"I'll be at Ma's if you want to crash there. I'll be asleep, so I will leave the door keys under the mat in the front hall for you to come in."

I slapped everyone five and left. On the way home, I realized that I was still a bit drunk. And, I was missing José. I couldn't remember the last time I'd spent a night away from him. I wanted to go to sleep to get the day over with and be closer to seeing him again. And when I got to Ma's, I went up those stairs opened the door and slipped the keys under the mat. Without waking anyone, I went straight to my room. I emptied my pockets of money and drugs and put it all on the dresser. Thanks to the booze, I fell asleep quickly and my last thought was that the pillow smelled like Jose. And, I was glad.

The next morning the distant honking of horns woke me up. I looked at the dresser. Two hundred dollars in cash and four fifty-dollar bags of coke were missing. A portion of the stuff I'd emptied out of my pockets and put on top of my dresser the night before were just gone

"Ma, have you been in my room?" I asked. We were both standing in the living room. Ma turned from the Jeopardy game show she was watching.

"No, I haven't been in there, but Rendell did stop by this morning. He came up for something and then left. I asked him, but he didn't say what. He just said you knew about it and that it was okay."

"Okay, Ma. Thanks," I said as I turned to go back to my room.

"Is everything alright?" she asked me.

"Yeah. Everything is good. Things are just moved around a little bit in here. It's fine," I lied and closed the bedroom door. I couldn't recall all the times I'd given Rendell coke or money just because he'd asked. There was no reason to steal. I got dressed in the same clothes I'd dropped on the floor before getting into bed and scooped up my phone. There were 20 missed calls and even more pages on my beeper. None were from Rendell.

I sat on the edge of my bed and took a couple of deep breaths to calm myself down while I dialed the number to the bar. Now that it was open, I wanted to see if Rendell had gone back there. As the phone rang, I realized my hands were shaking. The bartender picked up the line.

"It's Jeremy. Don't let him know I'm asking, but is Rendell there?"

"Yeah, he's here," the bartender said in a low voice, just above a whisper.

"How long ago did he get there?"

"He was waiting when I got here to open."

"Don't tell him I called. Don't say anything about me to him. I will be there in a few minutes." I got dressed, grabbed my gun and was out the door.

The walk from Ma's house to the bar happened in the blink of an eye. One second I was walking down the stairs of our building, the next I was turning to enter the bar. Rendell was seated at the bar. His back was to me. Seeing him calmly having a drink with money he'd stolen from me, his friend sent my hurt and anger soaring. I stood in the doorway for a second and just looked at him. I knew I couldn't let him get away with it. I couldn't let anyone steal from me. That would send a dangerous message to others who wanted to try shit. As I walked across the bar toward Rendell, I felt the .22 caliber gun inside my boot press against my ankle. I thought to myself, 'the part of me that is Noah loves Rendell and just wants to ignore this. But Jeremy has to handle his business.'

"How was your night?" I asked Rendell. He jumped and spun his upper body around to face me.

"Oh shit! You scared me, Jeremy." He laughed.

"When I didn't see you this morning, I figured you got lucky with them girls," I said.

"I did get lucky," Rendell said without looking me in the eyes. "But, I dropped by your spot for a second just to use the bathroom." I waited for him to say more. He didn't.

"You done with your drink? Take a walk with me. I have to meet some customers."

"Cool," Rendell said, putting his empty beer bottle on the bar. As he stood up, I couldn't help but notice that he kept playing with his nose and rubbing it with a tissue. "Let me just run to the bathroom right quick."

I knew he was going to be using more of the coke he'd stolen from me. As he disappeared into the restroom, I could hear my heart pounding. Rendell came back quickly, and I led him out of the bar. I hadn't thought it out, but soon I realized that I was leading him to the park.

"Jeremy, you alright? What's wrong?" Rendell kept asking me. I didn't want to spook him or make him run off, so I kept saying that nothing was wrong. That everything was okay. When we got to the park, I went over to the swings and Rendell followed. I pretended to bend down and tie my shoe. As I did, I looked around to make sure we were alone. I stood up with the gun in my hand and pointed it right at Rendell's forehead.

"Did you take anything from me when you came to my house last night?" I asked, hoping at least now he would come clean. Honesty would give me choices that his lying to me wouldn't.

"Jeremy!" he yelled and threw his hands over his head. "Noah... Of course not, Noah. I wouldn't do that to you. You my boy. You've given me everything. Why would I steal coke from you?"

"Funny," I said, " I didn't mention coke, you piece of shit." We stared at each other in silence. I watched drops of sweat gather on his forehead, then trickle down the side of his face. I lowered the .22 and enjoyed the second of relief that passed across his face just before I pulled the trigger.

Rendell didn't scream. He stood there and looked confused, as if he couldn't understand why there was smoke coming from a hole in his leg.

"You shot me," He whispered. "You fucking shot me."

"Yeah. And, I'll shoot you again if you say anything to the cops. I'll do even worse if you fuck with me again, Rendell." We stared at each other again in silence until I think we both realized that I was serious. As I turned to leave the park, I saw him drop to the ground and start to scream in agony. He would have to get himself to the emergency room. I just kept walking, asking myself why he had to steal from me. And, I imagined, Rendell was asking himself the same thing.

CHAPTER 34

"Alyssa, open up! It's me Noah." I couldn't think of anywhere else in the world to go. Maybe I needed someone familiar, an old friend who knew me before I became Ron Jeremy. Before the drugs and the guns. Maybe I just needed someone I knew I could trust. Even after my life got crazy and I was barely around, Alyssa Russo and I stayed friends. She never stopped calling to check up on me from time to time. And every now and then, I would stop by to see her and her family.

"What's wrong, Noah?" she asked as soon as she opened the front door. "You look like you just saw a ghost?"

"Rendell. I shot Rendell."

"You did what?" Instead of letting me into her house, Alyssa stepped out on to her porch and closed the door. The look on her face went beyond shock. Alyssa looked at me like I was a stranger, and I knew then that I couldn't tell her the truth.

"It was an accident," I lied. "We were playing around with my gun, and it just went off." After a horrified look crossed her face, she asked,

"Is he alive?" I nodded my head.

"Yeah. He'll be fine. I just needed someone to talk to, you understand?"

"Yes," she said, but I wasn't sure Alyssa really did. Hell, I wasn't sure I really did.

"Well, I won't tell anyone. You know that. But, I hope he will be fine. Noah, you have to be more careful." She hugged me. And I hugged her back. Her hands sliding up and down my back put me at ease. I needed that friendly embrace to let me know all was right with the world. The crazy world I was living in. The drugs, the guns, the sex, the lies about who I was and who I was fucking were catching up to me. Alyssa stepped back and looked up at me.

"Are you okay?" Still holding her, I just nodded and hugged her again. The truth, I knew, would make her think I was a monster. Would make her always look at me with that expression that said she didn't know me

"Thanks, Alyssa. I just needed to get my head straight after that crazy shit." My voice sounded different even to me. Suddenly, Jeremy was back.

"I gotta run. But I will come by again soon and stay for a longer visit." I made my way down the stairs leading away from Alyssa's porch and back to my life. Maybe I was a monster. As much as I wanted Alyssa to think nothing had changed, as much as I wanted to keep things the same between us, I wasn't sorry for shooting Rendell. He got what he deserved. I had to protect what was mine, or someone would try to step up and take it. Before I reached the end of Alyssa's block, my pager was buzzing with calls from customers. There wasn't another moment to second-guess myself. I knew what I had to do.

CHAPTER 35

"Look. Here's the deal. I can't pretend anymore. And, if what I'm about to say offends anyone, or someone just don't want to fuck with me because of this, then by all means, leave."

All my oldest and closest friends: Dog, Laree, Eddie, José, Caitlin, Alyssa, and Dianna looked at me and at each other trying to figure out what the hell I was saying. I knew I was rambling. I was stalling. I'd called this meeting to make an announcement.

"But, there ain't no coming back. Keep in mind, I'm the same motherfucker that works hard in the street, and ain't nothing changing for you guys. I am just trying to make myself more real."

I'd called this meeting because I couldn't live the lie anymore. I'd gone home with some girl the night before. It had taken forever to get hard, even longer than forever to make her come. And when I was with my boys, and girls tagged along, I'd have to front like I was interested. Who was I pretending for? I didn't want to pretend. So, I called this meeting with my closest friends to tell them the truth. And now I was stalling.

Dog bit the bullet. "What's going on, Jeremy? What up? I don't understand. What's wrong?"

I told myself, I could do this. I could be honest. I told myself, 'I'm a fucking gangster. A gun toting, drug slinging quick-to-slap-the-shit-out-of-you-mother fucker-gangster.' And then I told them...

"I'm gay."

They each responded with a blank stare almost as if they didn't hear what I had said.

"Stop playing," Dog said finally.

"Yea. Stop playing, Jeremy," Dianna said.

"What you mean, you gay. I seen you leave last night with that hot bitch, Alexis," Laree chimed in.

"Well, that's the last time I'm gonna be doing that shit," I said with a laugh. "I had to eat that bitch's pussy for an hour straight and make her cum three times before she would leave my house without a bad thing to say about me. I told her coke wouldn't let my dick get hard. But the truth is I've been messing with a dude for a while now. And the more I do, the less I want chicks. Now, I'm done completely. Tired of faking it."

"You lying," Dog said, shaking his head back and forth.

"I'm not lying. José is the one I've been messing with." Just as the words left my lips, José stood up and leaned across the corner of the table that separated us and planted a deep wet one on my mouth, in front of everyone. When he sat down, there were some shocked faces around the table.

"Anyone have a problem with it? Anyone have a problem with who I am?" There was silence. The next words came from Dog.

"Ah shit! Without you bagging the chicks, how we supposed to get pussy around here now?"

CHAPTER 36

"When was the last time you spoke to Roger?" I asked.

José looked at me for a few seconds. I could tell he was picking his words carefully.

"I only seen him one more time after we gave him the first package," he answered. "I gave him twice as much like you said we should. After that, I never heard from him again. It's been a few weeks."

"Let everyone know we're looking for him. There were a lot of our people in the bar that day we met, let them all know to keep a lookout for him," I said. "If we find him, I'll handle it. I want him brought to me."

José nodded and I continued giving orders. "Eddie is supposed to meet us here. He's been out of drugs for an hour already. So stay here and wait for him. This is ten thousand in twenties of blow and five thousand in dimes of crack. It should last him a few days."

"Also he's been doing really well, but the boy gets no sleep. Tell him I want him to find someone tough and trustworthy to work with him and split the day up. We'll pay him to oversee the kid, so it will make up for the money he loses giving up some hours."

I left José at the bar to wait for Eddie. I had $30,000 in cash on me that I needed to bring to James. My plan was to get all the business out of the way so I'd be free to chill and relax with everyone later that night. Things were going so good with me and José and the business. I felt like we both deserved the night off and trying out Ecstasy for the first time didn't sound like a bad idea. Dog had called me earlier and asked if we could hang later, said he had some good pot to try out.

As I left the bar, I dialed up Dog to tell him that tonight we could get fucked up without a care in the world and that José and I would see him at around ten. Then I called James. He told me that he was in the park handling some business and I could meet him there with the money.

"In fact," he said, "I'm gonna need a ride somewhere so come in a cab and you can take the ride with me when I'm done here." Twenty minutes later, the driver slowed down next to the park. It looked empty. I had to squint against the early evening shadows to make out a figure I thought it was James. I had the driver honk the horn to get his attention. What was he doing in the park? For a split second, I thought I could make out the silhouette of another person near James. But, when he started walking towards the cab, James was alone.

As he stepped into the light of the street lamp, the expression on his face made me stop breathing. He looked furious. Violent. And though I knew he was someone not to be fucked with, I'd never actually seen James upset. When he slid into the backseat with me, before I could ask what was wrong, his expression completely changed. He was all smiles. I slipped him the envelope filled with his money. He took it quickly and silently.

"What you getting into tonight, my man?" I asked before he pulled me into a hug. "You should come with me to party with some friends."

"First, you come with me to make a stop." He said. Then told the driver to take us to downtown Brooklyn. I decided not to ask him what he was doing in the park or about the person I thought I'd seen him with who suddenly dropped out of sight. I instinctively knew it was none of my business and if he wanted me to know, he would have told me.

When we arrived downtown, James directed the driver to the end of a street practically underneath the Brooklyn Bridge. James paid the driver a hundred bucks to wait and keep the meter running.

"Come with me, Noah." He hopped out of the car and walked briskly towards the river. I followed and had to jog a bit to keep up with him. I looked around and took in the quiet neighborhood with its big, expensive-looking apartment buildings.

"I think you understand now, Noah, that this business of ours is a dangerous one. You can't trust anyone. You have to be willing to fight for every dollar and kill for what's yours." James led me into what I thought was a park where he continued to walk. "I think you're like me, Noah. I think you're willing to do whatever it takes. And I trust you more than I trust anybody."

I was about to ask what was wrong. But before I could, he pulled a knife from inside the waist of his jeans. Even in the dark, I could tell it was covered in blood. James faced the river and, with a grunt, he hurled the knife towards the bright lights of Manhattan. It went spinning in an arc through the night air and disappeared silently into the darkness until I heard it hit the water.

"Take the cab back to go meet your friends. Enjoy your night."

Then he walked away -- down that quiet Brooklyn street. He never even looked back.

As I pulled up to Dianna's house I was shaking, but I had satisfaction in knowing that my workers were fully stocked with drugs, James was paid, and all my work for the day was done. I looked forward to relaxing for a couple of days.

Dog, José and Nancy were standing in front of the building waiting for me. Nancy was a neighborhood girl that sometimes hung around dog. Man she was hot!

"What's up, guys?" I said.

Dog nodded at me, jumped off the porch and headed to the side of the building. The three of us followed him past some garbage cans, then down the stairs into the basement. In the darkness of the hallway, José grabbed my hand. The basement was dimly lit. Once my eyes adjusted, I could make out the old ratty couch, a card table, a couple of chairs, and on a table were four gallons of water and four gallons of orange juice.

"We're going to need these," Dog said pointing to the water and juice. "Everyone does when they do Ecstasy."

Dog and Nancy sat on the couch and I pulled up a couple of chairs for José and me. As we circled up, Dog handed a pill to each of us. Without another word, we each swallowed them. 'It doesn't taste like anything,' I thought to myself. I wanted to ask how long it would take for something to happen, but decided to wait.

José turned on the radio. Dog produced some weed. We danced and smoked. After a couple of songs played, I started to feel really good. A warm tingle danced up my fingers and hands. The warmth spread through my chest. I wanted to be touched and asked Nancy to massage my shoulders. She happily agreed.

"I don't know if this is supposed to feel good to you or me, but it feels great on my hands," Nancy said, giggling. Out of the corner of my eye, I saw Dog and José talking seemingly about twenty words per second.

It was official: We were tripping.

José caught me staring. We locked eyes and he mouthed, "I love you." I thought I could feel my heart swelling inside my chest. I loved him too. A car horn beeped outside.

"I have a surprise for everyone!" I yelled. "Grab all yo' shit and meet me outside!"

I was the last to pile inside of the black limo parked in front of Dianna's. As we pulled away from the block, even in my Ecstasy high, I made a point to remember the smiles Dog, Nancy, and José had on their faces. That moment was what all the work was about. And, I was proud of myself. I was making a lot of money, and now it was time to spend some of it on my friends.

I told the driver to take us to the city and drive around until we decided to stop somewhere. For what I was paying him, he didn't object. About the time we crossed the Manhattan Bridge, Nancy and Dog were getting frisky. José and I were doing bumps of cocaine off my house keys when Nancy's moan caught our attention. She and Dog were kissing and he had his hand up her skirt, clearly fingering her. She moved her hips, eagerly matching the movement of his hands.

José and I sat back to enjoy the show. I guess she felt us staring, because at some point Nancy broke the kiss with Dog looked across the seats at us and smiled. Without a word, she discarded her skirt and panties. Then she undid Dog's jeans, pulled out his dick and went down on him. Dog leaned back into his seat, more than willing to let Nancy take the lead. In that position, Nancy's head was bobbing in Dog's lap, her ass was in the air pointed towards José and me.

"Oh my God," José whispered, as Dog, his eyes closed, ran his hand across Nancy's butt and slipped two fingers inside her as she kept blowing him. The thought of fucking a girl had not even crossed my mind. But watching Nancy blow Dog and getting a full view of him fingering her had my dick rock hard, this ecstasy was giving me just that If Dog didn't fuck her soon, I was pretty sure I was going to. As if he'd heard my thoughts, Dog pulled Nancy's hips and guided her so that she was now sitting upright, facing me and José, with her back to him. Lowering herself onto his lap, Nancy let out the sweetest hiss as Dog's dick slipped into her. The sound of her wetness drove me crazy. I wanted to join in.

"You're watching me. I wanna watch you," Nancy said. She scooped up her tank top and bra, exposing her tits and began tweaking her own nipples. I could see Dog kissing her shoulder and gripping her hips as he slammed into her. Nancy moaned and laughed.

"You're both about to pop out of them jeans," she said.

I looked down at José 's lap. He had a clear erection. I chuckled.

"You wanna watch?" I asked. I undid my pants and whipped my dick out. I was already leaking pre-cum so I used it as lube and started jerking myself off. José did the same. When Nancy saw what I was working with, her eyes widened and she winked at me.

"Play with your tits some more," José said. "And your clit. "I turned and looked at him, this was turning me the fuck on.

"I fucked girls before you," he said and shrugged, never taking his eyes off Nancy who was doing exactly as she was told. One hand was massaging the nipple of her breast. The other was fondling her clit. Then suddenly both her hands reached for the roof of the limo, she shuddered, and her mouth was wide open as if she couldn't breathe."

"She bustin'!" José whispered. "She so hot. Come on, Jeremy. "José slid across the seats. Nancy was still riding Dog who paused when he saw José get closer. José took one of Nancy's nipples into his mouth and began fingering her clit. Dog resumed his thrusting and Nancy cried out. Minutes later another orgasm sent Nancy bucking and rocking forward. José gave her room to collapse on the limo seat.

"Fuuuuuuuuck," Dog groaned, letting us know he climaxed too. He slipped out of Nancy and pulled his pants up.

When Nancy recovered she saw that I was still hard and jerking off, this ecstasy was driving me crazy. The way I felt from the ecstasy you could have called me tri-sexual, because I would have tried anything! Her lips parted and before I could say a word she was blowing me. The wet heat of her mouth was heaven. I managed to keep my eyes open just long enough to see José position himself behind Nancy. Her moans let me know when he entered her.

José threw his head back and lost himself in pounding her. Every now and then, Nancy would stop blowing me to tell José that he was hitting a spot she liked or not to go so deeply. She came for him two more times. The last time, while she came, she frantically jerked my dick, still wet from her mouth. My own orgasm was like a geyser. Thick lines of semen splashed over Nancy's fist and the seats of the limo.

Dog, who'd recovered enough to watch, laughed and pointed at my mess. José was lost, making his way towards an orgasm of his own. With one last push he buried himself inside Nancy who bit into my thigh as she took all of him.

"God, yo' ass is so good, Nancy," José panted as he moved away from her. Nancy raised herself off my lap and we all began putting ourselves back in our clothes. I reached for more coke to break up the silence.

CHAPTER 37

When I walked into the apartment, Ma didn't look up. She just sat at the dining table staring at a cup of coffee she cradled in her hands. Something was wrong. Dad? Was he in the hospital again? Did he get worse?

"What's wrong, Ma?" I rushed to the table. "Is Da-"

"Nothing is wrong, Noah. I just...I need you to sit down. I have something to say to you."

I didn't try to stop myself from letting out a sigh. I hated when she did this. Ma never seemed to understand that I was busy. That the money I slipped her on an almost daily basis, the money I used to pay their rent and bills, didn't just happen. I had to work. I couldn't just stop by EVERY time she called to spend time with her. I slouched into the chair across the table from her and pulled out my cell phone to see if any important calls had come in.

"Ma, do you need something? 'Cause if you don't, can we do this later? I got a lot to -"

"Cut the shit, I saw you this morning, Noah," she said. "In your room, sleeping. I saw you and Jose together... You were both naked. And he was holding you."

I closed my eyes, and my mind went blank. My mouth was dry. I couldn't find any words to explain away what Ma had seen. Careful. We had always been so careful to lock the door and not make any noise that would make Ma or Dad suspect anything. How'd she...? And it hit me. Jose had gone to the bathroom in the middle of the night. He must have forgotten to lock the door when he'd come back. And now she knew. She'd seen us. I couldn't look at my mother. I couldn't see her hate me. Hate what I was. What was she going to tell Dad? He'd kill me.

"I suspected it and have been waiting for you to tell me about you and Jose for a long time, but you never did." She said. "I guess I understand that. But, I want you to know that me and your father love you, no matter what and nothing is gonna change that."

"Shit, Dad knows…?" I stammered.

"Of course," she answered. "What do you think, we're completely stupid? Don't get me wrong. I'd love for you to have some kids and a wife. But I understand. Don't feel like you have to hide anything from me. And Jose is already like a son to us, Noah."

I lifted my head. Ma was looking back at me. There wasn't disgust or hate in her eyes. Ma was smiling.

"I'm sorry. I…I'm sorry, Ma. I never wanted to make you ashamed…" My own tears cut off the words.

"Noah, don't be sorry. God made you who you are. We're proud to say you're our son. I love you with all my heart and so does your father. Don't forget that. It's okay." And then she appeared around the table, by my side, hugging and kissing me. I cried, buried my face in the front her dress and hugged her back for a long time.

I just kept repeating, "I love you, Ma." And she just kept answering, "I know."

CHAPTER 38

"The guys from Martini's strip club said I couldn't sell here and they don't give a fuck who I work for," Eddie said. "Jeremy, they kicked me out and said not to come back."

"Did you get to meet the customer or are they still waiting?"

"Still waiting."

"Okay. I'll be right there." Rage made my jaw clench, and I was squeezing the phone so tight my knuckles cracked from the pressure. The girls from the neighborhood strip club hit up my work-phone when they needed drugs for themselves, or their customers. Eddie was responsible for taking care of them, but now the dick-head owner was saying he didn't want us running shit through his club. Apparently, no one told him this was my neighborhood.

After I hung up with Eddie, I dialed Dog as I walked into Dianna's house. I already had a gun on me, but it was small. I needed to make a bigger point to the strip club owner. Dog picked up on the first ring.

"'Sup, Jeremy?"

"Meet me at Dianna's. I need to solve a little problem with the club across the street." I half listened as he rattled off some minor shit about business. Through my anger, all that mattered was that he would be there in ten minutes. I grabbed a .45 caliber Colt from under the bed and threw the .25 Berretta in its place. I was already waiting at the door when Dog arrived with Laree.

"Let's go," I said, leading them across the street. At this time of night there would be a lot of people in the club. I didn't want to make a scene in front of witnesses. I thought it would be better to go straight to the office in the back and handle business in private. The club was on the second floor of a two-story building. Before we got to the top of the stairs, two security guards, black guys built like mountains, appeared out of nowhere and blocked the doors.

"Let's see some I.D. And, I'm going to have to search you boys," one of the guards said.

"You won't be checking no I.D. and you definitely ain't searching us. Get Vincent for me before I go on in and get him myself."

To his credit, the guard remained calm. "Who should I say is here?

"You shouldn't," I responded. "Now, go."

The guy looked at me, more worried than anything else and then disappeared through the door. I told Dog to go back downstairs and wait by the front door in case they called anyone. The guard came back, still looking worried.

"Vincent said to send you in. But just you." I turned to Laree.

"You stay here and watch the stairs. If I'm not out in 15 minutes, let yourself in." He nodded.

Inside the club, it was business as usual: girls on the stage, guys sitting and standing around them, throwing money to watch them shake their pussies and slide up and down the pole. Farther in the back of the club I could see girls giving lap dances and more in the Champagne Room. I passed the stage, the bathrooms, through the kitchen and straight into the office.

Vincent was seated behind a dark, wooden desk. He was fat, balding, and wore very thick glasses. I could tell his suit was expensive. The gold chains around his neck drew attention to the fact that he had more than one chin. Mounted on the wall to the right of his desk were video monitors displaying live feed from the club. He was still looking at them when I entered. They showed the street outside the club, the stairs, and inside the club. So, he knew I was not alone.

"Vincent," I said, taking a seat without being asked.

"Noah," he interrupted, "I've heard a lot about you. You actually work with some friends of mine in an after-hours spot."

I let out a frustrated breath.

"Here we go with this fake-ass mafia 'friends of ours' shit!" I screamed. "I'm not here to chat. My boys came in here to drop something off for me and were told they can't. I'm here to let you know I will be making those deliveries myself from now on. I expect there won't be any bullshit problems like we had today."

Vincent stared at me for a few seconds.

"Young man, that sounds like you're giving me orders...in my own establishment."

"Listen," I said, "You have a business to run, and so do I. I won't let anything get in the way of that."

"I appreciate and respect that," he said looking at me like I was a puzzle he was trying to solve. "I have no interest in letting things get ugly…and we do have some friends in common, so maybe we can come to an agreement."

"I'm listening," I said with a sigh, because it always came down to what I could do for these made guys, so they would let me do what I wanted.

"You can do what you need to do at Martini's," Vincent continued, "but you have to control the neighborhood and outside riffraff that comes in here. I don't even want a dime of the action." He said as his hand hit the desk.

"Fair enough," I started to say, but there was a quick knock on the door. I spun out of the chair, stood up, and pulled out my gun. Laree was standing in the doorway.

"You got a call on your phone, Jeremy. Laree said. They're holding that kid, Roger at the schoolyard a few blocks from here."

"Good. I'll be right out," I said, putting the gun back in my waistband. Vincent came from behind the desk and closed the door. Then he turned to me, staring at the place where I'd concealed my gun.

"What? You don't trust me?"

"I don't trust anyone," I said. "Starting tomorrow, I will have someone here to sell in-house. That will cut down on movement." Vincent nodded and we shook hands. I hurried out of the strip club. As I stepped back out on the streets of my neighborhood, I was smiling and my heart was racing. I was looking forward to getting to the schoolyard and making an example out of Roger.

"Come on, let's roll," I said to Dog and Laree.

The schoolyard was pitch black when I arrived. And I had to let my eyes adjust before I could see anything. When they did, I first saw Eddie there with one of his boys. In the little bit of light that reached us from the street lamps, I could see a tall solidly built Spanish kid with a deep, jagged scar that ran down the right side of his face. He was holding Roger up in a full nelson. With Dog and Laree behind me, I shook hands with Eddie then turned my attention to Roger.

"So, I guess you thought we'd never see you again, huh motherfucker?"

"Jeremy, you shoulda seen the look on his face when we pulled up to this nightclub in the city," Eddie said, laughing. "He was outside with his girl. We snatched her purse from here and took out her I.D. We told her if she called the cops, we'd be snatching her next."

"Good," I said to Eddie without taking my eyes off of Roger.

"So, answer me. You thought you'd get away with stealing from me?"

"I…I'm sorry, Jeremy. I was gonna p…p…pay you," he stammered.

He couldn't have known the first punch was coming. With all my strength I dug a few hook punches into his ribs like he was a heavy bag.

"Shut the fuck up wit' yo' lying ass," I growled through gritted teeth while I kept punching him. Far from calming me down, punching that fool just got me madder and madder as I thought about how he tried to take what was mine. How the money he was trying to take from me helped keep my family from going back to the lousy imitation turkey slices we had for Thanksgiving, or the tuna fish and macaroni dinners they were forced to eat before I became who I am today. Without this money they could not survive. Suddenly, I felt hands on me, and I heard Laree's voice.

"You're gonna kill him! Hold up. Hold up. Let him catch his breath!" With all my strength, I shrugged out of Laree's grip and scowled.

"Scar, let this punk-ass thief go." And he crumpled to the ground.

I could hear him groaning and struggling for air. I hoped I'd broken some of his ribs.

"What's your name?" I asked the dude with the scar.

"Jesse." He said in a tone that let me know he was ready for action.

"Well, Jesse, piss on this motherfucker." Jesse looked back at me and even in the dark, I could tell he thought I was joking or completely nuts.

"Did I stutter?" I barked and Jesse flinched. Then, he pulled out his dick and did as I ordered. Roger, sobbing, had managed to curl himself into a fetal position as piss sprayed all over him. I kicked him one more time, hard, making sure to dig the tip of my boot into his stomach.

"I'm gonna let you walk away with your life today, punk. I won't kill you over no bullshit fifteen hundred dollars. Consider yourself lucky. And consider your debt is clear. But never do I want to see your face anywhere again. Not ever. Or I will kill you." I dug a knot of money out of my pocket and tossed a one hundred dollar bill at Jesse.

"Hey Eddie, when you re-up, I got something for you." I always rewarded loyalty. So I would be sending a few extra grams his way and he could pocket the extra loot.

I turned and walked out of the schoolyard. Laree and Dog fell in line beside me. Now that the work was done, I felt like playing.

CHAPTER 39

I went back to Laree's house to set him up with his supplies and then headed out for the night. Laree had work, and I hadn't decided what I was going to do but I wanted to have some fun.

"My girl's going to a gay club tonight. She loves to dance with them gays," Laree told me. "She really likes the music and doesn't have to worry about any guys hitting on her."

"Oh, yeah? Where's it at?" I asked.

"Out in Queens."

"Let's go with her," I suggested. "I wanna get out of the neighborhood for once. Who knows, maybe we can make some money there. I'm sure we'll meet some people trying to buy."

"I would go, but I have some customers in Manhattan I have to meet." Laree said.

"Tell her I'll pick her up in a cab at midnight."

"Good. At least now I know she'll be safe with you."

I stood up and gave Laree a brief hug then headed out to my car. As I drove, I tried to imagine what a gay club would be like, and I really couldn't get a picture of it in my mind.

I pulled up in front of my parents' building, hopped out of the car, and looked around to see if anyone was following or watching me. Nothing looked out of the ordinary, so I hit the trunk button and pulled out my black duffel bag. Inside it, I had fifty pounds of weed I'd picked up earlier that day, but hadn't had a chance to unload.

I took the weed downstairs into the basement of our building, that we shared with the store on the first floor. It was for an alibi, so if the police ever did raid the place, I could deny that the drugs were mine. After the drugs were hidden, I made my way back up the stairs. My dog, Dutch, met me on the steps. To other people, Dutch might have looked like a scary-ass pit-bull, but he was really a lovable, loyal dog. When I got to the apartment the door was open. Inside the apartment, I went straight into the kitchen, pulled a bone from the cabinet and tossed it to him. He hungrily attacked it as if it had legs and could get away from him. The kitchen and living room were empty, but since the door was open, I knew someone was home. I found Ma in the bedroom, waiting.

"Hey, baby!" she said.

"Hey, Ma."

"I'm going to need some money for dog food and food for us."

I pulled a hundred dollars from my pocket and handed it to her. "I'm going to sleep at a hotel tonight. So, don't wait up and don't worry."

. "I'm your mother. I'll always worry," she said, leaving the bedroom and closing the door behind her. I loved her and hated this run-down stinking apartment. So many times I had wanted to move them but she always dragged her feet. 'It's okay,' she would say. 'Save your money.' I felt my cell phone buzz against my hip.

"Hey, Laree," I said, after checking the caller ID. But, it was Sarah, Laree's girl.

"Laree said you were coming with me tonight. What time you wanna meet up?"

"How about I'll be by you in thirty minutes. I'll grab a cab and call when I'm outside. I don't feel like driving all the way to queens."

"Sounds good to me. I'll see you soon," she said in a sweet voice. I picked out my clothes and hopped in the shower. With José handling business I could relax and have some fun. I took my time shaving and making sure my hair was on point. I wanted to look perfect. All I could think about was getting to this club. There had to be more guys like me out there, and hopefully I would find one. I was like a dog in heat.

CHAPTER 40

The lit-up sign read KRASH. And there was a line all the way down the block. A line, I decided immediately, that I wasn't going to stand on just to get into some club. When we got out of the cab, the people in line stared at us. I couldn't blame them. Sarah wore a very tight mini-skirt, knee-high stiletto boots and her hair was done to perfection. She looked like a model. Laree always liked the skinny white girls. And I made it a point to show off my body in my crisp tank top, and tight over the ass jeans.

As Sarah and I made our way to the front of the line, I couldn't help but notice that none of the guys carried themselves like I did. You could tell these dudes were gay from a mile away. The bouncers at the door were human mountains -- two black guys and a Latino.

"You're in the wrong place, my man," the Latino said to me.

"Oh, yeah? Why is that?" I

"This is a gay club," he answered nodding his head to the line behind us. I laughed.

"Don't worry. I'm in the right place."

"Really? Well the line starts back there," he said pointing down the block. From where we were standing, you couldn't see the line's end. There must have been over a hundred people waiting.

"I saw that. But, waiting on line isn't really my thing." I pulled a fifty-dollar bill out of my pocket and slid it into his hand.

"I don't blame you," he answered as he unlatched the rope and stepped aside for us.

Inside, the club was dark except for black lights, strobe lights, and flashing lasers that seemed to sync with the beat of the music. I could barely see Sarah next to me but she signaled me that she wanted to get a drink. On the way to the bar I could make out a load of hot young guys kissing and rubbing up on each other as they danced.

After waiting ages for a drink, I caught sight of a hot Spanish kid behind the bar. He wasn't wearing a shirt and with a body like his, he never should. Seeing him made me glad that I worked out! I made sure I caught his eye and waved a one hundred dollar bill in the air. He waved for me to come closer and leaned over the bar so he could hear me over all the insanity.

I yelled over the noise, "Get me an apple martini for the lady and a Hennessy and coke for me. Make it a double.". I watched his muscles and tattoos as he moved around making our drinks. Sarah was behind me, lost in the music.

"That will be thirty-four dollars," he said, setting our drinks on the bar. I handed him the hundred-dollar bill.

"I've never seen you here before. Is this your girl?"

"Nah. That's not my girl." I answered. "I'm bi, but definitely not looking for pussy tonight. I hope you don't mind me asking if you are into dudes." The bartender smiled. He had dimples.

"I'm straight," he said, turning to the cash register to make my change.

"What's your name?" he asked, handing me the money.

"Jeremy. You?"

"Jason. Well, Jeremy you could've fooled me. I thought you were straight. Nice meeting you," he said with a smile.

"Same here," I said, and placed the money he'd just handed me back on the bar.

"Keep the change." Jason looked at me like I was crazy and then looked down at the money on the bar. I smiled at his reaction.

"Do me a favor, though. If you see me waiting over here again, make sure to just hand me the same drinks all night." Jason winked at me. I winked back. I turned my back and took in the club. Of course, I'd never seen so many gay people before in my life. Black, white, Latino, Asian, fat, built, skinny, some in drag. All dancing and drinking and laughing. Free and having a good time. All over the place there were guys dancing with other guys, grinding and making out. I was amazed at what I was seeing and intrigued as well. I knew this wouldn't be my last time at Krash.

An hour later, I felt my phone vibrating against my hip. The music inside the club was too loud to take a call. But, I checked the caller I.D. in case it was someone I needed to talk to sooner rather than later. It was Eddie.

"Hold on a sec!" I screamed into the phone. "Let me step outside so I can hear you!"

As packed as Krash was on the inside, I was surprised to still see a line down the block of people waiting to get in. I noticed a few guys near the front checking me out. That made me smile as I put the phone back to my ear.

"Eddie, what's going on?"

"Jeremy, I think you need to get over here. We got a problem, and we can't handle it without you. Those guys you had a problem with a while back at Tommy's are out here, messing with José in the park." Since the cops had started watching the bar, we couldn't do business there and had been going to the park to make deliveries.

"I'll be right there," I said. I hung up the phone and ran back inside. Shoving my way through the crowd, I found Sarah on the dance floor and grabbed her hand. Leaning in until my lips were right next to her ear, I yelled over the music.

"It's time to go!" I led her off the dance floor and cut through the club. Most people, realizing I was leaving in a hurry, made room for us to get by as best they could. But when Sarah and I reached the end of the bar, I ran right into some fool who didn't get out of the way. In fact, it was like he was blocking us on purpose. I reached out my hand to push him when I looked up and realized it was Jason.

"You leaving already?"

"Yeah. I have a work emergency," I said. "I'll be back soon."

"Good," Jason said. "Maybe we can hang out more." And gave me another wink. I smiled and thought, 'Straight, my ass.' There was a line of cabs waiting in front. I put Sarah in one and gave money to the driver.

"Aren't you coming with me?"

"No. I have business to take care of, and you shouldn't be there." I jumped into another cab and told the driver where to take me. And fast. As we flew down the B.Q.E and approached the Prospect Expressway, I told the driver to head down Ocean Avenue and when he got to Avenue Kings Highway, make a right turn and he let me out a block from the park.

I walked into the park slowly, wanting to see what was going on before I jumped into anything but it was dark and hard to make out exactly what was going on. As soon as I approached, all I could see was arguing and fighting. There were three of my guys, Eddie, Dog and Cheddar and five of them. I didn't see Jose at first, but then I caught a glimpse of him out of the corner of my eye, backing away. I knew if shit went south and the cops came, he would try to leave with the drugs and money he was carrying. I recognized an older guy among them named Nelson. We'd grown up together and had been really cool. I figured I could reason with him.

"Let me talk!" I yelled as I pulled people apart and got in between them. "Nelson, whatever is going on here is just a misunderstanding. No one wants this shit to go down." Nelson stood down. "We all from the same place, basically." I continued. "It's not good for business to have my people getting hurt or having to hurt someone for fucking with my people."

"You ain't hurting nobody, you fucking pussy!" One of the other boys named Stretch yelled. Stretch was a tall black guy, much older than me and easily twice my weight. He rushed out from behind Nelson and I knew all hell was about to break loose. Just then I heard a car door slam and saw James come running into the park towards us. I knew he was cool with both us and this other crew of dealers, because James was their connect too. But none of my boys knew that. When I saw James, I was hoping maybe he could stop this from going too far.

Then out of nowhere, I heard a series of loud pops. The gunshots came suddenly, one after another. My instincts took over and I dropped to the ground, covering my head with my hands. Once it was silent, I looked up to see James and 3 others on the ground. I could tell by the way they were laying there – all sprawled out – they'd been hit and someone was probably dead.

What the fuck just happened? My mind wouldn't let me take it in. Something told me to run. As I started to run, I looked around but saw no sign of José. Had he already run? Was he okay? The next thing I was aware of was being at a train station about ten blocks from the park. Numb and on autopilot, I bought a token and took whatever train was heading into Manhattan. I found myself in Time Square and stopped in the first hotel I came across. Sitting alone in my room -- all I could think about was James. Was he dead? Sure the fuck looked like it.

CHAPTER 41

"Noah, what's going on?"

"I'm fine, Ma." Even though we were on the phone, I knew exactly the face my mother was making: the one that said she thought I was full of shit.

"You're fine? Really? Well, there are cops all over the fucking neighborhood," she cried. "They came here looking for you. They said you shot some people at the park. They're everywhere, Noah! Everywhere! Those hoodlum dealers from the other side of the neighborhood threatened your brother. They told him our whole family is dead, Noah. And Jose is missing!"

"Don't worry about them, Ma. I'm gonna deal with all of that. I have to get a lawyer and then turn myself in. It's all gonna work out. I know it will."

"What happened Noah?"

"I didn't shoot nobody. I just tried to break up a fight. The guy who got shot also came to break it up. But someone, I don't know who, didn't know who he was, got spooked, and shot him. I need a good lawyer. I'll call you back soon, Ma." I could hear her trying to stifle her crying.

"Please, be careful. Noah, I can't lose another child. I can't…"

"I'm gonna be fine, Ma. I promise." The sun was already up, throwing light all over my hotel room. I hit the button to lower the shades. In a couple of seconds, it was impossible to tell what time of day it was. I welcomed the dark.

I was in deep shit. My mind was spinning. What had happened to Jose? Was he okay? Screw him. He ran away and didn't have my back—I needed to take care of my family and myself now. Then, I made my next call.

"Hello," the voice on the other end answered in a flat tone

"Tommy? It's Noah." I knew he would know a great lawyer. Mob guys always do.

"You're lucky" I answered,

"I never answer phone numbers I don't know, but after seeing this morning's newspaper, I figured you'd try to reach me. What do you need?"

"This morning's paper?

What are you talking about?"

"What am I talking about? Pick up the Post, kid. Second page. It says you shot four people and tried to stab another. Some pretty wild shit. Got the whole neighborhood in an uproar."

"Look, I didn't shoot anyone!" Truth is I still have no idea who started shooting.

"Of course you didn't, kid."

"NO! I really didn't! Look, Tommy, I need a lawyer's number. A good one. And I...I need someone to come get me in a car that has tints. And I need a gun. I gotta come back to the neighborhood and get to the bottom of this."

"Not sure coming back here is the smartest idea, but anything for you, kid. Tell me your address and give me an hour." The sound of him shuffling around for a pen and paper reminded me to do the same, and I asked again for a lawyer's number.

"I know a guy. He's a Jew like you. Steinbaum. Give him a call, tell him I sent you and he'll take good care of you." He rattled off his number.

"Thanks, Tommy. I won't forget this." I gave him the address to the hotel. "You owe me one, Noah."

"It's not like I'm not good for it," I said. "I really appreciate this."

"Be safe, kid."

"I plan on it."

I quickly dialed 411 and asked for the number to the 68th precinct in Brooklyn. I dialed and nervously waited for someone to answer.

"Can I speak with a homicide detective please? It's Noah Braverman." I was put on hold for a few seconds and then a lady's voice came on the line.

"We've been waiting for your call."

"Look, whatever you think I did, I didn't do it."

"Why don't you come in, and we can talk about it."

"I will. I have to take care of a few things first, but I will come to you as soon as I do. I just wanted you to know that I didn't do it."

I hung up the phone. Everything about the lady detective's tone told me she didn't believe me. I'd watched enough cop shows to guess that they were probably trying to trace the call and find me. I jumped in the shower and collected my thoughts. On my way out I grabbed my key card off the bed and went down to the front desk to check out. While I was paying the bill, Tommy called. His guys were outside.

As I walked out of the front of the hotel, a black Lincoln town car with tinted windows caught my attention. The driver-side window rolled down to reveal three Italian guys. The bald driver called out my name and waved me over.

"Tommy sent us. Said to take ya wherever you gotta go. He also gave me something to give ya."

I climbed into the backseat. As soon as the door closed and the window was rolled back up, the Italian in the passenger seat turned around and handed me a blue steel .38 special.

"Be careful," he said. "And call Tommy if you need anything else." The driver steered the car south on Broadway.

"I need you guys to drop me off somewhere. I have to pay a little visit to some very disrespectful guys. They threatened my family, and I need to make sure people understand, I won't take that from nobody. Then, take me to turn myself in."

I closed my eyes as we pulled away from the curb and told them where I needed to go. The car was silent during the ride through Manhattan and over the bridge back into Brooklyn. I felt my body grow tense when I got back in my neighborhood, and we approached our destination.

"That's them right there. Pull over and wait here," I ordered.

"Wait here my ass, kid. Tommy told us to stay with you until we dropped you off at your final destination. Safely. That's what we gonna do," said the driver.

"Suit yourselves." I replied as I opened the car door and jumped out. Tommy's men followed, with their hands on their pistols. Slamming the doors behind them.

There were at least ten guys of mixed races standing in front of the subway station on Avenue King Highway. All part of, or friends with the dealers, from the other side of the neighborhood. I walked up, without hesitating and drew my pistol. Before anyone could react, I had it pointed right in the face of the guy I was able to reach first.

"You threatened my family?"

The entire group answered my question with shocked looks on their faces. I guessed they never expected me to show up on the block again. Especially not with backup aiming guns of their own. The guy I was aiming at made a move to back away. I slammed the pistol into his cheek as hard as I could. It sounded like knuckles cracking.

I loved the sound and got excited by it. It made me feel powerful and in control. I was a bad ass, that no one should fuck with. Then I whipped his face with the gun until he fell to the ground. Even then, when he was in the fetal position and covering his face, I kept hitting him. The only thing that stopped me was that I noticed a crowd started to gather. I'd been there too long. And realized someone could have called the cops. I turned to the rest of his crew.

"I had nothing to do with James' death. You guys knew him, but I did too. He was my boy. I would never hurt him. Stay the fuck away from my family!"

We ran for the car. As we drove off, the guys didn't say a word. Every minute or so, one them would turn back and look at me, as if they were trying to figure me out.

"Now, take me to the sixty-eighth precinct. I've got a date with a female pig."

As soon as I walked into the precinct, I knew I should have come with a lawyer, but it was too late. I had asked Ma to call Steinbaum and give him the details, but he wasn't available right away. Then I told her where a stash of cash was to take care of his fee, my bail and anything else that was needed.

I announced to the desk sergeant that I was Braverman, and two uniformed cops that didn't look much older than I was jumped up and escorted me to the second floor where the homicide detectives were located. Everyone I passed stopped what they were doing to watch me. I suddenly remembered Tommy telling me the shooting had been in the newspaper, and that everyone was talking about it. For whatever reason this particular shooting was getting attention. It was a big deal. I'd watched enough cop shows to know that meant the police had to pin it on someone, and fast.

When we got to the top of the stairs, a female detective greeted us. She was dressed in a suit that, despite her height and broad frame, managed to look a few sizes too big for her. She had a hard square jaw made more severe by the fact that she was scowling at me.

"So, you're the one," she said to me. "I'll take him from here, officers." She got behind me and placed her hand on the small of my back as if to guide me down a short hall and into the cell that stood just to the right of the detective squad.

"I'll be right back," she said after the bars clanged shut. And those were the last words I heard for hours.

The cell had no windows and no light of its own. What little light filtered down the hall from the offices was just enough to reveal how dingy the cell was and all the graffiti on the walls. 'Fuck you pigs!' Was written in magic marker over and over again. Names and gang signs scratched into the cracking paint and it smelled like piss and shit. How was I going to convince them I didn't do it? I would have to rely on the lawyer Tommy recommended to take care of that. When the detective finally appeared again, she was with a balding fat man just a bit taller than she was. He looked to be well into his forties. Standing outside the cell, she waved in my direction, "this is him." I didn't realize she was carrying keys until I heard them jingle as she unlocked the cell door.

"I'm detective, Alvarez," the man said to me with a smile as he reached out to shake my hand. Automatically, I shook his back.

"That's my partner, Detective Church. Don't mind her attitude. She's always like this."

Again, my education from hours and hours of New York Undercover and N.Y P.D. Blue let me know he was good cop and Church was bad cop.

"You want some coffee or a soda, kid?" Good Cop asked me.

"No, thanks." I just wanted this to be over.

They led me through a door with the words "Interview Room 1" marked on it into a small room with a table and two chairs. There was a mirror the length of one of the walls. I knew there were people on the other side listening and recording us.

"Ok. Now, your mother is downstairs. She gave us permission to talk to you, since you are under age." Detective Church said as she pointed to the chair I was supposed to take. Alvarez sat down across from me. He still had that smile on his face. Church stood just behind him.

"Now, do yourself a favor and help us help you," she said. "Tell us why you shot those people."

"I didn't shoot anyone. I told you before I didn't do it."

"So, who did? We know you were there." Snarled Church.

"I'm not denying being there." I agreed, "But, when I heard gun-shots, I dropped to the ground like everybody else and buried my face. I didn't see who was shooting. When it stopped, I ran."

"You're full of shit! Don't lie to us you fucking little punk! I should hurt you like you hurt those people!" she yelled, banging the table with her fist. But, her yelling didn't scare me. Not at all. And she knew it. That seemed to only make her angrier. She came around the table and stood over me. She bent down until her face was nearly touching mine.

"You're a killer! We know you shot those boys!"

Her spit was hitting me right in the face, but I had nothing to say. I had nothing else to say. Alvarez pulled her away and finally convinced her to go somewhere to calm down. He closed the door behind her and sat back down at the table. In a calm voice he said,

"I'm sorry for my partner's behavior. She just wants to get to the bottom of this. We're under a lot of pressure to solve this. Just tell me what happened. Tell me what you know, and we can all go home."

"I'm sorry, sir but I know nothing," I said with a shrug.

"I can't help you."

"You know what," he said, suddenly less calm. "I'm done playing with you!" His good cop had suddenly vanished.

"Okay, so can I leave now?"

"Leave?" Alvarez chuckled. "No. Stand up, turn around and put your hands behind your back. You're under arrest for murder."

CHAPTER 42

"Get up. Time to go to Central Booking."

I looked up and saw a uniformed officer opening the door of the holding cell. I must've dozed off and had no idea how much time had passed. At least a few hours. It was probably night-time by now. I stepped into the hall as the officer opened the cell two down from mine. He waved for the person to step out and stand in a spot a few feet in front of me.

When I saw the other prisoner, I thought the shadows of that dark hallway were playing tricks on me. I'd been thinking about where he was, since I ran from the park. But, once he stepped into the faint light that filtered down to us from the offices, there was no mistaking what I was seeing.

"José?" I called. He didn't answer.

"Yo, Jose. It's me, Jeremy!" Joy started to bubble up inside me. My voice raised and echoed off the cinderblock walls. Still no answer. I took a step toward him, but something made me stop cold. He didn't even look at me. He didn't say a word. Jose turned toward the officer like he didn't even know me. And then it clicked. That's why the detectives were so certain I knew something about the shooting. That's why they were convinced I was involved. Jose talked. He told them that I was there. He told them that I knew James. He told them how I knew James, that he was my cocaine connect.

"What the fuck did you tell them?" I screamed. I heard footsteps running before I saw the detectives come around the corner.

"Fake-ass motherfucker! Punk-ass snitch! Whhhhhyyy?" I cried.

Detective Church was the first one to reach me. Even in the darkness of that hell-hole of a hallway, I could see the cruel smile on her face.

"You need to shut up. You're only making it worse for yourself."

She stood in my way, blocking my view of Jose. I could make out Detective Alvarez's back and knew that he was leading Jose away from me.

"I told you to tell us the truth. Your little dealer there was more than willing to tell us what we wanted to know about you and the victim," she said. "He really helped us connect some dots. He told us that you knew the victim. In fact, he was your drug connect. So, was this a deal gone south? That's what we believe. We got your sorry ass."

"Fuck you, you fucking dyke pig!"

She lunged at me. Two uniformed officers held her back. Two others put me in cuffs.

"Get that little shit out of here before I kill him!"

They dragged me down the hall.

"And keep him away from his friend! Don't let them speak!"

I laughed. I laughed because she called Jose my friend. He'd been my lover. My love. And now, he'd turned on me. Friend. I laughed as those fucking cops dragged me down the hall and put me in the back of a car to take me to get booked.

When I walked in to Central Booking, a chill ran down my spine. It was cold. The walls were a dreary pale blue and the gates were rusted. It smelled like piss and body funk. Old, moldy cheese and green bologna were crusted on the floor and on the walls. I figured that meant the food wasn't very good. But I was so hungry by the time I reached Central Booking, I was willing to find out for myself.

When the cops dropped me off, they had a long conversation with the corrections officers before passing me over.

"Here it is," an officer said, shoving me towards the Corrections Officer.

"One body," the officer said with a smirk.

"So, this is the one, huh?" the C.O. said. "He doesn't look like much of a murderer. They gonna have fun with you in here, boy. They like 'em young."

I didn't respond. There was nothing to say as they laughed at me. The C.O. doing all the talking removed my cuffs and tossed them back to one of the cops who'd transported me.

"Later, fucko!" The cop said to me, and laughed.

Pigs.

As soon as that one left the quiet C.O. said, "I'm going to search you. Then you're going to see the nurse. Word to the wise, if you say something's wrong with you, it's just going to take longer to process you. It won't help you. You're not getting out of here. So, do us a favor, even if there is something wrong with you, keep it to yourself. Don't be a trouble maker."

They made me pull down my jeans and underwear, squat as deeply as I could and cough. They made me bend over and pull my butt checks apart for them to make sure I wasn't hiding anything up there. Then I emptied my pockets and they pushed me along to the nurse. It took less than ten minutes.

The nurse was a tiny little thing. Her eyes and hair were the same steel gray color. And like the officers, I got the sense that even if something was wrong with me her preference was that I keep it to myself. She looked me up and down, asked me if I had any pains and took my pulse. It took less than two minutes for her to decide I was healthy. Next thing I knew, I was pushed into a cell, handed some milk and two sandwiches. One of which I tore into before the cell door slammed shut.

I looked around as I ate. Almost everyone in this cell looked like one of my long-time crack customers. But some folks like the Rabbi who was arrested for soliciting a prostitute stood out. No one noticed me at first; which was good, because I didn't really want to be noticed. I wanted to find me a corner and be left alone.

But then, I heard someone call my name from the cell across the hall. I looked through the bars and recognized one of my customers from Sea Rise Houses out in Coney Island, a black guy named Darrell. A good customer. He usually bought weed by the pound.

"What up, killa? What you doing here?" he asked.

"Funny you say that," I chuckled.

"They got me in on a body that ain't even mine. They said I killed someone. What you in for?"

"They swept the block and I got caught up in it. I only had a bag of weed on me. So I'll be going home soon."

"I hope I will be, too," I said,

"Good luck," Darrell called, before he waved and disappeared into his crowded cell. I turned back to mine. A few feet away from me, there was an empty spot on a bench next to the wall. I took it and then leaned my head against the cold brick and closed my eyes. Sleep was waiting for me.

CHAPTER 43

"BRAVERMAN! BRAVER-MAAAAAAN! LAST CALL FOR BRAVERMAN!"

"That's me!" I called out, half-convinced I was still asleep and dreaming that the guard had finally come for me. I forced myself off the bench and towards the front of the cell. Pains shot up and down my neck and back, but I didn't care. I wanted to get the fuck out of there.

"You're up, kid. Let's go. It's your turn to see the judge." The Corrections Officer cuffed me and walked me up a flight of stairs that led to a row of narrow glass booths. I slid into an empty chair across from a man who looked exactly how you'd expect a mob lawyer to look: tailored navy blue suit, crisp white shirt, solid red tie, shiny gold cuff links, thin, designer glasses, and salt-and-pepper hair freshly cut and styled. I felt more confident and at-ease just knowing he was working on my side. He wasted no time getting down to business.

"Look, kid, don't worry about a thing." My lawyer, Steinbaum, assured me. "They don't have enough to indict you on murder so they will probably reduce the charges down to manslaughter. They just have to make it look good for the locals. It's all politics and show." He nodded with a sheepish grin. "The District Attorney lives close to the area where the shooting happened, and it doesn't look good for him, if they don't find the killer. Things like this aren't supposed to happen in areas like that. I'll get you bail and then we will talk."

163

"Braverman," the C.O. called. I didn't know what to make of the fact that after all the waiting, things seemed to be happening quickly.

"Okay, kid. Go with the officer. When we get inside, let me do the talking."

I followed the C.O. down a dark hall.

"Don't say a word when you're in the courtroom," my lawyer whispered as we stood in the doorway leading to a large, bright room. "The judge hates that. He'll throw you out for talking."

As I entered the courtroom it killed me to see my parents sitting in the second row looking pale and sickly and tears streaming down Ma's face.

I nodded my head as my eyes adjusted to the light. "Next case. This is number nineteen on the calendar. People versus Noah Braverman. The charges are murder, attempted murder, menacing, criminal possession of a weapon ..." The charges seemed to go on and on. Then I heard someone ask, "How do you plead?"

"Not guilty, your honor," Mr. Steinbaum answered.

"I'll hear you on bail." And I realized the person speaking was the judge. He was sitting on his bench, looking down at what I assumed was the file on my case. A tiny, bald white man with glasses. His face was so serious, I couldn't imagine that he ever smiled or laughed.

"Your, honor," the assistant district attorney said, "the people ask that bail be set at one hundred thousand dollars.

"One hundred thousand it is." The judge said, nodding.

"Your, honor," Mr. Steinbaum said. "My client is 17 years old, has no prior convictions, no record of being in trouble with the law. His family is present in court as a resource for him. They are on Social Security. Though these are serious allegations, he has the right to be considered innocent until proven guilty. A bail amount of ten thousand dollars would be more than adequate to ensure that Mr. Braverman will return to court."

"Fifty thousand," the judge said. "See you back here in two weeks, Mr. Braverman. Good luck." Fifty thousand dollars? Did he say fifty thousand dollars?

"I don't have that kind of money together right now, in total it's probably what I had with my stash of cash and the money I had owed to me for drugs that were on the streets," I whispered to Steinbaum.

"when you do get the money together, kid, they are going to want to know where it came from. How much can you get legitimately?" Before I could answer, the C.O. began pulling me away.

"Where am I going now?" I asked, hearing my own voice crack.

"They're taking you to Riker's Island. But, don't worry. I filing a motion for a bail reduction in the morning, it's your best bet since you really can't prove where you would have gotten fifty thousand dollars from. You'll be out soon. Let me earn my fee. It's a hefty one."

"Okay," I called as I was escorted out of the courtroom and the next case was called. Looking over my shoulder, I caught a glimpse of Ma. Her face was buried in Dad's shoulder, and she was shaking with sobs. Our eyes met. I saw her mouth my name as fresh tears rolled down her face. I mouthed, "I love you" and turned away before she could see me crying too.

CHAPTER 44

Riker's Island is the main jail of New York City, located in the East River between Queens and The Bronx, near LaGuardia Airport. Growing up, it seemed to me that everyone from my neighborhood knew or was related to somebody who'd spent time on "The Island." And certainly, after I started dealing, I met tons of folks who'd spent a good chunk of their lives going and coming out of Riker's.

I never thought I'd be one of them. And despite how much I'd heard of the place, I'd never really let myself think about it. For example, it didn't occur to me that Riker's Island was an actual island until our bus passed a sign that read: CITY OF NEW YORK CORRECTIONS DEPARTMENT, RIKER'S ISLAND, and veered onto a bridge.

After the judge set my bail and I'd left the courtroom, it took hours for the rest of the cases to be heard and even longer for them to load us on the bus and drive us from Brooklyn to our new home away from home. We didn't leave the courthouse until well after midnight, and I had no idea what time it was when we were crossing that bridge. The farther we moved across the bridge, the more I felt like I was disappearing into a whole other world. Even though I was probably just an hour's drive from my family, it felt like I may as well have been a million miles away.

For 30 minutes we drove around the island, stopping at different check points, getting waved through. I was shocked by the size of the place and the many buildings. I'd assumed Riker's was one big jail. Turned out, it was an island-city made up of jails for women, men, mentally ill people, inmates in protective custody, kids being tried as adults, and I think there was even a unit for gay or tranny inmates.

Finally, the bus stopped in front of a skanky looking building with a sign on the front that was impossible to read because the bright security lights kept most of the building in the shadows. I heard one of the guards say, "All for C-74, we're here."

A cheer went up from many of the inmates on the bus. They were actually glad to be back in this place? I had heard of C-74 and that it was specifically for anyone between the ages of 16 and 19. Throughout my 17 years I was told about some really scary shit happening there: rapes, robberies, gang beatings... Nothing I was looking forward to.

"Braverman!" I heard my name called in the roster of inmates to get off at this stop. When I acknowledged that I was on the bus, the guard walked down the aisle to me.

"What's your date of birth?"

I gave it to him and he looked down at his paperwork and nodded. I guess that was how they verified they had the right inmate. Inside the building, somehow it managed to be even brighter than the security lit area outside. Despite the blaring lights the place was dull, covered in grays and blues. And, it was hot as fuck. Which made it hard to breathe. Why would anyone be happy to be back here?

There was another roll call once we got inside. When I stepped forward, a guard asked me, "Braverman are you in a gang?"

"Nope." I said.

"You wanna kill yourself?" I said no again.

"Good. You go in general population.

I got my picture taken and was given a photo I.D. Then, the guards led me into a dull, whitish room furnished with only a waist-high table and an x-ray machine like you see at the airport. Also, in the room was a guard standing alone. He was a massive black man, stood easily at 6'6" and was muscular, even through the bulk of his corrections uniform. I'd never seen a man so big. Or so angry about everything.

"Step the fuck in, cracker. Take off everything you have. You own nothing in here motherfucker." He barked at me when I stopped in the doorway.

In silence, I did as I was told and threw my clothes into a bucket on a table. The guard snatched up the bucket, slammed it on the conveyor belt and sent my belongings into the x-ray machine.

"Now, turn the fuck around and let me see that asshole."

"Wha...Excuse me?" I asked,

"Did I stutter?" the officer said with an evil smile. "Did I stutter motherfucker? Turn. The fuck. Around. Bend over. And cough."

I felt my face turn red. I wanted to tell him that he didn't have to talk to me like I was stupid. I wanted to tell him having my butt searched was embarrassing enough without his attitude. I wanted to say a lot of things. Instead, I turned around, bent over, and coughed.

"Okay. Turn around, open your mouth, move your tongue around. Good. Now, let me see your gums. Good. Get dressed, motherfucker."

He handed me my shirt, my pants and my sneakers. Staring at my shoes, he said "I'm sure you won't have these long."

I dressed in silence. Another corrections officer came and escorted a bunch of us to our new "housing area." On the way there, I passed the first clock I'd seen in forever and learned that it was three o'clock in the morning. Fatigue from the day suddenly hit me. All, I wanted to do was go to bed. Upon entering the unit, a C.O. who'd clearly been expecting us was waiting at her gate. The officer who escorted us gave her a stack of colored cards with our pictures, names, and birth dates on them.

"They're all yours," he said and stepped back to let us pass through the gate.

"Get the fuck in here," the female officer said. "Stand by my side as I write your bed number on your floor card. I will call it out. Do not change your assigned bed, or you will be written up.

"I had no idea what she was talking about. The most I could make out was that she was going to tell me where to sleep. I didn't care about anything else.

"Braverman; what's your date of birth?"

It dawned on me that I was answering that question a lot. I guessed it was how they confirmed they had the right inmate.

"Go on in. C8 is your bed and I don't want to hear a fucking word."

"Oh, don't worry. You won't," I said.

Inside the unit, inmates were already sleeping. The lights were off, and it was almost too dark to see my way around. Another C.O. was right at the entrance to pass out pillows and blankets. In the dark, and trying to move quietly, it took me some time to find the bed marked C8. But when I finally did, I collapsed on to it, pulled the cover over me and didn't bother to take off any of my clothes. Not even my shoes. Sleep overcame me, bringing my first day as an inmate to a merciful end.

But morning came too quickly. I felt like I'd closed my eyes for a few seconds before the noise of gates opening and closing, men laughing, men arguing, and officers ordering people around pulled me out of my sleep.

It was daylight and the lights were on, so I had no problem seeing. Immediately I noticed that I was the only white boy there. To me, everyone looked suspicious of me, like they wanted to know who the fuck I was, and I figured that as soon as my feet hit the floor all eyes would be on me. Sitting on the edge of my bed, I scanned the unit until I saw what I was looking for: two phones at the front by the officers' bubble. I had to force myself not to run to the phones. I didn't want to seem weak, but I was scared. As I dialed, I couldn't help but notice that a lot of inmates were looking at me. And not just staring, they were looking at me like I'd lost my mind. Some guys were even shaking their heads in my direction. But, I didn't have time to worry about them

"Mom?"

"Noah! Thank God. I was worried sick. Are you okay?"

"Yeah, Ma. I'm fine," I lied. "What's up with the lawyer?"

"You have court early tomorrow for a bail reduction hearing. We got the ten money you told us about, but your lawyer says if he can't get your bail reduced that they would want a bail source hearing and would want to know where it came from. He is sure though that he will get the bail reduced tomorrow."

Before Ma was done talking, a robotic voice came on the line to warn me that I only had one minute left.

"Okay, Ma. I love you. I'll try to call later. If not, I'll see you tomorrow morning." She told me she loved me back and even in those few words I could hear the tears she was trying not to cry. After I got off the phone, I found the bathroom to wash up. At first, I didn't notice the three black kids following me.

"You're new here," the skinny leader of this little trio, said.

"So we ain't gonna fuck you up over it, but that's the Blood's phone you was usin'. So don't fucking touch it during the day or the night. The other phone is the Latin phone. You can use it during the day, but after eight at night, don't fucking touch it or we will ..." He didn't have to finish his words. The razor he pulled out of his mouth said it all. I was tough, but I wasn't stupid. I agreed to follow the phone rules, besides I wasn't staying here for long no matter what. After agreeing they left me to wash up in peace.

For the rest of the day I watched TV, stayed out of everyone's way and didn't talk to anyone. After dinner, or at least what they called dinner, all I could think about was all the money I had on the street that people owed me. I went back to my bed and went to sleep. Hoping that turning in early would make tomorrow come faster. It worked. At 3:30 a.m. a guard shook me awake, telling me I had court. They gave me two boxes of cereal and a box of milk. I was told to hurry the fuck up. So, I scarfed down my breakfast.

Even though they always tell you to hurry, nothing about being in Riker's happens quickly, was my next lesson. After I ate, I was escorted back to the intake area from the night before. I was asked again for my date of birth, and then I was taken into a pen marked Brooklyn Courts. I was in that pen for hours as more and more men with cases in Brooklyn arrived. In the end, there had to have been about 300 people packed into that pen.

It was 7:30 by the time I heard my name called and was asked my date of birth. I was cuffed and half an hour later was led onto the bus with the other inmates. When the bus finally lurched forward, I smiled for the first time in I don't remember how long. I just wanted to be at court even if I didn't get bail. Even if I just got to see my mother for a little bit. Anything was better than being on Riker's.

Shortly after we arrived at court, a guard from the court-house popped his head in and asked, "Do you have a Braverman with you?"

In no time, I was taken up to the courtroom. My lawyer was there, Ma and my brother, Adam. As I neared the table, my lawyer said, "Good news. I'm getting you out right now on 10,000 dollars' bail. Your mom already gave the money to the bail bondsman, so she actually only had to give them six thousand. So, you have more than enough left over to pay me."

"All rise!" The court officers called out as the judge walked into the room. I didn't understand, see, or hear anything else that happened in that appearance. It was all big lawyer words that meant I was going home.

I was going home. At least until the trial and then after that we would see.

Part 2

CHAPTER 45

I was now 19 years old and it had been a little over 2 years since the shooting of James in the park. It had been about eighteen months before I copped to a deal just before the trial started. Of all the shit-ass charges they had me on, in the end I pled to attempted assault.

The way my lawyer explained it to me, a plea for something minor was better than taking my chances at trial. For a first offense, I should have gotten just probation or some kind of community service. But they weren't going for anything less than jail time for me. A year to be exact, I only served 8 months and another five years on probation, once I was released. But I was done and it felt fucking great.

"Oh shit! Look who it is!" A voice came from behind me.

"What's up, Laree?" I said with a smile, grabbed my man's hand and pulled him into a hug. It was an early afternoon in July. I'd stopped by the pizzeria on Dianna's block where I used to hustle to see if I could find a familiar face.

"How's things with you Jeremy?"

"All good. Just got home from Brooklyn House."

"Man, I still don't believe you had to do eight months for that bullshit. You didn't even do anything."

"I know. But it could've been worse. At least I was out for the awaiting sentencing and shit. Gave me time to get shit in order before I went in, I said.

"Speaking of... you got something for me?" Laree tossed me a stack of cash and said there was more where that came from.

Because my sentence was so short, I didn't have to go to an upstate prison. I got to do my time in Brooklyn. Which was good because Ma got to come and visit me, but dad never came at all. During the time I'd been dealing with the case and my time away, he'd only gotten more ill. Which meant more hospital stays and more medications that his insurance didn't cover. And now, Ma's health wasn't the greatest either.

I'd tried to set things up so that my family would still be getting money while I was away. It was my hope that Ma wouldn't want for anything and that Dad's medical needs would be taken care of. That hadn't worked out as well as I'd hoped. A lot of the people I'd depended on to take care of my family while I was away just hadn't. Dog had run off to Florida to lay low after the shooting, so Laree was really the only friend left to take care of business while I was away, And business was the first thing I needed to address with Laree.

"Where is everyone?" I asked.

Laree looked at me for a second, as if he was trying to decide if he really wanted to say what was about to come out of his mouth.

"Listen, Jeremy. It's a whole new ball game out here. Since you left, everyone is doing their own thing. Me? I'm just surviving myself. With what you set up before you left, I've been barely able to keep sending you and your mom money. I know it wasn't much, but that's all that was coming in after people split up. It hasn't been good, Jeremy."

He was right. It hadn't been. As soon as I'd gotten home, Ma showed me the stack of bills, and there hadn't been much food in the house for a while. I'd pretended not to notice that she wasn't looking well herself. Ma was thin and tired all the time, with big dark circles under her eyes.

"Well, I'm home now and all that's going to change. After all the work I put into building this thing, I'm not gonna let my family be fucked up and broke. I have to get back to business or they will suffer, and that's not an option.

"Get me your connect," I said to Laree. "Tell him I want to meet. If there are lots of people out here doing their thing, then that means there's a lot of business for me to do. I need drugs to put on the street. Tell him tonight I want to meet. I'll be at my mom's. I'll hit you up later."

"Good deal." Laree said as he walked away.

"Hey, Laree," I called back to him, "when we meet later, bring me a gun. And make sure you have one too. We have things to take care of."

When Laree and I arrived at the after-hours spot, it looked closed.

The lights were out and everything was locked up tight. We were a bit early for our meeting with Tommy, but I still had expected somebody to be there. Tommy was one of the few people who kept sending me money when I was away, we didn't get to see each other because him visiting me wouldn't look good, but he always sent messages through inmates and always sent me money every week.

"Should we go back to the strip club and wait?" Laree asked.

"Nah. I got a key." Tommy had given me my own set just in case I ever had to be on the run again and needed a place to hide out. I opened up the door and headed down the hallway to the back office with Laree right behind me.

"Don't move motherfuckers!" Someone we didn't see yelled as we passed the bathrooms.

"It's me, Tommy. Jeremy."

"Don't you know how to knock or announce yourself? You scared the piss out of me."

"Good thing you were in the bathroom then," I said with a chuckle.

"Smart ass," he said as he lowered the gun he'd pointed at our backs.

"Glad you're early. Let's talk."

Inside his office, I sat and Laree stood by the door. Tommy poured me a glass of cognac. I wasn't in the mood for a drink but didn't say no to it either.

"One of my bars, the one on Ocean Avenue, is going down the shitter. It just isn't making me money," he said with a look of sadness. "But before I close it down for good, I thought I could give you a shot at running it and we split the profits fifty-fifty. It's legit money, you need that in your life right now since you just came home from jail and you can run the place any way you need as long as it makes money. Whaddya think?"

"Sure," I said. "But only if I can make it into a gay bar."

I wasn't surprised at the look of shock that crossed Tommy's face. A gay bar? In our neighborhood? He poured himself another glass of cognac before responding.

"I trust you, Jeremy. If you think it will make money, I know it will. I assume you understand people will talk. But talk makes them notice. And if they say the wrong thing, I know you will make them shut the fuck up... or I will. Either way, let me know when you're ready to start."

"As soon as possible," I said.

CHAPTER 46

"If you get the place, I'll get the girls. We'll split the profits fifty-fifty," Cheddar offered. He leaned back into Dianna's couch and took a pull on the blunt we were sharing.

I met Cheddar while I was in Brooklyn House. He'd been in on some drug charges and was one of the only black inmates who didn't give me shit for being white and Jewish. We hadn't been hanging out long before Cheddar revealed that though he dabbled in drugs, his real hustle was prostitution. Cheddar was a pimp. A twenty-three year-old pimp. I spent a lot of time listening to Cheddar tell me how he found the girls -- outside of group homes, homeless shelters and bus stations. He took them off the street, got them to fall for him and then put them to work.

Cheddar was young, in shape but skinny, tall, dark skinned and the most memorable thing about his face was the prominent gold tooth he sported. He was so charismatic and attractive. It was obvious why women fell in love with him. And would go on the 'ho' stroll, just because he asked them to. While in Brooklyn House, I thought he, like everyone else, exaggerated what his life on the streets had been like. Creating a reputation for yourself was just one way to pass the time when you were locked up.

Cheddar tracked me down when he'd been released sometime after I was. He needed a place to stay and a partner to get back into business with. It was perfect timing for me. I'd been staying with my parents mostly because I had to for my probation. But being under their roof again was getting on my nerves.

"I have the perfect place in mind," I told Cheddar. There was a house someone had told me about on Flatbush Avenue that I'd been looking at. Two stories, with a good size separate apartment I was planning on moving my into. But Ma was worried about being so close to my dealings and what would happen to them if I got caught and went back to prison. The house was a lot of space, but I figured I'd need it. My drug business was booming again, and people who worked for me might need a place to crash from time to time. Now it would work perfectly for Cheddar's proposal as well.

"I'll go by and see it when we're done here, and if it all checks out, I'll make the deal and we can get started," I said.

"Sounds good," Cheddar said as he took another pull on his blunt, his gold tooth glinting even in the low light of Dianna's apartment.

The next day I put down a hefty deposit on the house, made a cash payment schedule with the owner who held the mortgage, without even signed papers I was moving in.

CHAPTER 47

"How long d'ya think you can keep doing this, Noah?"

Scott was serious. I knew he was serious. We'd had this same conversation probably twenty times since my last arrest. This time we were having it at our parents' apartment at the dining table. I'd just given Ma money to do the grocery shopping so she was gone. Dad was in his own world in front of the television. And soon, Scott would be in his own world, high off the coke I'd just given him. But despite being one of my best customers, Scott still felt it was his duty as my older brother to tell me I was going down the wrong path.

"I know I ain't one to talk, Noah. You seen me get into my own shit. But that's why you should listen to what I'm telling you. I know this life. I've seen all the guys who do what you do come and go," he said with a sigh. "They get in the game, make some money. Everything goes good. They make some more money. Things go a little better, and they make lots of money. And then something fucks them up, and they get killed or they kill and get locked up."

The rest of this speech I could recite by heart. 'People snitch. Competitors get greedy and bold.' I knew all of that already. Jose was my snitch. He ratted on me to save his own ass. Before I could even put the word out about his betrayal, he and his mom, dad and brother skipped town. He got away. With everything. And people were trying me. It seemed like every other week people were testing whether or not I could control the territory I'd carved out for myself.

But, what Scott never included in his speech was the answer to what would happen to our family if I did get out of the business? Who would pay our parents' rent? Who would buy them groceries? Who would cover Dad's medical expenses that his insurance didn't pay? Between Ma, Dad, and my brother with special needs, they got about $1500 a month in social security income. That barely covered the rent. With the rest they bought groceries, I remember when we were kids and Ma would go to the neighborhood grocery store on the corner where she had credit and pay off last month's bill with this month's check always owing a month behind just to feed us. No way I'm letting them go back to that.

But Scott was my brother. So, I listened. I nodded my head and told him he was right. I was going down a path that only ended badly. And then I watched him walk away, knowing that he was going somewhere to snort the coke he'd bought from me at a discount.

Nope. No one could tell me how Dad and Ma would be taken care of, how anyone I loved would be taken care of if I left the game. So, I played. And as far as I was concerned I was going to stay winning.

CHAPTER 48

I was called by one of my guys, Cheddar he was completely crazy, I didn't want him to handle this himself. He was definitely one of the most violent, but loyal people id ever met. He told me some fool from Sheepshead Bay Houses was selling to my customers in my neighborhood.

To my customers?

"No don't do anything, I said to Cheddar, keep an eye on him and I'll be right there."

He was taking money out of my pocket and food out of my mouth. Out of my family's mouth. If I let him get away with selling in my neighborhood, it would send the message that anyone could do it. And they would until I was left with nothing. I couldn't have that. So, I got in my car and got there as fast as I could. Caught him right in the act on Ocean Avenue. I was on him before he knew what happened.

"Stop, man! You're going to kill the kid!" Cheddar's words hit me like a sucker punch. It was like I woke up from a dream and realized I was choking someone to death.

I'd been in shape when I'd gone into Brooklyn House. While there, almost all my time was spent working out. And I'd hit the weights even harder since being out. And that was on purpose. Because when I put my hands on someone, I wanted them to remember. I wanted people to look at me and know I wasn't someone to mess with.

Before I went to Brooklyn House, I think I'd been afraid of my anger. Afraid of how I could go into a rage. But while I was in, I'd learned to use it. To love it. People left me alone because they saw what my anger could do. Once a kid grabbed the phone during my time. He ignored me when I reminded him that it was my time. He just waved me off in front of all the other inmates like I didn't matter, like I was weak.

I gave the kid one more opportunity to get off the phone. He waved me off again and turned his back to me. I threw him into a choke-hold and dragged him into the nearest cell. He struggled and tried to grab at my arms, but my grip was tight. A few seconds after we got into the cell, he wasn't struggling. I gave him a few of the hardest punches id ever thrown to his face and ribs to remember me by.

I ain't weak. Nobody walks all over me. Nobody betrays me. Not like Jose did. Not like the punks who threatened my family did. Not like the punks who were involved in James' killing and then blamed me. They said I wanted to get rid of James because I owed him a lot of money and didn't want to pay up. Bull shit!

The truth was one of Dogs boys that night, a guy that I had never knew or even met before, had gotten spooked when James ran into the park. I didn't even know the kid and he didn't know James. James just happened to stop there when he saw what was going on and I'm sure was there to put an end to the situation. I am 100 % positive if those kids had never came to cause trouble that night that he would still be alive today.

If I let this drug dealing piece of shit who was selling to my customers get away with it, everything I had done, everything my family had been through and James' death would have been for nothing. I couldn't let it all be for nothing

"Jeremy! You're gonna kill him. People are watching!"

Cheddar's voice finally reached me. I wasn't in Brooklyn House. I was on Ocean Avenue. I released my grip on the guy's neck, and he fell to the sidewalk. His eyes were huge and bulging out. He looked at me like he'd never seen something like me before. On his hands and butt, he started scrambling back to get away from me.

"Don't let me catch you selling in my neighborhood again." I screamed as I watched him run for his life.

CHAPTER 49

"I can't believe there's this many people here!" I said. "This party is hot."

The music was blaring. The bar was packed. Again.

"Eddie, my man, I told you I could do it," I said as I bumped up against some hot dude's ass. It was scorching from all the dancing bodies in the tiny place. My parties had only gotten more popular with time. I'd done what everyone on the street said I couldn't: opened a gay bar in my neighborhood and got people – gay and straight – to come. I'd never doubted that I would succeed.

I was popular, a neighborhood celebrity. On top of that, my promotion for the Friday and Saturday night parties was great. The flyers I'd put out were really nice. I'd hired a couple of hot male strippers to do their thing. I had also gotten some of Cheddar's girls to come in and strip. Then they would provide some extra entertainment in a special VIP room I had set up in the liquor supply room. And I had special security posted near the VIP room to allow for privacy and to keep the dancers safe from drunk-ass customers.

"Jeremy! Jeremy!" A girl I recognized from the neighborhood but didn't know well – she was obviously drunk – got my attention.

"The strippers are so hot. Are they gay?"

I'd been getting that question all night. "I don't know, sweetheart.

Why don't you go test them out and see? For twenty bucks a song, they'll give you a lap dance in the VIP room." She giggled and went on her way. I agreed with her. The male strippers I'd hired were sexy as hell. But, one in particular had caught my eye. He was built similarly to me and had definitely caught me checking him out earlier, before the bar opened. Somehow, in conversation, he'd worked in the fact that he was straight. As soon as the words came out of his perfect lips, my dick got hard. I wanted him, and I liked a challenge.

"With a body like that, what do you need us strippers for?" he said to me, gesturing for me to lift my shirt so he could check out my abs. "You should be stripping tonight." I happily gave him a peek.

"Impressive." He said and walked away to get ready for the night.

Looking at him dancing on a little stage we had set up, letting patrons stuff money into his cute, red booty shorts, I couldn't resist any longer. I moved to the end of the bar where I knew eventually he would spot me. When we made eye contact, I waved a hundred dollar bill and nodded towards the VIP room. He nodded that he understood.

"I want more than a lap dance," I said once we were in the room.

"I've never been with a guy..." I grabbed his crotch and found what I was looking for.

"Why is your dick hard, then?"

"For the same reason yours is," he replied, grabbing me back. He started to stroke my dick through my jeans. We locked lips and started kissing like we'd missed each other. Suddenly, feeling him through the thin shorts wasn't enough and apparently he felt the same. He led me to the chair and sat me down. Then he undid my pants. While he was unbuckling and unzipping, he kissed my stomach, the hollow of my hips, and as soon as my jeans were below my knees...

CHAPTER 50

Damn cops. For a few weeks now, it had been obvious that the police were watching the bar and keeping tabs on everyone coming and going.

"There they are again," Eddie said. "You shouldn't even be in the car with me."

I was worried.

"I don't think they know where I live now, so don't go to my house," I said to Eddie, holding my breath. "Take me to the pool hall on Kings Highway. I'll take a cab when it's clear. Tomorrow, we'll look into finding you a new car. One they won't recognize."

Nearly a month ago, someone had come to cop drugs and when he left the club, the cops grabbed him. They'd offered to let the guy go if he gave me up. Me specifically. Unfortunately for them, I wasn't the one dealing in the club that night, and the kid they caught wouldn't snitch either way.

Eddie left me at Mickey's Pool Hall. Inside, there was the usual afternoon crew, shooting pool and hanging around the bar. If not by name, I recognized every face there. I took up a seat at the end of the bar that would allow me to see the front door and the emergency exit. I slapped a hundred dollar bill on the bar and told the bartender, a sexy older lady with long dark hair, named Veronica, to keep the Heinekens coming. She winked at me and I noticed, not for the first time, her breasts that were almost popping out of her tank top and her narrow waist that gave way to an amazing ass. But I really didn't give a shit. I just loved to flirt, and I gave her a wink.

As Veronica handed me the first beer, a guy came into the pool hall and sat at the opposite end of the bar. I pegged him as a cop in about three seconds. If the Boy Scout haircut and neat clothing hadn't given him away, the fact that he ordered a soda would have. It wasn't long before he was joined by another detective. They made a big show out of talking to each other and watching whatever bullshit game was playing on the hall's television. They even got up and shot a game of pool. But every now and then I would catch them glancing my way.

Fuck them, I thought. Fuck the games. So, I stared at them until I got someone's attention. When the first Boy Scout, who'd come in noticed me looking, he signaled to the other to look in my direction.

"I just want to make sure I give you something good to put in your report, you fucking pigs," I said and stuck up my middle finger. And that's what I did every time I caught one of those motherfuckers following me. I flicked them off and said, "Fuck you." Whatever I could do or say to let them know I saw them, and I wasn't afraid.

They couldn't touch me. I was smarter than them and would never be stupid enough to get caught in the act of doing something illegal. Word on the street was the cops were mad that I'd gotten off so easily for the shooting, a shooting I really didn't even have anything to do with. Considering how I was knee deep in the dealing game at the time, I should have left them alone, but my hatred for them was unboreable. They were on me with a vengeance. I noticed unmarked police cars, suit-wearing detectives, and officers in uniforms following me or watching wherever I went. The constant surveillance and harassing of my customers was getting old. We could play cat and mouse if they wanted. But I would show them that I wasn't the damn mouse.

CHAPTER 51

"That's bullshit!" I screamed. "You trying to play me Raul? I ain't some new kid to this game. Before I got locked up, a key cost twenty thousand! Now you wanna charge me twenty-nine?"

When I first got out of jail and started dealing again, I was only picking up small quantities of 50-75 grams of coke and turning them over for a small profit. For any other drug dealer that would have been a big deal, but for me it was chump change compared to what I was used to.

Now I had built up some cash flow and was ready to buy a whole key. I figured in the eight months of doing time and the few months I'd been running the bar, the cost of a key might have gone up a little but not what this cock-sucker Raul was trying to charge me. I had met with a few potential suppliers already but wasn't happy with their prices either. I was hoping that my fourth connect would be a charm and give me a good deal.

. "I understand that, Jeremy," Raul said, "But that was before 9/11." When I didn't respond he continued. "Since the Arabs took down the towers, borders have been closely guarded. You can't even mail a key like you used to. So take the price or leave it."

The douche bag looked at me like I was wasting his time. Before I got locked up, no one would have dared to take a tone like that with me. And even with his 9/11 bullshit excuse, I thought the price was highway robbery. But I had to take it. And the truth was, even at twenty-nine

184

thousand a key, it was a better rate than thirty-one to thirty-five thousand per key I'd been offered elsewhere.

I sighed, "I'll take it. But, how 'bout I pay for one and you give me one on consignment since you're charging me an arm and a leg."

"Deal," Raul agreed.

I didn't shake his hand. I turned and walked out, indicating he should follow. The cab I'd ordered for the day was waiting outside to take the connect to my new stash house on Flatbush Avenue. I would lead the way in my Infiniti, and he'd follow behind with the drugs. Of course, I had backup in three cars that would also follow. Anyone who tried to intercept us, even the cops, would find themselves in a car accident.

On the drive over, I thought about how easy it was to pick up where I left off. My only wish was that I didn't have to do it without James. Not a day went by that I didn't miss him. My new connect was someone I'd met through word-of-mouth. Actually, he'd found me through customers at the club. But, I didn't like him. Could never see myself being friends with him. It was all business, a business that would let me turn twenty-nine thousand into fifty thousand in a few days.

CHAPTER 52

Business was great! Life was great! My new connect was working out well, even though he was a douche-bag. I was happy. As happy as I could be, with having to look over my shoulder at every turn. Dog had finally returned from Florida and was helping me deal out of one of the bars; which made me feel more secure. Just to have a familiar face around was comforting. But I still needed more workers to grow my business.

"Another successful night, huh, Jeremy?" Eddie asked counting his money.

"Looks like it."

The register at the bar rang $3,000, the coke made $4,000, the girls brought in another $1,500, and I hadn't even checked on Laree yet to see how the phone sales were rocking.

Eddie kept counting. I'd let him sell in the bar because the cops were following us too hard on the street. When he finished counting twice, he looked up and smiled, "I made twelve hundred dollars thanks to you."

I nodded. That was a good haul for one shift. "I'd love for you to stay on working here at the bar. We need a big dude like you. And you need a place to crash, so come stay in an extra room at my house. Take this security position here; keep selling the coke on the side. It's a win-win."

Eddie shook my hand and gave me a hug as his answer. He seemed really grateful and surprised, but the truth was he was loyal. I was learning to reward loyalty. Plus, I didn't want to bring in any outsiders.

"Alright. We done here?" I said. "Get home. Get some rest. I'll see you back here tonight." It was almost six in the morning and we were burnt. "Take my key and make a copy. Be here right before six tonight so I can show you how to open."

"Thank you, Jeremy," Eddie said, taking the keys.

"Thank me by making me money," I answered.

I left the bar and headed home counting the seconds till I would be asleep. As I pulled up the block where I lived, something wasn't right.

I recognized the van immediately. It was the same plain white van with tinted side and rear windows I'd seen across the street from the bar two nights before. Now it was parked on the corner, half a block from my house. I knew it would only be a matter of time before the cops figured out where I lived. I drove past my house pretending like I hadn't noticed them.

I kept thinking about everything in the house that could cause problems: weed, coke, guns, hos, everything needed to cut and bag coke up for the street, the stuff to make crack.

What could they have seen? I didn't deal from the house. No one I bought drugs or guns from had been to the house. And the girls weren't working from the house. It was unlikely they had a warrant to search it yet. I'd only been there a few weeks. I worked hard to make this place a home. It had 2 floors and was 5 bedrooms 2 bathrooms. I spent thousands on furniture and big TVs, I didn't want to lose it. Fuck, it can't be. I had money to collect and a connect to pay. But, since they were following me, I'd go for a workout at the gym to get them off my back. I would go in the front, work out a bit, then call a cab, and sneak out the back door to go handle my business.

Parker's Gym was a short, ten-minute drive from my house. After I parked in the lot and while I was pulling my gym bag out of the trunk, I saw the van pull into the lot of a video rental store across the street. Either they were really bad at tailing people or just didn't give a fuck that I knew they were watching.

The gym was packed which meant that there would be a wait for the machines and plenty of guys to look at. I went into the locker and changed into my sweats. I was tired but nothing a bump or two of coke couldn't take care of, and I had to kill some time to get away from the fucking pigs.

Guys working out in basketball shorts had become a favorite obsession of mine. It was hard to focus on my own workout when I could see every curve and bulge of the hot guy pumping away across from me. And, I stared. When I saw I guy I liked, I looked at him hard so he knew that I was looking and exactly what I was looking at.

I was working on my triceps when I noticed that one guy I'd been checking out a few days before was checking me out now. He was built even bigger than I was. That turned me on. The guy was white and tall. His muscles were huge. He was on the machine working his shoulders. Watching his massive muscles contract had me grabbing my crotch because I was starting to get hard. I could tell he noticed my reaction because he smiled and grabbed at his own. That was all the invitation I needed. I nodded in his direction, got up from the machine and headed for the locker room. He followed. I was on him as soon as he walked in, grabbing him, spinning him around and holding him from behind. He didn't resist.

"I'm assuming it ain't a coincidence that you're in here at the same time." I said.

"Nope," he said, and I felt him press his muscled ass against my dick. I got rock hard. I took him by the arm and pulled him into the back of the locker room. There was a secluded alcove back there where the gym offered massages a few times a week. Right now, it was empty. Lucky me and soon lucky him. As soon as we realized we were alone, we starting pulling at each other's clothes. He ripped off my tank top and began sucking on my nipples. He kissed and moaned his way down my stomach, and yanked down my sweats. (I never wore underwear to the gym because I liked the way my big dick showed through athletic pants) He took me in his mouth all the way to the back of his throat. The warm, wet heat was amazing. When I felt his tongue caress my head, my knees quivered a bit.

"Yessssss," I encouraged him. And he responded just as I hoped. He began bobbing up and down on my dick, coating me with his spit and jerking me off. Then he grabbed my ass with both his hands wrapped around me and pulled me into him, forcing me to fuck his mouth. He was so strong. I loved it. I loved that he was big enough to move me and push me around. I felt myself getting too excited and pushed him off my dick. He yanked my hands away and kept going. I couldn't hold back if I wanted to. I leaned back against the wall of the massage room and had to close my eyes. I felt my body tense up just before I exploded. I couldn't imagine how much I must have shot into his mouth, but he didn't stop sucking and jerking me. It felt so good, I was so overwhelmed, I was shaking. When I could open my eyes, I found him still on his knees smiling up at me.

"Your turn," I said, helping him stand and then reaching for the crotch of his basketball shorts.

"There'll be time for that later. Let's exchange numbers."

It took me a second to understand that he didn't want me to blow him now. Wait? Why? But, I loved how he serviced me, and this was something I definitely wanted to do again. I gave him my number and took his.

"Where are you going from here?" he asked. For the first time I noticed his green eyes and deep dimples.

"Work," I said, pulling up my sweats. Where was my shirt?

"What do you do?" he asked.

I'd turned to look for my tank top, so my back was to him. The lie came to me immediately,

"Construction. You?"

"Cop," he answered.

I spun around and laughed. When he didn't laugh with me, I realized he wasn't joking.

"I hope that doesn't bother you. A lot of people don't like it, but when my uniform is off, I'm just me."

"It don't bother me," I lied. "Next time we meet up, you should bring your uniform. You can be bad cop, and I can be your perp."

"Deal," he said. "By the way, I'm Dylan."

"Noah." And we promised to plan another date soon.

CHAPTER 53

"Piss in this cup. If you dirty, I'm locking yo' white ass right back up."

Myles Jones from the New York City Department of Probation was a dick. I believed that every night he prayed that I'd give him a reason to violate me. If he looked hard enough, he could find plenty of reasons to put me back in jail. I committed at least one crime a day, hung out with convicted felons, carried fire-arms, and used drugs all the damn time. My weed habit was out of control. But my friends encouraged it, telling me the world was a safer place when I smoked, because it kept me calm. And the truth of that matter was that if I didn't sell it, I'd be some weed dealer's best customer, spending hundreds a week on it. I only smoked the best: Northern Lights, Silver Haze, Jack Herarra, Chronic. To beat the piss test, I drank a quick flush I bought at GNC. It gave clean urine for up to 8 hours. For it to work, you had to drink an ocean of water. By the time I had to piss in that cup, I was ready to explode.

"Let's do this," I told him.

We walked to the end of the hall and through a door on the right into the men's bathroom. It was puke green and even though I could smell the bleach used to clean it, it looked filthy. P.O. Jones pointed to a stall with a full-length mirror behind the toilet. I figured that was so he could see if I put anything besides my own urine in the cup. And, he was watching. I made a big show out of pulling out my dick. I hoped that motherfucker noticed how big it was. I felt the cup get warm as I filled it, and I had to hand it back to P.O. Jones while I was still pissing in the toilet. I felt his gloved hand take it from me. When I finished, I turned around, put my dick away (again giving Jones another chance to take a look) and saw that he was putting a stick into the cup. If it turned from white to bluish-green, it meant I was going back to Brooklyn House. My heart was racing. I started thinking that the quick flush isn't always a hundred percent, but has worked for people I knew in the past. Ninety seconds later, P.O. Jones threw away the cup and the stick with a look of disgusted disappointment on his face.

"You're clean. I'll see you next month." He held the door open, silently telling me to get the fuck out. Which was fine, because I didn't want to spend another second in that building

Coming out of the probation office my thoughts wandered to Dylan and how ironic it was that he was a cop. And the hot encounter we had in the massage room at the gym. Was I crazy? But I could not wait any longer, so I called him and told him to meet me at my house by now, I was finally alone for the night and told everyone to find somewhere to sleep so I'd have the place all to myself. I knew it was stupid to get involved with him but I couldn't help myself. I was already addicted to sex with him and perhaps a little arrogant.

I high-tailed it home and shortly after I arrived, there was a knock at the door. I guess he was just as anxious to see me. When I opened the door, there he was in a dark blue sweat suit. I took a second just to look at his broad shoulders and muscled chest that tapered down to his narrow waist. My eyes kept going, and I could see the bulge in his sweat pants.

"Happy to see me?" I asked, gesturing towards his dick. He blushed a little.

"I was thinking about what I would do when I got my hands on you," he said, as he stepped into the room, slamming the door closed with the back of his foot and pushing me back with his hand on my crotch before pushing me down on the bed.

As soon as my back hit the bed, we started kissing and pulling at each other's clothes. In no time, we had each other naked, and I felt Dylan's warm mouth wrapped around my dick. Warm and wet, he sucked me hard and deep using his right hand to jerk off as he worked his lips up and down over me. My hips had a life of their own and I fucked his throat.

I closed my eyes and concentrated on enjoying it but keeping myself from cumming. I wanted it to last. Dylan, sensing that I was holding back pulled out my dick, spit on the head of my penis for lube and jerked me until I moaned. Then he deep throated me. A few of those long strokes with his mouth are all it took to send me over the edge. I exploded into his mouth. Dylan moaned, I thought from swallowing my orgasm. But then I felt the hot lines of liquid heat shoot across my leg as Dylan jerked himself to an explosive orgasm of his own. Still panting, he crawled beside me and we curled into one another. As I dozed off, I was already thinking about what I wanted to do to him for round two.

I don't know how long we slept, but I don't think it was long. At first I thought I was dreaming, but realized Dylan was speaking to me. There was a banging on the door.

"They're calling your name," I heard him say as I opened my eyes. Fuck. What now?

I got up and slipped on some boxers, still not completely awake. As I put my hand out to open the door, I realized it wasn't my underwear I had on. The thought made me smile. I really liked this guy.

"It's me, Cheddar. Open up!" Cheddar stood in the hallway, looking both ways as if he suspected someone was following him. He nursed his right hand, which was sloppily wrapped in white blood soaked gauze bandages. Blood was running down his arms. His shirt was soaked.

"I stabbed him. I had to. He was stealing," Cheddar grumbled as he pushed by me into the apartment. "Somehow he turned the knife on me."

Dylan stared at Cheddar's bloody hand. And then at me. I couldn't think of any way to explain it. To make it worse, Cheddar scowled at Dylan, like Dylan was the one intruding.

"I think I should go," Dylan said, rolling off the bed and yanking on his sweats and then his sneakers.

I wanted to tell Dylan to stay. But the truth was he did have to go. I needed to take care of my boy.

"I'll call you soon," I said weakly. "I need to take care of this."

Dylan didn't make eye contact and hadn't even completely put on his sweat-shirt as he hurried toward the door.

"I understand, Jeremy. I really do. But I can't be around this." He kissed me quickly and softly on the lips and left.

Cheddar was screaming in pain. I dragged him to the kitchen and opened the freezer door and stuck his hand inside, which made him scream even more.

"Stay here." I screamed and ran through the house, frantically grabbing towels and tape. By the time I got back to the kitchen, my freezer was a blood soaked mess and he looked like he was ready to pass out. I ran his hand under cold water and then wrapped it in a towel and duct taped it tightly to stop the bleeding. With his hand wrapped, I sat him on a stool in front of the freezer and stuck his hand, back inside, so hopefully the bleeding would stop. I then put towels around the opening of the freezer door to keep the cold inside.

"I had that kid, Jack, work out of the strip club for me tonight. He cut the bags I gave him in half and was selling the other half for himself. Customers called me to complain about the cut product. When I got there,

I took him around the corner and asked him about it, but he lied. Right to my fucking face. I pulled out my knife and told him to empty his pockets -- he had two sets of bags. Our clear bags and his own pink ones."

Jack was a kid Cheddar hired to help take some hours each day to let him sleep.

Cheddar looked at me. I knew he expected me to say something. But what was there to say? I would have handled it differently. And it bothered me that he did this shit without asking me, but no sense in crying over spilt milk.

"I better not have to clean up behind this shit," I said.

I called a doctor that took care of my boys when they needed to be patched up or the hos when they caught something. He was cool, took cash and never reported anything to the cops. Cheddar was on the mend and was told by the Doc to take it easy at the house for a few days because he had lost a lot of blood.

A few days later I walked through the front door of my house and Cheddar was sitting on the new sofa struggling to play one handed video games on the new 60-inch-screen television. Three of the girls were cleaning the living room and I could hear another girl in the kitchen with Laree cooking something that smelled delicious. Eddie was in our new recliner, being straddled by a completely naked woman I didn't recognize. At least not from behind. She was brown-skinned with a thick afro. From the door, I could see Eddie's pants were around his ankles. He was gripping her ass with both hands and bringing her again and again into him. Even from the door I could tell her skin was covered in sweat. Their quiet moaning accompanied the wet, slapping noises their bodies made. Mounds of coke, joints, and pills I assumed were Ecstasy covered the coffee table. I wanted to jump on the couch and join the partying. But, I had work to do.

Raul my new connect, had run out of coke. Which meant that soon I would run out of coke. To me, that meant losing thousands of dollars a day. Dog told me about a connect that an old friend of his from high school dealt with from time to time who worked out of Washington Heights. Even though it was the cocaine capital of New York, I'd never been uptown. Mostly because I never needed to, I'd always had a local connect who'd given me the best price around. But now, times were rough.

I'd made plans for Dog, who was living back home with his family, to swing by the house. He'd arrive in a cab with his new boy Jake, who I didn't like at all, but Dog vouched for him. We'd take my car and the cab would follow us with money for the deal in its trunk. I had just enough time to shower and catch a quick bite before he arrived. I'd just finished the eggs and bacon one of the girls had made me when the doorbell rang announcing Dog's arrival.

"Right on time, my man."

"You know it. This is business," Dog said with a smile. He was wearing a Knicks jersey and baggy white shorts with white Nikes. I knew buried somewhere inside those shorts was at least one gun. Jake, a skinny, white kid all of 19 years old with blonde hair that was long and never looked combed, stood behind him. He looked at me and nodded his hello. I returned the nod, just to be polite.

Inside the car he told me that his boy, Juan, was going to meet us when we got there. As we pulled out of the driveway and I pressed down on the gas, I felt the weight of .22 Berretta against my ankle inside my boot. Once on the highway, the cab with the money close behind, Dog wanted to go over details. Juan wanted us to call when we were getting off the highway. We were getting close. Dog asked how much money I had brought. I told him: $27,000.

"That's it?" he asked.

After Ma's rent, the bar's rent, and my own rent – that was all I could come up with. I hated the first of the month.

"If your man will give us a key for $27,000, tell him I will be back in a few days for another. Just make the call."

The conversation was in Spanish. And I couldn't understand a word, except the part where he told them we were getting off the highway at 125th Street and what kind of car we were in.

"It's a go. Juan said to meet him at 145th and Broadway."

It was early afternoon by the time we arrived. Crowds of dark brown people were moving back and forth on the sidewalk. I figured that maybe this new connect was as afraid of getting robbed as we were; which was why he asked us to meet him in such a public place. Just as the thought left my mind, a minivan pulled up next to where we were parked.

"That's him," Dog said quietly.

Outside the car, the introduction happened quickly. Juan was a dark-skinned, Dominican with curly hair, very tall and skinny. He looked to be in his mid-twenties. I could see that there were other people sitting in the van, but I couldn't get a look at them.

Where's the money?" Juan said.

"It's in another car," I said. "Where are the drugs?"

"They're coming as soon as I see the money."

"Well, then we have a problem. Because you aren't seeing the money until I see the drugs," I said with an attitude.

The cab driver with my money drove past us when we pulled over as I had instructed him to do before we left. He parked a few blocks away and wasn't to come back unless I called him.

"Okay," Juan said, clearly irritated. "We will be back. Give us a few." He jumped back in the van and drove off.

"These guys are more paranoid than I am," I told Dog.

"Let's go get something to eat and tell your boy Jake to stay with our car."

We went to the McDonald's on the corner and it was packed. A few minutes later we were just getting our food when the cab driver called my phone. I picked up the phone to the sound of sobbing. "Jeremy...Jeremy! You there? Those fuckin' spics robbed me! They beat the shit out of me. My head is bleeding. They robbed me!"

I'd never hear one Spanish guy call another a spic before. The words detonated like bombs in my brain.

"What the fuck you mean? Robbed you how?"

And then it hit me: Those cock-suckers had to of followed us from the minute we got onto 125th Street. That's why they wanted us to call when we got off the highway. They must have noticed that the cab came off the highway and made all the same turns we did.

"Head back to Brooklyn," I told the cab driver,

"Meet me at the bar." And I hung up. I looked at Dog. His eyes were the size of saucers. He took a few steps back from me.

"You fucked up. You fucked up big. Let's go," I screamed.

CHAPTER 54

"Get the fuck on the floor!" In the dark, I felt hands grab me and yank me off the bed. I hit the floor in a tangle of sheets and blankets. At least two men were holding me down on my stomach, pinning my arms behind me. I felt what must have been someone's knee in my back.

"What the fuck is going on?" I yelled as handcuffs pinched into my wrists. Someone flicked on the lights. Men in street clothes wearing bulletproof vests were everywhere, searching my closet and dresser drawers. They even flipped over my mattress.

"Where the fuck are the guns and drugs? Your boy already told us they were up here!" This came from the one with his knee in my back. I turned my head as much as I could to see him.

"I don't know what the fuck you're talking about."

As soon as the words came out of my mouth, a detective came in the room, apparently from downstairs where Cheddar and Eddie stayed. He was carrying two pistols. Fuck. Eddie had only been staying with us a few weeks. Ever since he moved in, I'd noticed more cops around more often. Was he a snitch? How else could they know there were guns and drugs in the house?

Even though I could hear some in other parts of the house, there were at least ten detectives in my room. How'd they know to focus there? It was as if they knew exactly what they were looking for and where to look. But,

I'd never told Eddie -- or anyone -- not even Cheddar. I had a carpenter cut out the floor in my closet and make a hidden trap door. He'd even used the original wood chips that chipped off to make it look perfect.

After nearly an hour of searching while I was on the floor, all they found was half an ounce of Chronic, (probably some of the best weed I'd ever had), left over from what I had smoked before I went to bed and a thousand dollars I had laying on the bedside table. I did, however, have two pounds of haze stashed in the hidden compartment along with about five guns, a couple grams of coke, and $5,000, the last of my money. Cheddar and Eddie were brought upstairs and into the bedroom. They were in cuffs along with the three girls that were in the house.

"No one is talking," the cop leading them said to one of the detectives who was clearly in charge. But, if no one talked, how the fuck did they know about me having drugs and guns.

An hour later, we were at the precinct. I was put in a cell alone with Cheddar and Eddie. The girls were put somewhere else. When I was sure no cops were listening, I turned to them.

"HOW did this happen?"

"I...It...I met a customer outside the house," Eddie said. "I thought..."

"You. Did. What?" I said but couldn't believe what I was hearing. "Eddie, I took you off the phone so you didn't HAVE to deal with customers outside any more. I gave you a spot in the bar and a place to live. And you fuck me like this?"

"I was just trying to make us more money," he said. "I didn't think..."

"Shut the fuck up. Of course you didn't think, you greedy, lazy fuck."

I didn't even realize I'd gotten up from the bench until I felt Cheddar holding me back. I had to calm down. The cops were staring.

"You're going to own up to this you little fuck," I said trying to keep my voice down. "The only reason they came in the house is because you sold outside the house. They didn't have a warrant. Did you let them in too?"

"Jeremy, they said if I didn't let them in the house they would kick the door in and come upstairs. So, I did. I didn't think they would go up to you. They said they wouldn't."

"Well, they lied to you, you fucking idiot. You are taking the fall for this one. If they find all that shit in my room, we're fucked."

And as if they'd been waiting for me to say that, two cops walked in carrying the box I'd hidden in my closet.

We were fucked.

CHAPTER 55

I spent two nights in Central Booking. Steinbaum again came to the rescue. Luckily because I was only on probation, I could fight the case from the street. And our bail was set at only $5,000 each.

Obviously, I couldn't go back to the spot that was raided. So, I went back to where I always went when shit turned sour: Ma's house. No matter how much trouble I got into, Ma was always glad to see me. She was happy to have me living under her roof again.

I needed to clear my head and figure out my next move. I had to come up with a way to get my hands on some blow, and fast. Tommy loaned me money, for a fee of course. He was a loan shark at heart. And I agreed to take $22,000 from him.

My brother's old friend Slavic, who first introduced me to dealing the day I quit school, had heard about my situation and was coming up from Florida in two days to help. I hadn't seen him since I used to sell drugs for him back in the day. He had moved to Miami and in Florida, coke was a lot cheaper, and he was doing me a favor by not charging me for transporting it to New York. Hopefully this would be exactly what I needed to get back on my feet. With nothing to do but wait for my coke to arrive, I decided to call Dylan. If he was free, I could use some playtime.

He was happy that I called and invited me to his apartment where he wore his NYPD uniform especially for me. I loved the way the dark blue fit over his broad shoulders and tapered down to his slim waist. I'd come over expecting just to fuck. But Dylan insisted on feeding me. Roasted chicken. Baked potatoes. Carrots. Some wine I couldn't pronounce. After he cleared the dishes, he stepped away and came back into the living room wearing a little less of his uniform, he lost the belt and shirt, man his ass looked great in those dress blues. I didn't wait for him.

I crossed the room and wrapped my arms around him. I forced his mouth open and filled it with my tongue. I needed to taste him. I pressed my hardening dick into him and ran my hand down his back and over his ass. I squeezed his cheeks and pulled him into me until I was lifting him. I carried him into the bedroom. On his bed, I laid him on his back. His hard-on strained the front of his uniform pants. I stroked it through the fabric until he moaned. I slowly unhooked his belt and unbuttoned his pants. He moaned again when I slid them down his hips, over his erection, down those sexy man thighs, and tucked them around his ankles. I licked the palm of my hand and jerked him until his hips started moving in time with my stroke. I told him to roll over onto his stomach.

The sight of his muscular back and that ass exposed, turned up towards me made me squirt pre-cum that dripped down my thigh. I dropped my jeans quickly. My dick was wet and I rubbed my own liquid over the head of my cock. That was the only lube I used to mount him. Dylan moaned as I pounded into him. He kept repeating my name, urging me to take him there. "Noah, Oh fuck, Noah, please fuck me deep"

I did just that.

"You're so deep. Oh my god. Yes. So. Thick," he gasped. I forced all my length into his tight heat. Again and again. Pounding him, I sucked his neck then his ear, I began biting him on his neck just enough to let him know I was man and it was driving him crazy. I couldn't take it anymore "I'm cumming, oh fuck I'm cumming." I roared like a beast, and finally I emptied myself into him. Almost at the exact same time he came while I continued to pound it out of him.

"Fuck your dick is so good, I'm cumming." He exploded all over the bed.

I rolled off him onto my back. I hadn't even come down from the orgasm before I felt his lips around my cock. I was still sensitive the way you get after you come. His touch made me tremble and laugh. It was almost too much, but he wouldn't be pushed away. And then I started to get hard again. His mouth was hot and wet. He took me down his throat, hard. I fucked his face at a pace that had me biting my lip. I used my hand on the back of his head to steady him. And before I knew it, I was erupting again. He took every drop.

"I was glad you called. I've been wanting to see you again," he said. I was still panting, nearly passed out from the amazing blow job he'd just given me.

"I've been wanting to see you, too."

He kissed my neck and started lightly stroking my dick. Did he want a third time? I'd needed a minute. Instead, I reached for his and he pushed my hand away.

"Why do you keep taking care of me without letting me do it back?"

"Satisfying you does it for me," he said, shrugging his shoulders. "There is something so manly about you, Noah. Something so masculine. Like you should naturally be in charge. A man like you should be taken care of, and you should let me be the man to do it."

I smiled and kissed him on the lips. The idea of being with Dylan -- coming home to someone every night -- excited me. But, I couldn't hide who I was from him forever. And my business came first. As much as I would love to have a man, it couldn't be him. I could not ignore the fact that I was falling in love with him. It was a powerful feeling, but one I had to fight.

"When can we see each other again?" he asked.

"Soon," I said with a yawn. "Real soon."

Then I passed out.

"Your phone is ringing." Dylan's voice pulled me from sleep. My phone was in the pocket of my jeans, which were in a ball on the floor by the bed. I fished it out.

"Yo, it's me, Slavic," said a familiar voice on the other end.

"One sec, my man."

Dylan was turned on his side and I could see his eyes were closed. I'd finally forced him to let me make him cum. Twice to be exact. Maybe he was a little tired too. But in case he wasn't sleeping, I walked out of the bedroom. He was used to me stepping away during our dates to take a work-related phone call. He'd jokingly complained about it a few times. I left the bedroom and went into the bathroom, where I turned on the shower. And even then, I chose my words carefully.

"How is everything? You in town yet?"

"No. But, I will be in a few hours. Get your shit together and meet me in New Jersey."

"Okay. Should I come prepared?"

"Yes. Do that."

I called Eddie and told him to get Dog and meet me at the pizzeria.

"We're taking a trip and you don't need to come strapped." The money and my boys was all I needed for this deal. Because if anything went south during the deal, I didn't want to be caught with guns not in NJ. I heard what they did to out of towners there that came to commit crimes, they practically put them under the jail

"You sure no guns and you want Dog to come," Eddie asked, "after he fucked up with the cab getting robbed uptown?

"He's got a debt to repay," I said. "so, yeah. His ass HAS to come," Slavic's call made me start to feel better. I had coke on the way and customers waiting for me. I stripped off my boxers and hopped in the shower. Before long, Dylan joined me. He washed and rinsed my back. And then, with a soapy hand, started jerking me off. He couldn't get enough of me.

Slavic's instructions were for us to meet him at a Motel 6 off of a highway in New Jersey. Cheddar and Dog were silent on the drive. I guess they could tell I was on edge. As we approached the exit, I saw a state trooper in my rearview mirror. Before I could say anything, lights started flashing.

Fuck, I thought. Thank God we had no guns on us for this one. I knew this kid since grade school, could he fuck me? Nah. I didn't have anything illegal on me so I was cool, and the cash was, as usual, in a cab following us. I pulled over. And the state trooper zoomed right by. My palms were sweaty on the steering wheel and it took everything I had not to show the fellas I was shaking. Without a word, I continued driving.

Once we were off the highway, I called Slavic's cell to let him know we were nearby. I pulled into a shopping center across the street from Motel 6 where we were to meet, and the cab pulled up about 50 feet behind me. I signaled for Dog to go get the money from the cab. For some reason, I didn't want to go straight to the motel; as much as I trusted Slav, I had a strange feeling. It was a busy area. If anything went down, we could get lost in the crowd.

Slavic said he would be in the parking lot in a Cadillac truck. I spotted it as soon as we walked into the lot. Slav jumped out of the truck immediately and headed my way. I told Cheddar and Dog to wait as I walked closer to Slavic. Alone.

"What's up, bro? Long time, no see," I said with a smile. " How you been? How's business in Florida?"

"Great!" He said. "And if all goes vell, things vill be great for yo' ass, too."

"That's good because right now things aren't so good," I said.

"You got the money?" he asked, something about the way he said it, the way his eyes never really met mine, the way he was fidgeting, made me nervous. I didn't like it. Was I being paranoid?

"Yeah, I got it." I waved Cheddar over. He showed Slavic the money. I told him to take Dog and grab us a room. As soon as I saw them walk into the motel at the front desk, I turned to Slavic and asked. "So where is the shit?"

"Oh, I got you. It's right over here. Follow me." He led me to a Cadillac truck. Before we reached it, a tall skinny blonde guy jumped out. His hair was pulled into a long pony-tail, and he looked like a redneck.

"You were supposed to meet me alone, Slavic. Deals off. I'm out of here."

But, before I could take a step to leave, an army of men in black hoods and masks jumped out from behind cars. They carried small machine guns. Cars and trucks pulled up simultaneously and surrounded me. A helicopter buzzed overhead. It all happened too quickly for me to see anyone clearly. But, I knew that this wasn't the regular police. This wasn't some D.A.'s task force. And then I saw it, written on their jackets and across their vests, D.E.A.

Fucked by the Feds.

At the precinct, I overheard a D.E.A. agent thanking an NYPD detective and someone from the Brooklyn D.A.'s task force for the joint effort. Apparently, they'd worked together to capture me. I was in some serious shit. I thought the only thing I had on my side was that I hadn't actually made an exchange for goods. I could say that I came to buy a car and that Slavic had tricked me to save his own ass. Clearly, he was the one who set me up. Eventually, two D.E.A agents came to talk to me. They were both men and looked almost identical: dark, close cut hair, wearing dark suits. They had me handcuffed in a tiny office with no windows. They set up a video camera. One of them read me my rights, something that the cops had never done, and asked me if I understood "on camera."

I said that I did. The other agent told me that they were going to give me just one opportunity to help myself. "Tell me who you know that sells drugs. Come work for us or we fry you. We know who you are, and there's a lot of people that would love to see your ass go to prison for a long time."

"I didn't do shit," I said.

"Let me explain something to you, tough guy. We got you on a conspiracy charges. We have you on tape admitting that you were going to transport and sell the shit back in New York. We didn't need you to buy anything you fool. We got you to do exactly what we wanted you to do. Exactly where we wanted you to do it. This state don't play and unless you rat, you will go to prison."

"Fuck, you. Prison it is."

"No, fucko. Fuck your mother 'cause you ain't gonna see her for about twenty years." The agents got up to leave. But before they left, one turned to me.

"By the way, Dylan said to give you his best."

Before I could help it, my mouth dropped open.

"When we first made contact with him, he actually believed you worked in construction. Didn't take long for us to convince him of the truth. Then he was helpful in all kinds of ways. Guess he liked his job more then he liked you, he filled in the blanks of your moves."

The agent threw a file on the table and when I opened it, it had pictures of the two of us and also pictures of me and some of my customers.

"While you were playing house and falling in love, Dylan was helping us build our case against you."

Hot tears slid down my cheeks. The agents left me with their laughter, the sound of my world, caving in.

CHAPTER 56

"Get the fuck up!" Some asshole guard was yelling. "You're going to see the judge."

I must have dozed off. And thank God, because staring at those four walls and the bars left me with nothing else to do but think. I was thinking about what the agent had said, and he was right. I was involved in a conspiracy. I knew guys that were doing ten years and more for that. I missed Ma. I thought about how long it could be before I got to really see my family again. Twenty years? Ma and Dad might be gone by then.

"Let's go. You're up," that asshole guard said, shoving me through a door. The guard stood right behind me holding the chain of the cuffs, I guess so that I could not run.

"All rise. The Honorable Jack Frederick presiding."

I was already standing. The packed courtroom got up as well.

"Let's get this show on the road," the judge said as he sat down in his chair. To me, he looked young for a judge, but serious. He didn't look at me.

"Your, honor, the defendant was caught attempting to buy two keys of cocaine from undercover officers." The prosecutor stated. "It was a joint effort from the D.E.A, the Burlington County prosecutor's office and the state police. He is already out on bail in New York, has a prior felony charge, not to mention multiple arrests. One witness in this collaborative investigation is an officer in New York. We're asking the defendant to be denied bail."

I couldn't help but still be in disbelief, they were talking about Dylan. How could I have been so stupid! I held my forehead. He fucked me just like the feds did and I let him. My heart stopped. No bail? I wouldn't even get to spend time home during the trial?

"First things first, counsel," the judge said. "How do you plead, Mr. Braverman?"

"Not guilty, your honor." They'd assigned me a public defender. She was an older black woman. She hadn't said much when she came to interview me in holding. And she wasn't saying much now. I wished Steinbaum could have come to the rescue. But he wasn't licensed in Jersey, so I was stuck with who they gave me. "Your honor, everyone is presumed innocent until proven guilty. On behalf of Mr. Braverman, we'd be asking for the court to set a bail of $10,000 please."

"Bail is $300,000 and I want a bail source hearing. I want to know where this money is coming from. Case adjourned until one week from today."

I didn't hear anything the judge said after that. I felt the court officer drag me out of the courtroom because my feet wouldn't move. My lawyer said something about a bail reduction. And told me to be patient. As if I had a choice.

CHAPTER 57

I had been locked up for six days, and I was already tired of the shit.

"Count-up, mother fuckers!" It had already been a long afternoon, and I was not in the mood for these asshole C.O.s. They were so fucking disrespectful.

"We've only been in the yard forty minutes. We're supposed to get an hour," I yelled to the guard.

"You go in when I say you go in. Now, count-up mother fuckers, before I give you a 'disrupting the court' charge, and another for 'disrupting an institutional movement.'"

Fuck it. At least I'd gotten in a good work out. I had to work out every day to keep my head clear and somewhere else. The waiting was driving me crazy. But, I just had one more day to find out if I'd go home. I hadn't spoken to my mom or dad in a few days. But I got money dropped off to my account that morning so I could finally call them. As we trailed back into the building from the yard, I asked a lady officer if I could use the phone before lock-in.

This jail was unlike the one I'd been in before. It was two-tiers, which was nothing new, but it was twenty-three-hours-a-day lock-in. We only got one hour out each day. Both tiers couldn't be out at the same time.

"Sure you can use the phone, sweetheart. But, hurry." She was the only nice one out of all of them as far as I could tell.

I jogged to the phone, picked it up and dialed the number. I punched in my inmate ID when the automated voice told me to and the same voice reminded me that the call was recorded.

I heard Ma pick up. The voice told her that she had a call from an inmate in a New Jersey County Jail. With a touch of a button from her end, we were connected. Instantly, Ma was crying. Her pain put a lump in my throat. I didn't know what to say to comfort her. I said nothing.

"Noah," she finally managed to say through her tears, "this is serious. The lawyers and bail bondsman, everyone I speak to tells me you're facing some serious charges. They're saying that in Jersey the max could be twenty years and, even as a nonviolent offender, you would have to do at least twelve years of it."

Twelve years? I was barely holding on after six days! Ma's words dissolved into her crying again, and this time I couldn't hold back. Hot tears rolled down my cheeks.

"I don't know what the fuck I did to myself. I feel like my life is over," I said holding my head. "The whole reason I started doing what I did was for you and the family. Look at me now. Ma, I got greedy. I fucked up. And now...I might not see you guys for twelve years...maybe even twenty..." I heard myself sob into the phone. I had to take a deep breath to try to pull my shit together. When I looked up to see if anyone noticed my breakdown, I saw the female C.O. waving me off the phone.

"I have to go, Ma. I don't want to let go of this phone, but I have to. I love you. More than you can ever know."

"This is my fault," she insisted.

"No." I cut her off. "I did this. You tried your hardest over and over again. No one is to blame here but me. I will handle this like a man. I'll be okay. I love you."

And with that I hung up. I couldn't take hearing or saying another word. The next day I was hopeful that I would at least get out on a reasonable bail, but life had another plan for me.

"Your motion is denied, but you may file again in thirty days." I was the first case called. I wasn't even in the courtroom for five minutes. It was clear to me that this judge didn't want me out.

"I think what they're trying to do, Noah, is make sure you miss your court date in New York," my lawyer explained to me before they led me away.

Oh shit! My court date in Brooklyn was in just a few days.

"If that happens, there will be a warrant out for your arrest. Or maybe the court there will want to remand you for getting arrested while on probation with a pending case. Either way, when you finally do make bail here, you will likely have to be extradited back to New York, and then you will be locked up there."

I didn't understand all of what I was hearing. But, I knew the bottom line was that I was fucked. As I finished my thought, the guard began pulling on my shackles signaling me to get moving out of the courtroom. As I stood, I saw my parents in the back, crying their eyes out. Ma yelled that she loved me. Again, her tears falling were like punches to my gut…because I'd done it to her. I was breaking my Ma's heart.

Part 3

CHAPTER 58

"Braverman, get up. It's moving day! It was the tall, skinny blonde corrections officer with a buzz cut, banging his baton against the bars of my cell as if his barking at me wasn't enough to pull me out of my sleep. He doesn't speak often. Usually just scowls. I am used to the barking and the banging. I almost welcome it, with the news that I am leaving this shit-house, I don't mind.

It's moving day! That's what they call the day an inmate gets to leave Riker's Island. For me, it meant that the authorities from New Jersey were there to get me so I could finish my case in Newark.

Finally my wait was over. I was free of this crap hole. And even though I knew I was facing more time in Jersey, getting out of Riker's still felt like I was free. Even if just for a little while

Of the one-year sentence I'd been given on my New York cases, I'd done eight months. But, because I had a case in another jurisdiction, there was a hold put on my release. Instead of letting me go from Riker's, I was taken to this boat docked in the Bronx that was also a jail. At the time, I couldn't have imagined anything worse than Riker's but the boat was worse. The corrections officers were more dangerous than the inmates. They would beat prisoners relentlessly and make us sit on our knees for hours if someone pissed them off. Then they would send some of the unlucky bastards back to Rikers Island.

I kept to myself. Which was easy to do when I thought that I was only going to be there for a week, waiting for transportation to Jersey. That week turned into a month.

The lawyer I was assigned to in New Jersey kept in touch with me. She'd never stopped working on my case and had gotten me a deal. I would plead guilty in exchange for a sentence of six years with no minimum. That meant that, if the judge agreed, it would be up to the parole board of New Jersey to decide if I got out early. With any luck, I could do as little as two years. But, even the six years was less than the possible twenty I'd been facing.

I packed my things quickly, not putting them in any order. I was surprised by how quickly they processed my release. Maybe because they wanted to get rid of me or out of respect for the guys who needed to get back to Jersey, they got shit done faster than usual. After the paperwork was done, I was led to two guards from New Jersey. One of them was holding shackles. I signed a final piece of paper, and one of the guards signed his name undermine as the other cuffed me.

I rode in the back seat of a plain, navy blue sedan with one guard sitting next to me while the other drove. I could feel some weight lifting off of me as I looked out the window. The sun was just starting to rise as we crossed the George Washington Bridge. It's amazing how freedom from incarceration or the illusion of it makes you see and appreciate things you never really noticed before.

The guards were nice. They bought me a Big Mac and fries at some rest stop in New Jersey. One talked about his kids; the other about the woman he was planning to marry. They were lucky. They had a life, a normal life. They asked me about my time and how I came to get into so much trouble. I gave them the half-honest answers I figured they wanted to hear. They said I am different than they expected. They'd heard I was real jerk. And dangerous. Am I really different than what they expected?

I am not sure, but I think I am starting to become different than what I expected myself to be, too.

I was taken straight to the courthouse. And after a brief meeting with my attorney, I went before the judge, the same one I saw many months ago.

"Your honor," the prosecutor started, "Mr. Braverman has just been produced in this courthouse from Riker's Island in New York City where he just served most of his one year sentence a for drug-related convictions. He is a dangerous criminal and a flight-risk. Mr. Braverman has a warrant history in New York. He is not from, nor does he live in the state of New Jersey. We'd ask that his bail be revoked, and he be remanded to ensure that he appears in court."

The judge looked down, reading something, while the prosecutor spoke. This wasn't the same judge as last time. Then the judge looked at me. Directly at me.

"Mr. Braverman, from what I am reading you have a deal in place now for 6 years flat. Correct?"

"Yes your honor."

"You posted bail on your charges here. And the fugitive warrant issued out of New York was because you missed court as a result of being held here. Correct?"

"Y...Yes... sir, uh, your honor," I stammered

"Then, I assume you turned yourself into the authorities willingly in New York

"Yes, your honor."

"Then, I have no reason to believe you will do any differently here. So if you're ready to proceed pleading guilty, then I will allow you to go out on bail until your sentencing in 30 days. Are you ready?"

"Yes your honor," I happily answered.

"Counsel, your application to revoke Mr. Braverman's bail is denied," the judge decreed. After my lawyer and the D.A. signed a few legal papers about my plea deal, my lawyer returned to my table. The next words I heard were music to my ears, the feeling of excitement that ran through my body was unexplainable.

"Defendant is free pending sentencing in 30 days. Don't make me regret this, Mr. Braverman."

My lawyer turned to me and smiled. I don't think I had ever really seen her genuinely smile at me before. She gave me a hug and said she would wait for me to get released.

I was in shock. Happily in shock.

I'd expected to come to court, be remanded for a week until I came back to take the plea deal, then get sentenced and do my time. I never let myself believe that I would be released for any time in between. My family wasn't there. They still thought I was on that boat in the Bronx. I had no money in my pocket and no idea how I was going to get home. Maybe my lawyer would spot me. But, I was free. For the time being. That's all that mattered.

Part 4

CHAPTER 59

Life goes on outside while you're in jail. Nothing waits for you. People don't stop. They do what they have to do without you. They go to work. They hustle. They wake up every day. Eat. Fuck. Break up. Make up. They get older.

'Life will go on without me.' That's what I'm thinking as I watched my friends, family, drug customers, connects, guys who dealt for me and others dance and eat and clown around. They had thrown me a going away party at a strip club they rented out for the occasion. They went all out. There's food. And a DJ. It's bigger than any party I'd ever seen. Bigger than any birthday I've ever had. The place was packed. Dog and Cheddar; who pled to lesser charges and got out on probation. Eddie. Laree. Alyssa. Caitlin. My brothers. Dianna. Even people I don't know were there having a good time and letting loose. It had been a couple of hours since I arrived. I was high and drunk. I was in a white tank top and slacks because the button-down I wore was God knows where. Probably the same place I lost my belt.

"Jeremy!" An older lady, over fifty, who I don't know well that one of my guys sells to on a regular basis. She's short with reddish-blonde hair. Thin. She stumbled towards me in such a way that I was actually getting ready to catch her if she fell. She made it to me and leaned against me, putting her hand up on my shoulder.

"I'm gonna leave soon, hun." She said. " I just wanted to make sure I wished you good luck. I'll be prayin' for ya, but I know you'll do fine. I heard you got six years."

I just nodded. "My boy got ten years upstate," she continued.

"Got mixed up with a crowd doing robberies. Nasty business. But six years, you're gonna be fine. Seems like time flew when you had to do that year in Riker's right?" I nodded again. And kissed her on the cheek, because I wanted her to leave. Time flew. I have heard that a lot about my being away at Riker's. For people on the outside, except for maybe Ma, time flew. I felt every damn second. It was the thirty days the New Jersey judge gave me on the outside till I returned for sentencing that flew. And I know that even if I am lucky enough to just do the two-year minimum on my six year sentence, I will still feel every painful second. My friends were dancing. They were laughing. They were holding drinks in the air. Some, I know, were even in the bathroom doing coke. Some were on the roof of the building smoking weed. I knew would join them. All of them. I knew I would drink some more. Get higher. I would dance. And before the night was over, I would fuck. Fuck like it was the last time I would ever fuck.

But right then, as the red-haired lady stumbles off, I turned away from the dancing and celebrating. I look out of the tinted window of the strip club on the second floor. And directly across the street I saw the Cyclone – the famous wooden roller coaster in Coney Island. There's nothing more Brooklyn than that damn roller coaster. How long would it be before I was back here? Before I got a chance to prove to Ma and Dad that I could take care of them legally?

In just a few short hours from then, I would say good-bye to my parents for the last time, for a long time. Eddie and Cheddar offered to drive my parents and me to the courthouse in Jersey to start my sentence. Every time someone, like the redhead, came up to me to say goodbye, I knew I was getting closer to that time. Each goodbye made me feel like I was never going to see these people or this place again. Yes, life goes on without you.

I turned away from the window before the tears started to fall. I put the Jeremy smile back on my face, and ran into the middle of the dancing crowd. And I partied like it is the last time I will ever party.

CHAPTER 60

No one was talking but there really wasn't any silence because Ma was crying. She had been crying since we left Brooklyn. And I couldn't think of anything to say to her to make it easier.

It is what it is.

Eddie was at the wheel driving us back to the courthouse where I took my plea. We were almost there and for the last hour of the ride, I had been assuring myself that I could do this. That I will be home soon.

As we pulled into the parking lot of the courthouse, I sat up to say something to my Dad who was in the back seat with me and Ma. And I realize he is also crying too.

"Dad." Whatever words I had to say stuck in my throat. Eddie parked and we all get out of the car. I hugged my father. I hugged and kiss my mother. She sobbed relentlessly. And when she let me go, I couldn't help but notice how tired she looked, and then she pressed her hand to her chest. I allowed myself to believe that it's merely emotional pain that makes her look like this. She is just worried about me. And, if I am fine, she will be fine. I believe this because I have to.

"You take care of yourself, Lady," I said to her, giving her another hug.

"Don't worry about me," she whimpered. "God don't want me, only the good die young." And she forced herself to smile for me.

"I love you," I said.

As my parents got back in the car I turned to Eddie and Cheddar. Without a word, they gave me exactly what I needed. I did a huge bump of coke and chugged a few gulps of Hennessy. My boys hugged me. They cried silent tears that they tried not to let me or each other see. I was done crying. A clock somewhere chimed nine times and I broke our hug. As I approached the doors of the courthouse, I called over my shoulder, "You guys be safe, I took one last bump, one that could have killed an Elephant, tossed the empty bag on the floor. Look out for each other," And I was off to prison.

Part 5

CHAPTER 61

I've been away over a year and a half now and can't help to think about what I will do and how I will survive when I get out of here. I want a different life for myself. So, even though I dropped out of school in 7th grade, and education has never been my thing, I got my GED in the time that I've been locked up. I also got a certificate in culinary arts and another for computer repair. I figured that for me to make an honest life for myself, I need proof that I know how to do something that someone will pay me for, proof that I have skills.

And, I have another plan. I am part owner of a store that my brother Scott runs in Bensonhurst, repairing vacuum cleaners. I was planning for the store to be my source of income when I finally got out, but business hasn't been good. The store is hanging on, though.

I have applied for the state's halfway house program. This is a program that allows convicts who've served a portion of their sentence with no major problems an opportunity to be supervised in the community and transition into being on parole. In order to be considered, I need proof that I can work and earn a steady income. Being part owner in a legal business that's staying afloat in a bad economy, I think, will make me a shoe-in. I call

216

my brother every week or so just to see how things are going.

In Southern State Correctional Facility, where I am doing my time, the phones are in the back of our day room. The day room is where we prisoners have our meals, watch television, play cards, talk, and spend the day. The phones are like pay phones, except you don't put money in them. You can only make collect calls or prepaid calls. When I sit down to call Scott, the area is empty. I choose the phone closest to the wall, because for some reason I feel like this gives me even more privacy. I sit down, pick up the phone, and punch in the number to my prepaid account, and then Scott's number.

The computerized voice tells me to say my name and then hold. I hear Scott's number being dialed. He picks up and the same voice tells him that he has a prepaid call from an inmate in the Southern State Correctional Facility. He presses whatever he has to press to connect my call.

"Hey, bro! How are you? How is everything going?" I ask. There is silence. Scott is never silent, so I think maybe we have a bad connection. I am about to ask him if he can hear me when he says,

"I have something to tell you but you have to promise not to flip out." The store. He lost the store. WE lost the store. He is about to tell me that we've lost the store. I close my eyes before I speak and let out a deep breath.

"I promise not to flip out. What's up, Scott?" My entire body tenses up. I lean forward, holding the phone tight to my ear and put my elbows on my knees to brace myself for the horrible details. What the fuck are we gonna do without the store? I need a job. Scott needs the money even more because he has family to support. And, why didn't he tell me things were THIS bad sooner so I could have...

"Mom passed away," he says.

The three words come at me like punches. An ache rips and twists its way from the center of my chest up to my throat, choking me, leaving me unable to breathe or speak. Ma...Mom...my mother can't...yeah, she's been sick, but she's the strongest person I know. Ma hasn't sat still a day in her life. No! No!. No!

I think of the last time I saw her. She made the three-hour trip to visit me here. I had been so happy to see her that maybe I let myself ignore how tired she looked. Or the bruises from dialysis that stretched all the way up her arm and even on the left side of her neck. My world goes black as I curl against the wall, quietly shaking with sobs, so none of the other inmates or guards in the day room can see me.

"Noah, talk to me!" Scott calls again and again, but it's like I am hearing him from under water. His voice seems like it's coming from another world.

And, I am here alone. I want to speak. I want to say something to him, but I know if I talk right now, it will be a scream and that I won't be able to stop screaming. After what feels like an hour but must have been ten minutes, I manage to speak.

"How? How did she pass?"

"We really aren't sure." He says. "Her kidneys were shot and you know she was in a lot of pain. She's in a better place now, Noah."

He tells me that our brother Adam woke up in the middle of the night and found her sleeping with her head at a funny angle and blood on her chin. Adam called Scott. And by the time Scott got there, Dad was in some sort of shock and was convinced that Ma was going into a diabetic coma. Scott caught Dad trying to feed Ma chocolate to wake her up...not wanting to believe his wife of over 50 years was gone. We run out of time on the phone. And, really, there is nothing left to say because my mother is dead, and I am in jail and because we are Jewish, she is already buried by the time this conversation is happening. And I was not at her funeral.

Before the call is disconnected, I tell Scott I love him. He loves me too and makes me promise not to lose it. I promise and hang up the phone. I get up from where I am sitting and walk out to the yard. I've spent at least part of every day of my sentence in the yard: weight-lifting, doing push-ups, sit-ups, and running, all for recreation and to pass the time. But now, I am not going to the yard for any of that. I am going to be alone. I am going to find a place to hide this pain for now. My thoughts are scattered, and I hurt. Somewhere in my mind I make the choice not to tell anyone that my mother has died. If the prison finds out, I will be placed in administrative segregation -- also known as The Hole, The Bing, Solitary Confinement, Isolation -- so they can keep me from hurting myself or someone else. And being placed there would keep me from being discharged to a halfway house and would keep me from my family even longer.

I have to hold it together. So, I walk around the dirt path that circles the yard called the track. Four times around the track is a mile. I walk there until it is dark, and I am told to come inside for evening count. Once evening count is down, I go back outside and walk some more. I need, at least, the illusion of freedom that being under the naked sky gives me. If I look straight up, I see the moon and a few stars that have begun to appear. I pretend that there are no walls or fences keeping me away from the people I love when they need me most.

At some point in my walk, I start talking to God,

I need him to make me understand why my mother had to go through so much. Why did she have to die while her baby boy was in jail? She had already endured so much in her life, a lot of it because of me. She raised us with no money. Had to deal with seven kids who did almost nothing but get in trouble all the time. She even had to deal with losing my sister, Rachel.

Thinking of Rachel makes me smile. I never met her. But, Ma always showed me pictures of her. And me and Ma shared this game where at night she would make me look up into the sky and find the brightest star.

"That star is Rachel," she'd say, "See her up there? She is watching over us, keeping us safe."

These memories make fresh, hot tears run down my face. And I look up. I look for the brightest star. I look for my sister and my heart stops in my chest. There are only two bright stars in the sky tonight, and they are near one another. I swear that they are the brightest stars I have ever seen.

Rachel and Ma.

I speak to them. I tell Rachel that I never knew her, but Ma talked about her all the time. I tell Rachel that Ma is with her now and that she is lucky to have our mother by her side. I ask Rachel to take care of Ma and keep watching out for the rest of the family. They need her now. I tell my mother that I am sorry for all the times that I hurt and disappointed her. I thank her for loving me and always being there. I thank her because there wasn't a day of my life that she didn't show me that she loved me with all her heart. Even after she found out I dealt drugs. After everything, she accepted me. And, I promise her that I am going to get out of this life that put me in jail. I promise her that I will make her proud of me. I tell my stars that I love them. I say it over and over and over again, until more tears come and I can't talk.

I wipe away the tears. As I turn and walk back inside, I promise myself that I will never again be in a situation where I can't be there for the people I love. I promise myself that I will survive prison. I won't die having the last thing I ever am be Inmate 700455EE. I promise to be a Noah Braverman that my mother would have been proud of.

Inside I do not notice anyone talking to me. I do not notice anyone asking me to join a card game or look at some hot girl on television. I do not notice anyone asking me if I am okay. I find my cell and climb into my bunk and close my eyes.

I think of my mother in a better place and my family in Brooklyn, grieving without me. I think about the life waiting for me on the other side of my bid. And, I think of the life I led that put me here. I think about the drugs, the money, the parties, the trips, the sex, the violence, the guns, the power -- all that power -- and how I would trade it all in for just another hour with Ma. I pray for sleep. And when it finally takes me, I have a heavy heart and many promises to keep.

EPILOGUE

It's hard to find stars in the sky over Brooklyn. At least harder than I remember it being when I was a kid. More lights? More pollution? I'm not sure why. But on a night in February, despite the cold, I need to find the brightest star in the sky.

I have something to say.

A good friend suggested that I write a letter to Ma. At first, the very idea of writing down and then reading all the things I never got to say to her put a lump in my throat. But, the idea stayed with me. I wasn't sure I'd ever do it. But, at some point, I realized that my mother spent the last years of her life hoping I'd turn things around, hoping that I'd make something of myself. And, if I managed to even do a little bit of that, she deserved to hear about it.

I'm on the roof of an apartment building in Bay Ridge. At first, no star in the sky grabs my attention. They all seem small and far away. And then, there is one, bigger than the rest. Brighter. I don't know how I missed it. There she is.

Dear Ma...,

I wish you were here today so I could say these things to you face-to-face rather than writing you this letter. I love and miss you and I want to thank you for everything you've done for me. Not a single day goes by that I don't think about you and wish I'd had more time with you.

I want to tell you that I'm sorry for all the things I put you through. And I understand why you and dad beat me; to keep me from going down the wrong path. But I always wondered why the beatings were so harsh. I know it was hard to control us any

221

other way, but at times they got so bad that I wondered why you had me. I guess I'm looking for answers I'll never get. But I just want you to know that I do forgive you.

I also want you to know that you gave me the confidence I needed in life to achieve all I have. I only wished I had made good choice's instead bad ones. You always believed in me, always thought I was special. And you always believed I could change. Even when I went to jail and promised that I would do better, when I got out, you didn't doubt me. There's so much going on in my life now that I'm thankful for and I think would make you proud.

I've been home several years now from prison. Since I got home, I have been working on a book about my life and the inspiration for writing it was you. I want the world to read my story, our story, and see that it's never too late for good things to happen if you change your ways. I hope parents can learn from us about what to look for in their own behavior and in their kids' behavior that shows they might be going down the wrong path. And for kids to see that there is nothing good that comes from taking the road I took.

I've been working since the day I came home from prison. First with Scott at the store and now on my own. After two years working at this club I bar-tended at, they made me manager, since then I've started some pretty successful business ventures. I'm still not where I want to be in life and my career, and I'm not even sure if it's I want to do forever, but it pays the bills. Also, Ma, I went to college – for a while it wasn't really for me although I was doing really well. I remember you always told me I could do if I put my mind to it. You were right.

And, last but not least, Ma, I'm married. My husband's name is Michael, and you would love him. He's wonderful to me. I honestly think he helped bring whatever good was left in me out. I tell him all the time that if you were here now, you'd approve. Not only is he a military man like dad, but he's also handsome extremely talented, smart and caring. He cares for me like no one has ever cared for me. He never lets me leave the house without knowing how much he loves me, just like you used to do. So, there's another Braverman in the world.

I have to confess something to you, Ma. When I found out that you died, my heart stopped. Nothing in the world mattered to me. Nothing I had done and planned to do to make a better life to make you proud – none of it was worth anything to me. I felt like I didn't deserve a better life because I wasn't there when you needed me. I can never forgive myself for not being there. It haunts me still. I cry sometimes when I think about how much I fucked up and how much of my life I wasted by not listening to you.

But even with the guilt, when I really wanted to give up and check out for good, I could hear your voice telling me to keep pushing. So, I've been pushing. And things are turning out so well, Ma. I won't stop making you proud of me. Again, I'm sorry for how I disappointed you and for not being there when you needed me most. The thing I realized from writing my story is that I started selling drugs so you and Dad wouldn't have to worry about money. I told myself I was doing it for my family. But somewhere along the way, I got greedy. I forgot why I started. And the greed took me away from what mattered to me most. I just need you to understand that there's no place else in the world that I would have rather been than by your side, holding your hand when you were passing. Because I would have wanted to spend every last second telling you how much I loved you and appreciated everything you ever did for me. And, you did your best. I honestly don't know if I can ever forgive myself for not being there for you when you needed me the most, but that's something I am trying still to this day to come to terms with. Now, it's time for me to do my best and keep on doing things that I know would have made you proud. I love you, Ma. I always look for your star in the sky.

Love always,
Noah

ABOUT JEFFREY WACHMAN

Since his release from the Southern State Correctional Facility on May 5, 2010, Jeffrey has succeeded in keeping the vow he made to change his life. Immediately after his release, he began working sales jobs and has since become a successful model, entrepreneur and club manager in New York City. Jeffrey owns BuffBoyzz Entertainment and runs multiple businesses under that umbrella.

He married the love of his life, Matthew, on January 13, 2013 and they reside in New York, New York with their dogs Daxter and Hammer. Both Jeffrey and his husband, Matthew, are avid supporters of numerous LGBT organizations as well as organizations focused on under-privileged youth.

ABOUT TRAVIS MONTEZ

Journalist/poet/activist, Travis Montez, is a Brooklyn-based juvenile rights attorney who represents children in the Family Court system of New York City. Born and raised in Nashville, Tennessee, Montez came to NYC in the late 90s to attend New York University where he pursued degrees in journalism and Africana Studies. It was there that he was first introduced to spoken word poetry and writing.

His work has been featured in a number of anthologies and international publications such as Bullets & Butterflies: Queer Spoken Word Poetry. Montez recently released his fifth collection of poetry, Full Disclosure.

CPSIA information can be obtained
at www.ICGtesting.com
Printed in the USA
FSOW04n0254200616
21759FS